# All That Glitters

by

## Nick Hilliard

Visit:

NickHilliard.com

# Dedications

To all the men and women of the past who weren't allowed by society to love and live as they chose. Thank you for blazing the trail.

To Robert - Thank you for all your help and your vicious editing pen.

Once again, a special thank you to Myra and Sharon for taking hours out of your life to beta read my work.

To Dvorak: my constant companion even when the sun didn't shine and there were squirrels to chase.

# 1

The gatekeeper at RC's estate must have seen us coming, and even in the dark remembered the sleek red Mercedes Roadster that had raced the electric gates' abilities the last time it was there. Before we even got close, the massive gates began to swing open. The tires screeched to a stop in front of the gatehouse. Because the Mercedes was an English drive, I was across the car from the gatekeeper himself.

"Good evening, Curtis."

The man looked taken aback and then beamed. I was fairly confident it was the first time ever anyone had used his name.

"Good evening, Miss Desmond, Mr. Wainwright." He grinned and tipped his hat.

"Okay if we head on up to the party?"

"Yes, Ma'am! From what I hear you two are the guests of honor." And he waved us on with a flourish.

I drove through the entry and up the drive a short way, then pulled to a stop again.

"Hugo, be a dear and help me get this cape back over my shoulder."

Hugo did as I asked. If anyone saw us, they would think we looked like two monkeys at play, our arms and hands flailing in the air and batting at each other. My right shoulder was farthest from him, and the gear shift and handbrake were between the seats. When the deed was finally done, we sat for several minutes just laughing.

"What women won't do to get noticed."

"Oh, my dear, the correct line is: What a movie star won't do to get noticed. Just wait. You're only getting started." I put the car in gear. I hit the throttle hard enough that we both jolted back in our seats. Gravel flew up behind us as we shot down the driveway.

We rocketed to the front of the house. I pulled the little red car up to the red carpet so quickly that some of the photographers actually jumped back a bit. All eyes turned to us. Most, if not all, of the other guests had arrived in their chauffeured limousines. I was certain no automobile had been driven by a woman. Flashbulbs popped the second the photographers recognized us. The young valet in his tuxedo with tails, the same one assigned this task every time I had been here before, opened my door. The roadster's door swung open at the front, placing me in full view of the photographers.

The valet proffered his hand. I took it. Stepping from the roadster, I said, "Thank you, Bobby."

The young man looked at me with an astonished look. "You are so welcome, Miss Desmond. I can't wait to see your new picture." The smile he gave me was dazzling.

I palmed Bobby the five-dollar bill I had pulled from my purse while we were stopped back down the driveway fussing with my cape. "Would you mind seeing that my car gets parked since I don't have a driver tonight?"

"You bet Ma'am," he said excitedly with a quick bob of his head.

"And Bobby, I am so grateful for you taking care of this matter for me that I'll make sure you get two free tickets to

*Samson and Delilah."*

"Ma'am, that's not necessary."

"It is necessary to me. If I don't get them to you tomorrow, call my house and talk to my secretary, Cecilia. Tell her that crazy actress boss of hers promised you two tickets and you're guessing she forgot."

Bobby chuckled. "Yes, thank you, Ma'am."

I stepped away from him and stood posed as I'd been instructed, except I just couldn't seem to look bored. I could not keep from smiling as the flashbulbs popped. I tilted my shoulder, the cape dropped. Out of the corner of my eye, I saw Bobby reach to grab it, but it fell into the palm of my hand and my fingers closed around it. There were audible gasps and a new volley of bulbs popped. I dragged it behind me about halfway up the walkway and turned back as if to say to Hugo, *I'm waiting.*

I noticed that Bobby had closed the driver's door to the Mercedes. Using the top of the windscreen and the back of the driver's seat, Hugo lifted himself into the air, pulling both feet up. He extended his legs across the auto until he was standing in the driver's seat, raising his hands in the air waving to the photographers. Flashbulbs popped and some of the reporters were even clapping. With his arms outstretched, he bent his knees. Suddenly his entire body was in mid-air. He landed flat footed on the red carpet amid a torrent of flashes and applause. Straightening his legs, he pretended to dust himself off and stood while photographers went wild. He nodded to the photographers before bounding down the walkway to my side.

"Why, Mr. Wainwright, I do believe you are enjoying your new job." I gave him a wicked grin.

"Why, my dear Miss Desmond, I would say that is an understatement. I am loving my new job."

He slipped his arms around my waist, leaned forward and

kissed me. Photographers went into a frenzy. The space around us was instantly as brilliant as day. I thought that surely the photographers would run out of flashbulbs.

As we turned and moved toward the open doorway to the house, he leaned close to my ear. "Besides, I didn't want some movie star goodie-two-shoes upstaging me." And his face split into a wide smile.

"We are going to be in so much hot water tomorrow when that picture hits the papers across the country." Then I winked mischievously up at him.

"I'm sure you're right. Without a doubt, we will most certainly be called to the headmaster's office."

"Don't you mean the throne room?" And I winked again.

When we were within earshot of the front doors, I could see they were flanked by the same two doormen as before.

"Good evening, Oscar, Tom." I nodded to each of them.

They both smiled broadly. "Good evening Miss Desmond. Good evening Mr. Wainwright," they said in turn.

As we stepped through the doorway the scene was familiar. It was almost indistinguishable from the first party I had attended in this house. The coat check stand had reappeared, music floated down from upstairs, and there were people everywhere. And many of those people were the same people who had been at RC's party for the Duke. This was getting easier.

Hugo guided us towards the coat check. He lifted my fur from where it trailed behind me and handed it to a coat check girl in a geisha costume. She handed me the ticket. It was then I remembered I still had the little handbag.

"Thank you, Tilley," I said, as I took the ticket. "I would like to check my bag as well."

As she took the tiny purse, she looked bewildered. "You know my name?"

Before the words had finished leaving her lips, RC's butler

was at her side.

"Yes, Tilley, Miss Desmond knows everyone's name it would seem." He gave me a curious smile.

"Thank you, Tilley," I said, holding up my ticket stub. "And thank you too, Samuel." I smiled and gave the butler a quick wink as I tucked the ticket into Hugo's jacket pocket. I slid my arm through Hugo's and leaned against him. He began to maneuver us into the crowd.

When we reached the staircase, I pulled my arm from his to better navigate the stairs. As I pulled free, Hugo's hand slipped around my waist. I lifted the hem of the heavy dress to avoid tripping as I climbed. Stepping slightly in front of Hugo, I took the first step. This put Hugo directly behind me, and as I mounted the second step and he the first, his hand moved almost naturally down to my bottom.

*Oh, God!* I thought. I started doing long division with double digits in my head, willing my body NOT to react to his touch. The thought had never crossed my mind as to how intimate that particular touch could be. *Divide four thousand three hundred and twenty-four by twelve. Twelve goes into forty-three 3 times, leaving seven. Bringing down the two makes seventy-two.* It was during my calculations that I took in the identical twin staircase on the far wall. I had never paid any attention before, but that staircase seemed to be the "down" staircase and we were on the "up" one, just like the escalators in some of the large department stores. Funny what your mind chooses to notice when it's trying desperately not to notice the elephant in the room. I snickered slightly to myself, thinking what that might imply as I mentally thought of my own very well hidden and tightly secured elephant's trunk.

"What's so funny?" Hugo asked, smiling and giving my bottom a squeeze.

And now I was back to long division.

At the top of the stairs, we stepped into the massive ballroom. My father, Bertram Standish, stood next to his now-constant companion, Gertrude Myers. Gertie had been my father's secretary since he opened his office some twenty-five years earlier. She had known me all my life. I would have never imagined my father, who had intimate knowledge of almost every actress in Hollywood, ever having more than a business relationship with Gertie. Yet here they were, together and pretty much inseparable. And right now, the inseparable duo was staring sternly at both Hugo and me and headed our direction at a marching pace.

It was my father who spoke first when they reached us. "Have you lost your minds? What in the devil were you thinking, kissing each other? It's gotten all over this room in less than five minutes. It'll be all over the world by morning."

As if to acknowledge my prophecy, Hugo gave my bottom another squeeze as he took my father's rebuke.

"And get your hand off his bottom." He barked out in a hiss.

*He had said <u>his</u>. Oh, God!*

"I don't have my hand on his bottom?" I said indignantly, covering my father's faux pas.

"I meant to say, Hugo take 'your' hand OFF Theodora's bottom," he amended with a stutter.

For the first time ever, I wasn't sure whether it was my father or my agent talking. I cocked an eyebrow. As if in answer to my question, my father cocked his as well. I smiled. It was the protective father I was seeing. And like a young man caught getting too familiar with his sweetheart, Hugo removed the offending appendage instantly.

"Come on, the both of you. RC has asked me twice where you were and why it was taking you so long to arrive." He spoke in a stage whisper, like we could be overheard amidst the cacophony of conversations and music.

As if on cue, Gertie moved around and took Hugo by the arm, with my father following suit with me. And just like that the misbehaved children had been separated. I looked up at Hugo and a smirk shot across his face.

This time, as we made our way across the room to where our host was holding court, I found it a great deal easier mingling with the rich and famous people clustered in their cliquish clutches.

"There you are at last!" RC exclaimed, in delight.

He gave me a hug and what had become his trademark kiss on the forehead. He moved to Hugo and shook his hand vigorously.

"Well, well, well, Mr. Wainwright. Perhaps instead of playing leading man to Hollywood's newest temptress, I should cast you as a swashbuckling pirate. It would appear from tonight's entrance you think you might rival Fairbanks." RC's tone was both bubbling over and chiding all at once.

Still clasping RC's hand from the shake, Hugo turned the back of RC's hand skyward and bowed his forehead to it. "Your wish is my command, My Liege." His face radiated sincerity, accepting the reprimand for jumping out of the Mercedes in front of the press, but not apologizing for it.

In response, RC clasped his other hand around Hugo's and pumped even harder. RC's cheeks turned rosy and the smile that lit his face made him look more like jolly ole Saint Nick than the head of one of Hollywood's largest motion picture studios.

"You are going to make it big, my boy," he said, almost laughing out loud. "Now both of you get over here, I have some gentlemen I want you to meet.

We didn't really have to move so much as re-orient ourselves. My father and Gertie had placed themselves next to the Duke, who stood just behind RC's left shoulder, while

Nick Hillard

to RC's right were three men lined up in a row. All three were in tuxedos, but one stood out. Tall, slender, and ruggedly handsome, he was wearing a black cowboy hat with his tux; and instead of the usual loafers or wing-tips, his feet were clad in shiny black cowboy boots with a high heel that made him even taller.

*If I ever get to be a man again, I might need to buy a pair of those.*

"I'd like to make some introductions." RC started with the gentleman closest to him. "This is Ezra Blum. Ezra is a diamond merchant from New York City."

Mr. Blum nodded to us.

"Next to Ezra is Grady Chesterfield. Grady owns about half the state of Montana. He deals in cattle and thoroughbred horses. More than one of the horses he's bred and trained has won the Kentucky Derby."

"I can only take credit for breeding and training them. I have to give all the credit for the races to their current owners and jockeys."

His humbling words didn't exactly ring sincere.

"And last, but far from least, is Raymond Housley Overholser. Mr. Overholser is an oilman from the great state of Texas." RC sounded like a politician introducing a candidate from Texas at the Democratic convention. "Gentlemen, I'd like to introduce Colossal Pictures' most adored actress and soon to be America's most sensual temptress, Miss Theodora Desmond. This is her co-star, our newest leading man, Hugo Wainwright."

Hugo was the first to shake everyone's hand and then it was my turn. Like most perfunctory handshakes, it was an extension of the arm, a clasp of hands and a single firm pump. At least with both Mr. Blum and Mr. Chesterfield it happened that way. However, when I extended my hand to Mr. Overholser, he held it.

"You can call me Tex," he drawled out, with a Southwestern twang. His voice was almost as oily as his profession, and he was still holding my hand.

"I have acquaintances who own a rather large ranch in Texas. Their names are William and Margaret Morgan. Do you know them by chance?" I was trying to make polite conversation.

He gave a slight laugh. "Oh, honey, Texas is a mighty big place. No, I'm afraid I don't." He was still holding steadfast to my hand.

"Well, Tex," I drawled back, mimicking his accent, "they have a mighty big ranch."

I didn't like him calling me *honey*.

"Well, little filly, in case you haven't heard it before, *everything's* big in Texas."

The corner of his mouth turned up into something that was between a grin and a sneer. He gave me a wink. Then he rubbed his thumb slowly up and down the back of my hand. I nearly cringed in revulsion.

Instead, I dramatically feigned embarrassment, with a slight turn of my head. I caught my father's eye. He had that look. Then, I noticed so did the Duke as well as did Mr. Chesterfield. And to my pleasant surprise, so did Hugo. And I would bet that my own face mirrored that same expression. I'm not talking about a look of rightful indignation because the man had brazenly propositioned a woman in public. I'm talking about the look of challenge.

Most men would tell you that the fairer sex consists of complicated creatures. But I find men equally baffling. A band of men will gladly concede which man is the wealthiest, which is the most handsome and which is the strongest. They will even concede, as to which has the greatest prowess when it comes to the fairer sex. But let one man in that band boast about the size of his credentials and suddenly there is an overwhelming need for proof. And at this very moment, there were five men within earshot ready to throw down the proverbial gauntlet of challenge to this braggart, and I was one of them. If this had not been a public forum and had we not been in mixed company, I'm sure there would have been a wager followed by a laying down of the cards, so to speak. And quite confidently, my money would be on the Standish boys.

Feeling an almost uncontrollable desire to fight, I snapped my head back abruptly and locked my eyes with the arrogant cowboy. "Well, then Tex, I guess all it will take is one of those Texas-sized checks invested in my next movie to throw that big ole Texas-sized hat of yours into the ring." And I gave him an exaggerated wink.

"Now why would I do that, Li'l Filly?" A tight, almost wicked smile creased his face. "Just so old RC over there can overpay his cute little pet actress?"

"My dear Tex, I have now made seven films. My very first movie was wildly successful, and each one thereafter has earned more than the one before it. In *Samson and Delilah*, Theodora Desmond the commodity has gone from being America's sweetheart to America's most wanton femme fatale. Do you know what that means, Tex?" I hissed his name and landed hard on the X.

I took a step in, holding on to his hand tightly. "It means, with the release of this new talking picture, every red-blooded American male will LUST after Theodora Desmond, the sensual siren, and every red-blooded American girl will long to emulate Theodora Desmond, the sexual goddess. And that translates into dollars and cents."

My voice was nearing a low growl now. I stepped even closer and glared up at him. I squeezed his hand as hard as I could. Due to my judo training, I have a very firm grip. His eyes popped open wide. He tightened his own grip in return.

"And it only takes the slightest bit of business acumen to know, the smaller the group of investors in a sound and successful venture, the larger the profit for said investors. So Tex, know that I, Theodora Desmond, have three more years left on my contract with Colossal Studios. If you are not seeing dollar signs by now, you are never going to see them. And you need to understand this, Tex. No matter how much money I get paid, I'm worth *every* penny!"

I immediately regained my composure and extricated my hand from his. I looked over to Hugo.

"Dear Hugo," I said as sweetly as I could. "I am truly parched after all this business talk. Would you escort this li'l filly to the bar on the veranda? I would just love some fresh air and a glass of champagne."

Hugo nodded his good-nights to each man in turn, moved over to me, and proffered his arm. I slipped mine through his, slunk against him as I had all evening, and we moved away from RC and his money coalition.

"I think I'm with Theodora," Gertie said. She was right behind us as my father shook every hand before scurrying to catch up with her.

# 2

The four of us reached the bar on the far side of the swimming pool without saying another word. The bar itself spanned nearly the entire length of the pool. Once we had positioned ourselves at the far end, well out of ear shot, Hugo whipped around to face me.

"What in the devil was all that about?"

"Keep your voice down boy," my father shushed. Then in a much gentler tone with a huge grin on his face, he said, "That was Theodora, securing three very prodigious investor checks on RC's behalf. One, of course, will be much larger than the other two."

"What?" Hugo looked puzzled.

It was my turn to continue enlightening him.

"Hugo, let me share a bit of advice a sage mentor once shared with me." I winked at my father. "The entertainment industry is only twenty percent entertainment. The other eighty percent is politics. RC needed those men to understand that investing in a Theodora Desmond film was a sound investment, a sure thing. What I just did in that brief exchange of barbs would have taken RC days, if not weeks, to accomplish. He will have their commitment, if not the actual check in hand before they leave here tonight."

Hugo looked a bit dumbfounded. Our conversation dipped, and the bartender took that opportunity to approach.

"We'll have three Champagnes, and I'll have a Scotch on the rocks," Hugo told him.

"Make that two Scotch rocks," my father amended.

"No, make that three," Gertie said, holding up three fingers, punctuated with a heavy sigh.

The bartender looked over at me with a slight smile.

"I'm sticking with the champagne, Lawrence, thank you," I said, politely returning his smile.

He nodded and was off to pour our drinks.

"I don't think I'll ever get this." Hugo was shaking his head. "I thought Overholser was being a complete ass."

"Oh, that's being nice about it. I would say Mr. Overholser was a pompous pandering prick, and Theodora artfully turned the tables on him." My father was positively bursting with pride.

"And as your client, I will expect you to negotiate a raise on my behalf for it," I said to my father with a grin.

Lawrence returned with our drinks.

"Thank you, Lawrence," I said, as he set the flute of fizzing champagne in front of me.

"You are most welcome, Miss Desmond. Is there anything else I can get you?"

"No, thank you, Lawrence. I think this will do us perfectly for the moment."

When Lawrence moved back to the other end of the bar to help a newcomer, my father leaned into me.

"What in the world is up? You've known the name of every servant, waiter, and bartender you've come in contact with tonight. And they are all talking about it. Do you know how unusual that is?" His voice was barely above a whisper.

"Do you remember telling me that every servant in every household was pretty much expected to know every one of

Hollywood's movie dynasty by name?  Well, I wanted to see if I was as clever and talented as they are.  I had Seedy compile a list last week of everyone who would be working at tonight's party.  And you know Seedy!  I not only got the list of names but a brief background, as well as a picture attached.  Don't ask me how she got them.  After that, it was no different than learning a movie script.  I must say, I really have enjoyed watching their faces light up as I call them each by name.  You know, that same sage mentor who taught me the eighty-twenty rule also once told me, 'To use someone's name is to honor him.'"  As mentor in both instances, of course, he again smiled with pride.

"I see Thomas Hicks over there," my father said, turning to Gertie.  "He's the new up and coming Western star.  For some reason, RC turned him down, but Horace at Monumental Studio's picked him up.  I think I should wander over and say hello.  Do you think, if we leave you two alone," looking sternly back and forth at both Hugo and me, "that you can stay out of mischief?  Or if not, at least out of harm's way?"  Then shaking his head, he chuckled, "I really should know better than to ask that."

*"Et mon lion arrive sur le champ de bataille,"* Gertie said, as she slipped her arm into my father's and allowed him to spirit her away.

Gertie knew I didn't speak French.  She also knew that Hugo did.

"Well?" I asked, as I turned and glared at him.

"And my lion enters the battlefield."  He lifted both arms up in the air in mock surrender adding, "Don't shoot the messenger."

Hugo's raised arms framed a group across the pool.  At the center was Charlie, the Viscount of Kintyre and Lorne.  He was with Regina Banks, his current lady friend and a fellow actress, whom I supposed had just become my rival.  With a successful nearly decades-long career as a movie temptress, she also had the reputation of marrying much older, wealthy men. So far, Regina had been widowed five times, a fact that had everyone in Hollywood wondering why she had taken an interest in a man several years her junior. But even as the question arose in my mind, there came the answer as well: money. Charlie appeared to be frowning, and Regina looked angry with the world. Earlier when they were at my house, before the movie, I thought she was jealous because she thought I had designs on Charlie. Now I wasn't so sure.

"Do you think the Viscount has done something to anger Regina?" I asked Hugo, nodding as inconspicuously as possible towards the couple.

Hugo lowered his arms and turned to look. Just then a glass of cold champagne appeared in front of me, and the old one was whisked away.

"I haven't the foggiest," Hugo shrugged.

"You haven't heard?" It was Lawrence speaking.

We both turned to looked at him. "No, I haven't heard anything," I said.

"All the staff is talking about it. Two days ago, Mr. Crawford gave Regina the sack. She had four pictures left on her contract. Her latest silent film was due to be released the first of next month. Mr. Crawford told her the day of the silent movie is dead and gone. He said he was pulling the film because it was just throwing good money after bad. Apparently, Regina's voice hadn't tested well."

"I would have thought that if something of that magnitude had happened, everyone here would be talking about it." Hugo sounded as if he didn't believe Lawrence.

"It hasn't been announced yet. Regina is only here tonight because Mr. Crawford made her come. And everybody *is* talking about it." He grinned. "Just not in the group that you are a part of. Samuel would shoot me if he knew I'd said anything to you."

"Thanks for the information, Lawrence. We will most certainly keep your confidence." I smiled at him.

Lawrence gave me a thumbs up and moved back to the other end of the bar to fill a tray of champagne glasses for one of the waiters serving the pool area.

"Wow! What do you think of that?" I stared at Regina, feeling a little sorry for her.

"Do you mean, what do I think of a nasty woman who openly chases older wealthy men getting the ax? Or what do I think of you gaining entry into an inner circle that most of your peers consider invisible? Personally, I think the latter is much more impressive." Hugo grinned at me with delight, like I had done something astounding instead of just noticing the people around me.

I excused myself and made a beeline for the lady's room. I wanted to listen in. I had an overwhelming desire to give Hugo's conjecture a try, but perhaps more importantly was that I wanted to get off my feet for a few minutes. These heels were killing me!

When I reached the sanctum of the powder room, I found an empty chaise lounge and managed to get my aching feet off the floor. I felt like I might never be able to stand again. With congratulations on the new movie coming from everyone walking through the door, I could barely listen in on any of the other conversations. But it seemed as though no one was talking about Regina.

The last time I was in here, I hadn't noticed the attendant at all. New to RC's staff, Mary Colter was a fidgety girl who appeared to be in her mid-twenties. I was guessing Samuel had placed her on this detail for two reasons. First, she was new. How hard could it be to dispense hand-towels, refill lotions, lipsticks and facial tissue containers? But I also suspected she was possessed of excellent hearing. This room alone would be an abundant source of inside information and gossip.

The room had cleared a bit. While there was a lull, I thought I would give Hugo's theory a go.

"Mary," I called, beckoning her over.

She did a double take and pointed to herself. I nodded in affirmation. She left her post in the corner behind the door and moved warily over to me. If the room had been empty, I would have asked her to sit, but as it was, that would have been grounds for her dismissal. I motioned for her to come close. She did, leaning forward to hear what I was going to say.

"Just nod, don't answer," I whispered in her ear. "Do you know anything about Regina Banks?" Her eyes popped open wide. I had my answer. "Have any of the women in here tonight mentioned it?"

She shook her head no.

"Thank you, Mary," I praised, in a normal tone. "You have been quite helpful," I added, just in case anyone thought it odd I was speaking in whispers to the bathroom attendant.

It was time to head back into the fray. I stood up, and immediately winced.

"My dogs are killing me too, honey," commiserated a rather hefty woman in a black lace and sequined gown. She had one leg crossed over the other in a very un-lady-like fashion, the offending shoe off her foot, and she was massaging her pudgy toes through her silk stockings.

I hobbled to the door. Then I turned back toward my new sore-footed friend, stood erect, and threw one arm in the air with my index finger pointing skyward, looking for all intents and purposes like the Statue of Liberty.

"Beauty knows no pain," I declared, and she was treated to my best pose-for-the-camera smile. "The show must go on." And with that, I glided gracefully out the door.

When I reached Hugo, he was sitting alone looking a bit forlorn, his Scotch glass empty.

"Have you reached your limit?" I asked, gesturing down at his glass with its melting ice cubes.

"No, but I don't seem to command the same attention of the staff that one Miss Theodora Desmond does." He lifted the glass to his lips and sucked the water off the melting cubes with an audible slurp.

"You could just yell down to the end of the bar and ask Lawrence to bring you a new one."

Hugo turned, looking a bit surprised.

"Hey Lawrence, when you get a minute, could I get another?" Hugo held up and jiggled his empty glass.

"Sure thing, Mr. Wainwright. Coming right up," he called out with a big smile and a quick thumbs-up.

"I find that works every time," I grinned.

"You know, it is amazing." The corners of his mouth quirked up. "Six months ago, if I'd been having a drink with my friends on the police force, I wouldn't have hesitated to call out to the bartender. I don't know what's happening to me."

"Entitlement comes easy, doesn't it?"

"I can't believe it, but you're right. Damn, you are right," he said as if he had just made a monumental discovery.

The new Scotch and a fresh glass of champagne arrived. Lawrence picked up the empty rocks glass.

I looked down at the bubbling golden liquid and then back up at Lawrence.

"Thank you, Lawrence. That was so thoughtful of you."

And there was that smile again.

"Is there anything else I can get for the two of you?"

"Unless Miss Desmond needs something, I think we're stellar. Thank you, Lawrence."

"Whatever you need, I'm here," was Lawrence's reply, and

he moved back to the other end of the bar.

I looked over Hugo's shoulder to see the Viscount standing alone, and he didn't seem quite so miserable as he had earlier. He caught me looking, and he waved. I waved back. I beckoned him over. When I did, Hugo looked to see who I was motioning to. He gave Charlie a nod of acknowledgment as he moved in our direction.

"You are looking absolutely breathtaking this evening, Theo," Charlie said, giving me a hug accompanied by the European kiss on both cheeks. "Good evening, Hugo old man," he greeted, extending his hand.

"Where is that lucky charm you usually have on your arm?" asked Hugo.

"She's in the powder room. I'm afraid she's not feeling very well this evening. But neither of us would have missed your premiere for the world. You both gave quite the performance. But Hugo, I have to say, for my money, Theodora stole the show." He grinned.

"Well sir, it was your money that financed the movie. Therefore, your opinion is always the correct one." Hugo straightened up and gave the Viscount a hearty pat on the back with a wink. "But you are one hundred percent correct. Theodora Desmond's radiant light outshines us all." He finished his rather melodramatic soliloquy by placing his hand first on his heart and ending with his arm extended to the sky.

I slapped Hugo on one of those massive biceps.

"That wonderful performance just goes to show how ill-suited you were for your former career as a police detective. You were born to be in front of a camera, which is exactly what my father and I are banking on," Charlie added, raising his champagne flute in salute.

As if on cue, Regina Banks appeared at the far end of the pool, saw Charlie, and quickly started closing the distance.

Strangely, she was now sporting a full-length mink coat, and it was not draped off her shoulders and hanging in the crook of her elbows, as the proper fashion in the evening at a Beverly Hills party dictates. It was drawn close, held tightly as if she were freezing. She scowled when she recognized the company Charlie was keeping.

When Regina reached us, she slipped her arm around Charlie, pulling him in close. When she did, the coat moved a bit and I saw a small bright red streak running down her soft pink silk gown.

*She must have dropped lipstick on herself while she was in the powder room. I would have gotten my coat and worn it to cover my faux pas too.*

"Oh Charlie, would you mind taking me home. I seem to have caught a chill on top of everything else."

*Oh, Lord, I think she actually batted her eyelashes as she looked up at him. Talk about melodrama.*

"Of course, my dear," answered Charlie, patting her hand. He looked back at both of us. "Please excuse us. We should get together for dinner soon. All four of us if you'd like." He smiled brightly.

We nodded our agreement, and the two of them walked away, Regina clinging to Charlie and her coat tightly, as they moved back towards the house.

"It really does look as if poor Charlie is about to become husband number six," I said with a sad pout.

"How do you think dear Regina will fair in the highlands of Scotland in wintertime if she has to wrap up in a mink in June in California?" His bold laugh was followed with a snort.

I almost snorted myself. My mind immediately pictured Regina Banks wearing her mink coat, standing next to Charlie in his dress kilt, both knee-deep in snow in front of Charlie's beloved castle in the middle of a Scottish Highland winter.

"Hugo," I said, with a heavy sigh. "Why don't we follow their lead and go. I don't know about you, but it has been a very, very long day."

"Oh, Theo, do you think we can?" His tone was wistful. "I thought maybe since we were the guests of honor, we'd have to stay until the bitter end."

"Look around, dear boy. Do you think our leaving will be noticed at all? Besides, I have had about as many congratulatory handshakes, hugs, and kisses as I can take. Come on!" I grabbed him by the hand. "Let's go say our goodbyes to our host and get out of here."

Twenty minutes later I had retrieved my cape and purse and we were walking out the front door. I was expecting Bobby to have brought around my red Mercedes Roadster, but instead I found him holding the door open to my shiny black Daimler. I must have looked puzzled because Bobby answered my unspoken question.

"Your man, Wallace, called Samuel and told him he was sending your car and driver. He figured you would be tired after such a long day and thought you'd rather ride than drive."

"And he was so, so, right. Don't forget to telephone my secretary about those tickets to *Samson and Delilah*, Bobby."

"I won't, Miss Desmond. Thank you so much! You have a great rest of your evening." He smiled broadly.

I noted Bobby had given me the servant's names in his explanation of the automobile switch. By just learning a few names, I indeed had become one of the inner-circle of the invisible people. I climbed into the big comfortable motor car next to Hugo, Bobby closed the door, I acknowledged Randel, and we were gone.

# 3

My eyes popped open. Without moving, I surveyed the room. Morning light filtered by the sheer blue curtains gave the place a dappled look. I started. Standing across from the foot of my bed was Reginald Montgrieve. Well, the portrait of Reggie hung there anyway. The blasted painting always gave me a fright. The dang thing was so lifelike.

I had moved into Theodora's bedroom after the filming had finished on *Samson and Delilah*. Having no need for an extra-large bed, I had movers crate the swimming pool-sized beast originally in the room and had it shipped off to Texas, via Oklahoma, of course. Molly had meant the bed for Will and herself, and now they had it. I had a beautiful letter thanking me, along with a photograph of my new nephew.

With all the space that was left after the removal of the monstrous bed, Claudette and I had created a sitting area. It had promptly become the spot where Claudette, Seedy, and I would take our morning coffee. We went over my calendar for the day and my attire. But most of all, we used the time to catch up on any gossip. And with the number of evening soirees that I attended, there was always gossip. I turned my head and looked at the clock. It said two o'clock, and I sat bolt upright in bed.

# All That Glitters

*It couldn't be that late in the afternoon.*

I reached for the clock.

*I had three, maybe four glasses of champagne. But I had only a couple of sips out of each glass. I hadn't felt the slightest bit tipsy.*

"It can't be two o'clock," I said, shaking the clock.

I put it to my ear. It wasn't ticking. It had run down. I guess, with all the excitement yesterday, Claudette had forgotten to wind it. I breathed a sigh of relief. Not that it would have mattered that I had slept late, but I just hate sleeping the day away.

I hopped out of bed and hurried to the bath to use the facilities. I stopped to brush my teeth and slip into the man's bathrobe that hung behind the bathroom door, a wonderful gift from Wallace, my butler. I pulled the belt tight as I sat down in one of the three new chairs. The three chairs made a semi-circle of sorts around a beautiful chrome and glass art deco coffee table. Thanks to the much smaller bed, the sitting area nestled comfortably between the new bed and the dressing table. I sat in what had become Claudette's chair, the one that faced the portrait of Reggie. She just loved looking at him. Seedy and I had each told her that lusting after a dead man was rather macabre. To which she always replied, "*Âne!*" with a shrug of her shoulders.

Perhaps I would give the portrait to Claudette to hang in her room. I was looking directly at Reggie, but I was seeing Hugo. Last night, Hugo had kissed me. I thought it had been a publicity stunt, but when Randel dropped him off at his villa, he moved to kiss me again. This time there were no cameras to catch the moment. I rebuffed his advance, telling him that we were colleagues and we needed to make sure we could maintain a long-standing business relationship and not get caught up in the heat of the moment. For my part, it was a complete load of poppycock. I wanted him to kiss me, but I knew he thought he was kissing Theodora and had no clue that Theodora was really Eddie. As much as I didn't want to, I had to keep him at bay. Besides, he would be over me in no time as soon as every girl in the country began throwing themselves at his feet.

I was torn from my musings as the bedroom door burst open. Seedy marched in with a stack of newspapers cradled in her arms and her clipboard perched on top. Claudette was right behind her carrying the silver coffee service with its now familiar three robin-egg-blue porcelain cups clacking in their saucers as she hurried in.

"Good morning, ladies," I said, a bit startled.

"Good morning?" Seedy boomed. "Have you lost your mind?" Her voice was escalating with each subsequent syllable.

She pulled the first newspaper from under the clipboard she had balanced on top of the stack. She had it folded to highlight the nearly quarter page photo of Hugo kissing me.

"This one has my favorite headline. 'Desmond's back, and she talks,' then in all caps, 'AND SHE KISSES TOO!'"

She threw that paper on the bed and pulled out the next one. It was a different angle of the same kiss.

"This one is short and sweet. 'Boy Howdy! Is Desmond ever back! And Wainwright's got her.'"

She discarded that one to the bed as well. The next one had a different picture. It was the shot just after I had dropped the cape and caught it at the theater.

"Ah, it's a shame. That paper must not have had a photographer at the party," I said, in my most mockingly sorrowful tone.

"It's a fashion article," she snipped out matter-of-factly. "'The last time this reporter saw Theodora Desmond at the opening of *Passions of the Night*, she was wearing a sweetheart pink satin evening gown designed by New York City designer Nino Rossi. Last night for the opening of *Samson and Delilah,* Miss Desmond was bedecked in a white beaded sheath and white chinchilla fur cape by an undisclosed designer. She was also wearing the now renowned Rose of Kintyre ruby mounted in its newly designed diamond choker created by the Blum Brothers Jewelers of New York City. Simply stunning. However, after seeing *Sampson and Delilah,* I thought perhaps Miss Desmond should have considered wearing all red.'"

"What's wrong with that one? That's the response we wanted. Theodora can't be the siren and a goody-two-shoes all at the same time."

"I know, but I loved the old Theodora."

"Thanks a lot! And just so you both know, that was Hugo kissing me."

"That may be so, but it appears that you were kissing him back," Claudette snickered, never looking up as she poured the coffee.

"And some guy named Bobby," Seedy was reading from her notepad now, "called first thing this morning. He asked for me and informed me that you had promised him two tickets to the movie. And that he would like those for this Friday, if possible. Do you know how hard it was to get tickets for this Friday night? Especially to get seats good enough for Theodora Desmond to give as a gift?"

"Why was it so hard?" I asked, reaching for my cup and saucer.

"Because most theaters in Hollywood are already sold out."

It was my turn to smirk as I lifted the cup to my lips. After six more newspapers, all with some version of the same picture, from each of which Seedy quoted the headlines, she exhausted her commentary and joined Claudette and me for coffee.

I began to lay out the juicy bits I knew they would want to

hear about last night's party. I told them all about Regina getting the boot. I described how I had used all the servant's names from the list Seedy had compiled. How some of the staff had begun to open up and talk with me, and that it was one of the servants who had taken me into his confidence and informed me of Regina. I explained how no one outside the staff seemed to have had any knowledge of Regina's fate yet, and also about my little experiment in the lady's room to test Hugo's theory. Claudette was stunned that I would talk to the staff as equals. Seedy didn't understand the gravitas of the situation, having never been in service to anyone but me, and I was pretty sure that really didn't count either.

I gloated a bit about my interaction with the three investors. I gave them my appraisal of Mr. Blum the diamond merchant, Mr. Chesterfield the thoroughbred breeder, and of course the pompous ass Mr. Raymond Housley Overholser.

"Oh, well that explains it. I almost forgot. I got so caught up in the gossip." Seedy popped out of the chair and shot out the bedroom door into the hall. She was back in a flash carrying a huge crystal vase full to bursting with yellow roses.

"This came for you first thing this morning." She set the enormous bouquet on the coffee table in front of us.

She had to push the tray holding the silver coffee service to the side just to fit the overflowing vase onto the sleek glass surface. The display was so big that once it was in place, I could not see over the arrangement. I could only make out Seedy's hands as she picked up her clipboard. I watched her hands as she pulled a small envelope free from the clip, opened the flap, and pulled free a small card. She stood so she could see my face as she read the note.

"My dear Miss Desmond. I'm sending you the yellow roses of Texas. As beautiful as they are, they pale in comparison to the red rose of Hollywood. I have written that Texas-sized check and my big ole hat is officially in the ring. I look forward to spending time with you in the very near future so that I might share with you my 'Texas-sized' hospitality. Tex."

I shuddered.

"There are four dozen of them. Seedy and I counted them twice to make sure." Claudette's face puckered like she had bitten into something sour as she waved her hand dismissively.

I took it she was not impressed by the gesture.

*I was in trouble now.*

The telephone rang. Claudette pushed her chair back and moved to the dressing table to answer it.

"Hello, Desmond residence, Claudette speaking." She listened for a moment, "May I tell her who is calling?"

Claudette looked puzzled. She put her hand over the mouthpiece.

"It's Samuel, Mr. Crawford's butler." she said, with an expression akin to horror on her face. "He wishes to speak with you."

Now it was my turn to look puzzled. I stood and made my way to the telephone.

"Hello, Samuel. How may I help you?"

"Please Miss Desmond, come immediately. Mr. Crawford must speak with you as soon as possible." His voice was urgent.

*I was being summoned for the kiss. Well, it had only been a matter of time, I knew.*

"Yes, Samuel, I will be there within the hour."

"Yes Ma'am, please hurry." And he hung up.

I breathed a heavy sigh, and my shoulders slumped.

"What is it?" Seedy asked.

"I've been called to heel," I said, gesturing to the

newspapers on the bed.

Seedy squinted and drew her mouth wide as if saying, "Yikes!"

"There is nothing for it then. Go take your chastising and get it done." Claudette shot into my closet.

When she returned, she was carrying a dress I'd never seen before. It was very official looking, black with pinstripes.

"Georgie has replaced your going to the lawyer suit." She said recognizing my confused look. "Today you need to look professional. Looking like a businesswoman might cause RC to think that the kiss was just a business maneuver to gain publicity and not the careless act of a love-struck starlet," she said, her eyebrows raised.

My face took on a look of righteous indignation.

"Don't use that face on me, and get yourself bathed." With that, she shooed me into the bathroom.

As I closed the door behind me, I heard her tell Seedy, "You get dressed as well and go with her. It might soften the sharpness of his rebuke."

When I exited the bath, everything was laid out on the bed, and the ridiculous behemoth of a bouquet was gone.

"Sit," Claudette commanded.

I sat, and in less than thirty minutes I was dressed. The pinstriped suit looked severe. Claudette had paired it with a white silk blouse cut like a man's dress shirt, complete with a separate starched collar. She hung a red silk man's tie around my neck and adroitly fashioned it into a full Windsor in moments.

"I'm impressed. I have a hard time tying that knot when I'm the one doing the tying. How did you ever learn to tie it backward?"

"It is only backward if the wearer knows how to tie the knot himself. To a valet, it is the only way he knows to tie the knot," she said as she tightened the tie's knot and shaped the dimple into the center.

"And you've been a valet?"

"No. But I have had more than one lover who was the young master of a household."

"Claudette, you are shameless," I said, grinning.

"Shameless yes, but not ashamed. Now let's get you gone before you receive a second call."

Claudette draped a fox stole over one shoulder and put a wide-brimmed black hat with a small veil on my head.

"If you tilt your head down and look up from behind the veil you should look sufficiently cowed." Then she pushed me out the door.

"I look positively funereal," I complained, as I stumbled into the hall.

She gave me a devilish smile. "Good! Then look penitent as well!"

# 4

The Daimler pulled up in front of RC's home not twenty minutes later. Randel helped me from the automobile. I stood on the wide sidewalk leading up to the massive entrance. It always seemed so much smaller when a red carpet ran down its center, and red velvet ropes held back the reporters and photographers. Parked just in front of the Daimler sat a Mercedes Roadster just like mine but in a brilliant cobalt blue. I really liked it in this color too.

*I wonder who it belongs to.*

Once Seedy was out of the automobile, Randel closed the door.

"Shall I wait here, Ma'am, or over by the garage?" He asked.

I frowned. "I'm not sure. Wait here, and if we are longer than fifteen minutes move over to the garages. I wouldn't want to be on Samuel's bad side as well as RC's."

"Yes Ma'am," he replied, tipping his hat.

I turned to Seedy. "Well, ready or not, let's go."

We turned toward the house and made our way to the front door. As we reached the porch, it dawned on me that this might be the first time I'd ever seen the imposing double door entry not standing wide open. Before Seedy could reach for the bell, one of the enormous doors began to swing open. I was expecting to see Samuel standing before me. Instead, it was Mary, the fidgety maid who was working in the lady's powder room the night before.

She bowed her head and gave a slight curtsy. "Please come in, Miss Desmond. Samuel will be with you in just a moment." She gestured, extending her arm for us to enter.

As I entered the room, I could see that the house had been converted back to a residence once again. The coat check stand was gone, and the massive mahogany table once again stood between the curved staircases. In front of that table stood two men, one of them I now understood to be the owner of the blue Roadster out front.

"Good Morning, Hugo," I said brightly.

"Good morning, Miss Desmond. Good morning, Miss Schofield," came his chilly reply. So, we were back to Miss Desmond, were we?

The young man standing next to him looked vaguely familiar.

"Miss Desmond, Miss Schofield, I'm not sure if you remember former police officer Willard Densmore. Young Mr. Densmore has taken up the position of my personal secretary and valet."

"Glad to officially meet you both," he said, extending his hand to me.

Hugo pushed his arm down instantly. "You don't shake hands with a lady. Especially one above your station. You slightly bow to each in turn, the higher-ranking one first," Hugo commanded.

He immediately bowed first to me, then to Seedy. A little too deeply, if I was honest.

"Officially met?" I asked.

"Yes, Ma'am. When Miss Schofield's fiancé was being held for murder, you gave me your autograph at the station house."

"Please forgive me for not recognizing you. That was a very harried evening."

"That's quite all right, Ma'am. I'm sure you give out hundreds, maybe even thousands of autographs and meet twice that many people. You surely can't be expected to remember everyone." He gave me a broad smile. Turning his attention to Seedy, he asked, "Have you and Mr. Herndon wed yet?"

Hugo coughed and covered his mouth, fighting back a grin, while Seedy turned bright red.

"I'm sorry to say, after that ordeal, he lost all affection for me." Seedy stammered, trying hard not to look as if she might cry.

"I am so sorry to hear that." Willard's words were sincere, and he gave her a warm smile.

"Thank you." She returned Mr. Densmore's smile with a shy one of her own.

Samuel emerged through a door between the two staircases. Designed as part of one of the oriental landscape murals covering every wall of the massive foyer, the door had been hidden so cleverly that I had never noticed it before.

"Miss Desmond, Mr. Wainwright, if you will follow me, please. Mary, please take Miss Schofield and Mr. Densmore to the visitor's parlor and see to any needs they may have."

He moved back towards the hidden door.

"RC is not in his office?" I inquired, looking over to the closed office door.

Samuel stopped and turned back to me, a pained look momentarily crossing his face. One second it was there, and the next his stoic features had returned.

"No, Ma'am, he is not." He turned again and moved once more towards the mysterious door, this time with both Hugo and me in tow.

# All That Glitters

*Well, so much for using Seedy as a buffer. It seems Hugo was using Mr. Densmore the same way, but it looks as if both our heads are about to be on the proverbial chopping block.*

As we passed through the tiny unassuming door, it was if we had been transported into another time and place. We stood on a balcony outlined with carved sandstone arches and polished white marble balustrades. The room below rivaled that of any of the old European castles I had seen in photographs and newsreels. The entire back wall was glass and looked out on a lower terrace, then across the lush green lawn to the two palm groves and gardens beyond. The entire effect nearly caused me to gasp.

Samuel motioned us toward a door. He opened it, and we stepped into the boxy confines of an elevator. It was a lavish luxury to have one elevator in a house, but this one made two. We stepped inside. Space was tight for three, and I stood close to Hugo. So close, I could smell the spicy sandalwood scent he'd taken to wearing. I liked it. I liked it a lot. In just moments, we had reached the floor below and Samuel opened the door. Cool fresh air rushed in. Samuel extended his arm, bidding me to exit first. I did, and Hugo followed.

The elevator spilled us out into a cavernous chamber that seemed to be a collection of many rooms in one open space. There was a parlor, a library, a billiards room, and of course a private movie theater. The centerpiece of the parlor portion was a monstrous rough gray granite fireplace, the opening so large that at least five grown men could stand shoulder to shoulder at their full height. I couldn't even imagine seeing it lit. Six matching Davenport sofas, all with brown leather ribbed backs, rolled arms, and deep rich burgundy cut-velvet down-filled cushions, stood guard around the fireplace's gaping maw. A plush Persian rug of ochres, aubergine, and soft faded blues mixed with claret stretched out in front of the hearth. Small craftsman occasional tables dotted the rug in front of each sofa.

Looking to the other side of the massive room, I saw a curving wall of bookcases rounding out the corners of the room, creating a library. The bookcases were topped with thick crown molding, their shelves filled with leather-bound volumes, most of a uniform size that seemed to be collected together by color, like sets of reference books. Centered in the library was a massive hand-carved burlwood desk covered with a deep green leather top, its border embossed with a gold-leaf laurel pattern. The desk was so big I fancied it must have been built right where it sat.

Farther around from the office area and closed in on three sides was a theater, complete with silver screen and a dozen chairs arranged in two rows of six with an aisle down the center, all upholstered to match the six sofas. Between the theater and the windows sat a billiard table.

Closest to the windows sat two comfortable William Morris lounge chairs, both with ottomans, and a small craftsman table huddled between them. Each chair had its own Tiffany glass reading lamp. Directly behind the table stood a beautiful radio in a contemporary art deco cabinet. Seated in one of those chairs with his feet propped on the footstool was our host, RC. One elbow rested on the arm of his chair, his head lolled in his hand. His perpetual smile was gone, and he looked lost in thought. He did not even look up as we approached.

In fact, he took no notice of us until Samuel touched him on the shoulder and spoke. "Sir, Miss Desmond and Mr. Wainwright are here."

It was only then that his head slowly lifted, and his puffy glassy eyes tried desperately to focus on us. He gave us a half-hearted smile.

"Have a seat, won't you." He gestured languidly with his

other arm, never lifting his head from his palm.

Hugo nodded for me to sit in the other chair, then Hugo sat on its matching ottoman. As we settled in, RC nodded off. We sat for a moment looking at the sleeping man.

I turned to Samuel, who was standing perfectly still beside my chair. "Samuel, what in the world is wrong?"

"I am so sorry Miss Desmond. I'm afraid his physician has given him laudanum to calm his nerves."

"Laudanum?" Hugo sounded horrified. "What could possibly have caused him that much anxiety?"

Samuel looked torn, but he remained silent. So, there we sat for several long uncomfortable minutes, all three of us staring at the unconscious RC.

I finally broke the silence. "Samuel, do you know what RC wanted to talk to us about?"

He hesitated. "Yes, Ma'am, I do but…." He glanced down as he trailed off, reluctantly.

"But you feel it's *not* your place to say?"

"That is correct, Ma'am." He sounded almost relieved.

"Did RC, before he was given the laudanum, tell you by chance that he was going to take us into his confidence? That he was going to tell us what you already know?"

"Yes, Ma'am, he did."

"Then it would appear that we have only two choices at this time. We can return once RC has slept off the effects of the opiate. Or you can tell us what he was going to tell us. Your choice should be based solely on the urgency of the matter."

"The matter is definitely urgent, Ma'am."

"Then your decision should be simple."

Hugo and I waited patiently as Samuel thought this through. I could see on his face the moment he made up his mind.

"There has been a death."

"A death?" Hugo asked, surprised.

"Yes, well, actually it's a murder."

"Murder!" Hugo jumped to his feet, and RC moaned.

Samuel looked over at his employer, but RC didn't stir again.

"Yes, sir. It is Mr. Clayton Foster, Mr. Crawford's personal secretary and lead attorney. His body is in Mr. Crawford's study."

"Have the police already been here?"

"No, sir. They have not."

"How long ago did you notify them?"

"They have not been notified as yet."

"What? Why?" Hugo bellowed, and RC moaned again.

"Keep your voice down," I said in a loud whisper.

"Mr. Clayton appears to have been killed last evening sometime. Mr. Crawford wanted to talk to the two of you before he telephoned the police. He especially wanted to speak with you, Ma'am." Hugo looked a bit offended. "He said you would certainly understand the meaning of a delicate situation and most assuredly would know how to handle it discreetly."

"Good God, man, there is nothing discreet about murder." Hugo's voice was rising once more.

I put my hand on his arm, but he jerked it away.

"Show me his body and telephone the police."

"Yes, sir." Samuel moved back towards the elevator.

Hugo turned to me and snapped, "You stay here."

"I most certainly will not." I stood, stomped around him, and got right behind Samuel.

# 5

The three of us piled back into the elevator, the smell of sandalwood almost overpowering. Clearly Hugo's body temperature had risen, and his cold brash demeanor told me his blood pressure had risen as well. The tension in the tiny moving box was palpable and the short ride seemed to take forever. I stood at Hugo's side, but he kept his face forward and never looked down.

When the elevator reached the top, Samuel led us back out into the foyer. Mary stood at the large round table as if she were keeping guard. Samuel walked over and spoke softly to her. "Notify the authorities, Mary."

She bobbed a curtsy and moved away. Our little party then moved quickly on toward the closed, and I was wagering locked, door of RC's office. I had guessed correctly. When we approached the door, Samuel produced a small set of keys from his jacket pocket. As he fitted the key into the lock, Hugo and I lined up side by side behind him. Neither of us was going to allow the other into the room first.

The door swung open. Clayton Foster's body was situated behind RC's desk on the "Throne of Power," a large gilded movie prop encrusted with paste jewels of various sizes and colors and upholstered in a garish royal blue velvet. The razor-sharp tip of a long blade protruded from his chest. His face bore a mixture of horror and pain, his once-brown eyes glazed over with the white film of death. His black suit and white shirt were stained with thickly congealed blood, now turning a dirty, rusty brown. I stood frozen to the spot. Hugo moved carefully across the room. He placed his palm lightly over Clayton's face and slid two fingers over the man's eyelids. When he removed his hand, Clayton's eyes were closed.

I took in the room. On the bookshelves behind the man, only one thing seemed out of place. I recalled an antique ornamental Chinese sword on a black lacquered stand occupying the long lower shelf. The stand was on the floor, the empty scabbard now lay flat on the shelf, stretching nearly the entire length of the space.

"I'm guessing that's the murder weapon," I said, pointing to the empty scabbard. "Well, maybe not," I corrected, taking in a long blade that lay on the floor in front of the bookcase next to the lacquered stand.

Hugo saw my look of consternation, and even though he was angry with me, he gave a slight grin.

"It is the murder weapon. That's a double Chinese Shuang Jian sword. It has two blades in one scabbard. Look closely at the handle." He pointed to the blade on the floor. "See the unadorned flatten backside of the hilt. It lies flat against its companion. Together, when they are sheathed, they look like one piece. The other one is currently residing in Mr. Foster's chest. Whoever did this was a total low life scoundrel, literally stabbing the man in the back."

He addressed his last comment primarily towards Samuel. It was a man's comment on the cowardliness of another man. Ladies, of course, were excluded.

"I take it then, you think the crime was committed by a man?" I asked.

"Yes, almost assuredly."

I could tell by the look on Samuel's face that he agreed with both statements, and my gut told me it was the work of a man as well. However, since we were now speaking, I thought I might as well play devil's advocate.

"Why must this be a man's crime?"

"First, because knives aren't generally a woman's weapon of choice, and especially against a man. But in this case, my second reason is the one I believe shows proof without a doubt. Whoever murdered Mr. Foster held him by the neck just so." He straddled the pool of blood on the floor behind the throne and placed his arm around poor Clayton's neck, taking great care not to touch the body itself.

"He then thrust the sword all the way through the back of the chair," he continued, "and entirely through Mr. Foster's body. That would take a great deal of strength. Plus, if you look at the sword's hilt, you'll see it's aiming downward." He imitated the downward thrust. "Unless our murderer was over six feet tall, the blade would have come up from below." Again, he demonstrated the maneuver.

Having moved nearer the sword on the floor, I was looking at Hugo's demonstration from the side.

"Why is Mr. Foster's back arched?" I asked.

"I would say it was his last-ditch effort to pull free of the sword."

"But why is there no blood on that section?" I pointed to the open area on the sword between the chair back and where the sword entered Mr. Foster's body. It was completely free of blood.

"Maybe he arched his back when he first felt the sharp blade pierce his body."

I nodded my understanding.

The painting on the wall next to the bookcase was hinged and standing away from the wall. There was a safe behind the painting and its door stood open. Within the safe, we could see two leather-bound ledger's, several stuffed brown paper envelopes, and various other loose papers.

"Samuel, do you know if RC kept money in the safe?" Hugo asked.

"Yes, sir. It was his petty cash. Generally, there was around ten thousand dollars or so."

Hugo let out a long whistle. "I'd hardly call that amount of cash *petty.*"

"Neither would I sir," Samuel gave a rare chuckle, "but I'm not the head of a million-dollar movie studio either. And before you ask, yes, the money is missing."

"I know you have no real evidence, but do you feel this murder was committed as part of a robbery?"

"I would have absolutely no way of knowing that, sir."

"I know. I know. But give me your gut."

"My gut sir," he paused, "is no. I'm not sure why, but I think the murder was first and foremost. The money was simply, well, convenient."

"That's my gut too." Hugo smiled at him.

There was a knock at the front door. From my position inside the office, I watched as Mary, the fidgety maid, moved across the hall to the massive front door and slowly opened it, revealing a police officer and a detective. She showed them in and then across to the office door. The detective had his badge out, prepared to identify himself.

"Sean, how the devil are you?" Hugo boomed.

The detective first looked surprised, and then a smile split his face. Hugo began to step back over the pool of blood to greet the man when the knee of his raised leg hit the hilt of the sword still embedded in Clayton's chest. He teetered in the air for a moment, grabbing for the top of the throne to keep from falling. Although he saved himself, the rocking motion scooted the feet of the throne into the pooled blood, causing the throne to slip sideways, then topple to the floor, taking Clayton's body along with it. Still hopping with one foot in the air, Hugo tipped into Samuel's arms.

"Good catch!" barked the Detective and howled with laughter.

Samuel helped Hugo right himself. Hugo brushed himself off, turning red with embarrassment.

"Way to screw up a crime scene, Lister." The Detective was still laughing. "Oh, I forgot. Hugo Wainwright, the movie star."

"Has the green-eyed monster got hold of you, Sean?" Hugo moved to shake the man's hand.

"Nah, I'll let you keep your new job. I like the one I've got," the man retorted, clasping Hugo's hand and giving it a firm shake.

"Well, let me make the introductions then. Theo, this is Detective Sean O'Flaherty. Sean, this is Theodora Desmond."

"Oh, I know who you are, Miss Desmond. You sure look a far cry different than the last time I saw you."

I thought back to the last time I had anything to do with the police, certain it was during the Reginald Montgrieve case. "Oh, how did I look the last time you saw me?"

"Well, you were dressed in a lot less than that, and you were telling this ugly mug over here that you would love him until the stars turned cold." He had both hands over his heart and batted his eyes at Hugo.

I laughed, "I don't think I said it quite like that. So, you were at the opening last night then?"

"I sure was. Won a pair of tickets at my barbershop. I came the closest to guessing how many peppermints there were in a big jar the barbershop had in its front window. Eight hundred and twenty-eight was my guess, and there were eight hundred and thirty-three in the jar. I was sitting in the bleachers when you and Hugo got there." Again, he gave

Hugo one of those guy looks then a sharp clap on the back. Turning back to me, he continued, "Catching that fur coat was a pretty swell trick. Did you practice that?"

"As a of matter fact, I did." I already liked Detective Sean O'Flaherty.

"I told my girl you did. But she said that a famous movie star wouldn't have to plan something like that."

"Tell that sweet girl of yours that is what is known in the movie industry as marketing."

O'Flaherty laughed. He had a rich, infectious laugh. Unlike the tall and very muscled Hugo, O'Flaherty was slender with a sharp angular face. His features were, of course, very Irish. He had ginger hair, pale skin, and eyes the color of a four-leaf clover, flecked with end-of-the-rainbow gold shooting around the edge of the irises. They even sparkled with the mischief of a leprechaun.

"If you will move out of the way, Mr. Clumsy Movie Star," the detective chided Hugo, "the sergeant and I are going to set our murder victim back up. Then, Lister, I want you to tell me everything you observed before I got here."

The detective turned to Samuel. "I'm also going to want to talk to the staff and to Mr. Crawford." He then looked around, asking, "Hey, where is Mr. Crawford anyway? Looks like he'd be here too."

Samuel looked at me.

"Mr. Crawford has taken this news very badly." I pointed at the dead man saying, "Mr. Foster... Mr. Clayton Foster," I corrected, "has worked for Mr. Crawford for many, many years. Mr. Crawford's doctor has given him a sedative, and he's resting in his chambers at the moment."

"His doctor? How long did you know this man was dead before you called the police?"

"A couple of hours, maybe three?"

"Why did you wait so long to telephone the authorities?"

O'Flaherty barked.

"We," I said, gesturing at Hugo and me, "did not wait to notify you. Mr. Crawford practically collapsed upon finding Mr. Foster's body this morning. Samuel and Mr. Crawford's staff were concerned for the health and well-being of their employer, as well they should be. After all, there was nothing more they could do for poor Mr. Foster at that point, except lock up the room and preserve the scene. We," I gestured to Hugo and me again, "telephoned the police as soon as we were informed. And you do have my apologies, Detective, that Hugo and I failed to preserve the scene as well as Mr. Crawford's staff had done."

The inspector looked over at Hugo, the corners of his mouth turning up. "Hugo, you've found yourself quite a girl. She's smart, she kisses you in public, she is quite the looker, and she just took half the blame for your cock-up. I'd say you'd better keep this one."

"She is all of those things, I'll give you that. But Sean, what you see in public is a lot like that catching of the fur coat. It's all for show. Miss Desmond and I have a working relationship only. The public sees what we want them to see."

My heart sank. But as much as that cut me to the quick, I knew it was how it had to be.

"It was a fur cape, not a coat." I looked at Hugo with an annoyed expression. "But Hugo's right, Detective O'Flaherty, it is all for show. We have a working relationship only." I echoed Hugo's words for emphasis as if to finalize the issue, and we both nodded at each other curtly.

"Well, Lister, you are turning out to be a much better actor than I ever thought you'd be. If that kiss on the front page of the paper is all for show, then you have finally found your true calling."

"What picture on the front of what paper?" Hugo looked

puzzled.

"On the front of every newspaper in Los Angeles. And it's the picture of you kissing Miss Desmond here, right in front of this very house. Come to think of it," O'Flaherty added, staring straight at Clayton Foster's body, "this is the second murder at this house in less than a year."

"That isn't quite the case," Hugo quickly retorted. "Martin Musgrove's death was ruled an accident."

"Accidental with extenuating circumstances," O'Flaherty pointed out, holding up a finger.

"Be that as it may, there has only been one murder. But that wasn't the point I set out to make. Like the incident with Martin Musgrove, Mr. Foster's death occurred in the evening, an evening when there was a party going on in this house with no fewer than three hundred people in attendance, just like the night Mr. Musgrove met his untimely end. I'm bringing this up right now because, if you follow proper police procedure, you are about to try to interview three hundred of this city's most influential people. It will be no small task, and it will create plenty of hard feelings towards the police. And you—yourself—will receive at least fifty complaints against you from those same people and an equal number from their attorneys. So, speaking from personal experience, you might save yourself the grief and headache that brings by narrowing your list of suspects and witness pool before following 'proper police procedure.' But do as you wish; it's merely a suggestion."

O'Flaherty's brow creased. I could tell he was deep in thought.

"Excellent point." He pursed his lips and stroked his chin.

Then he was back to business. O'Flaherty sent Samuel to round up the staff, and Hugo suggested that he take them all upstairs to the ballroom.

As Samuel turned to leave, Hugo called out, "Samuel." He

stopped to listen without turning, "would you please send in young Mister Densmore?"

"Densmore?" It was O'Flaherty's turn to look puzzled.

"Yes, Willard left the police force to become my personal secretary and valet."

"A valet and personal secretary? What the hell do you need one of those for? And what does Densmore know about being a valet?" scoffed O'Flaherty.

"Very little sir, but the pay is much better," Densmore called out cheerily from the far side of the foyer as he and Seedy strode across. "But currently it would appear that you could use someone familiar with police procedure, and I can guarantee you, sir, I know a great deal about that." Nodding toward Hugo and then to me, he added, "I hope you will forgive both Seedy and me, Miss Desmond, Mr. Wainwright. We were going stir crazy cooped up in that parlor. We could hear all the commotion going on. This front hall echoes something fierce."

"Perfect then, Densmore; get in here," said O'Flaherty, nodding to him. "Miss Desmond, that will be all for now, but if we have any further questions we will be in touch," he added with a nod.

Hugo nodded at me and smirked. What was up with all this infernal head bobbing? I started to protest being dismissed, but as Samuel exited the room, passing in front of me, he too gave me a slight nod. However, his head bob was one of those "follow me" nods. So, rather than cause a squabble, I decided to acquiesce. Densmore and the sergeant were already in the process of righting the Throne of Power, bringing poor Clayton's body, still attached by the sword through his chest along with it. I nodded gracefully, looking down my nose toward both Hugo and O'Flaherty. I didn't care which one I was addressing, but I was going to get my nod in too. I turned and marched after Samuel, my heels clacking loudly on the marble floor of the tomb-like foyer, with Seedy following close behind me.

# 6

Seedy and I were right behind Samuel. As he moved across the foyer closer to the far staircase, he called out softly, "Mary."

The fidgety woman jumped up from a small sitting area hidden by the curve of the staircase and rushed over to him. She stood bolt upright and didn't speak.

"Gather the staff in the ballroom. Tell each one that you are speaking on my behalf and that they need to be there within the next fifteen minutes. Now, tell me of Mr. Crawford."

"I called in two of the gardeners and had them assist him to his bedchamber, sir. Mrs. Brumley was there, sir, and she removed his shoes and got him all nicely tucked up, sir."

"Good, now be off with you." He gave her a shooing motion, and she hurried away.

Samuel was the "RC" of his realm. No one questioned his authority nor balked at his command. He proceeded across the hall back toward the parlor where Seedy and Mr. Densmore had previously been sequestered.

I hurried up next to Samuel and asked, "How did the gardeners get Mr. Crawford upstairs? We were in the office. We would have heard, if not, seen anyone coming through the foyer. This room is like an amphitheater."

"They used the elevator, Ma'am. It goes to both the second and third floors as well." And he continued to lead the way toward the parlor.

Once inside, he closed the door. He didn't motion for us to sit, but instead turned to us and spoke directly to me.

"I am so very sorry, Ma'am, but I must be brief. I'm sure the police will want to question me as well. However, before they do, there is still another urgent matter that needs to be handled. Normally, Mr. Foster would handle anything that had to do with the studio in times such as these, but... " He stopped speaking abruptly, taking several seconds before chokingly adding, "but he can't." His eyes brimmed with tears. "I have worked for Mr. Crawford and Mr. Foster for soon to be eighteen years. This tragedy is exceedingly difficult for me as well. Please excuse me."

He paused for a long moment, pulled a handkerchief from an inside pocket, dabbed at his eyes, then finally regained his composure. "There is a crucial meeting scheduled for today. It is with the investors for your new movie. It cannot be rescheduled because one of the investors says he is leaving town tomorrow morning. It is the presentation of the prospectus showing how the investors' funds will be used. Normally, Mr. Crawford moderates these types of meetings, and Mr. Foster would do the presentation and talk about the numbers. I am telling you this because, without the guidance of Mr. Crawford or Mr. Foster, I need someone's help and I know Mr. Crawford trusts you implicitly."

"Oh Samuel, as much as I greatly appreciate your and Mr. Crawford's confidence in me, I'm not sure what I can do. I know nothing of the numbers associated with this or any other production."

"The numbers have already been calculated, Ma'am. The originals are on Mr. Foster's desk, and Edwina, Mr.

Crawford's secretary, has the copies for the investors. All that is needed at this point is someone to moderate the meeting, present the figures, and ensure the investors that their money is in good hands."

"Is that all?" I gave him a mirthless chuckle.

Samuel just stood there, his eyes imploring. Seedy hadn't said a word up to then. When she spoke, her voice was almost a whisper.

"You can do it, Theo. I'll help you. I'm pretty sure I can read a prospectus. If you'll moderate the meeting and mollify the investors, I'll present the figures."

I looked at her with a smile. She was one of the bravest people I'd ever met. It would seem there was no challenge she wasn't up for, and that decided my course of action. If Seedy could do it, so could I.

"All right Samuel, we'll take care of it."

"Wonderful, Ma'am. That door between the stairs was only ever used by one person, Mr. Foster. It was his shortcut to Mr. Crawford's office. The office you saw downstairs in the private quarters is…was Mr. Foster's office."

He pulled out his key ring and removed one key.

"This is the key to the door between the stairs. As I said, the original prospectus is on Mr. Foster's desk. That door is self-locking, so you'll need the key to get both in and out. The meeting is scheduled for 1:30 today."

"Oh, my Lord, that's in less than ninety minutes!" exclaimed Seedy.

"Then we'd better hurry." I snatched the key from Samuel and started for the door. Turning back as we left the parlor, I called, "Ring for my car please, Samuel. We'll need to leave within the next fifteen minutes. And please make my apologies to Hugo for leaving without saying goodbye."

I was almost through the door when I turned again. "On second thought, forget about talking to Hugo for me."

"As you wish Ma'am," came his reply.

I barely heard it as we rushed toward the little hidden door.

# 7

As we passed through the door, Seedy gave an audible gasp.

"I know," was my automatic response. "Amazing, isn't it?"

I showed her over to the elevator, but the door wouldn't open. At first, I didn't understand and pulled harder on the knob. Seedy reached across me and pushed the call button.

"I still can't believe RC has two elevators in his house," she said.

We heard a lock click. I turned the knob once more and the door opened easily, revealing the tiny box. Seedy and I climbed in and closed the door. There were only two buttons.

*I could have sworn Samuel told us that the elevator went to the two floors above as well. But it couldn't. If it did, it would open right in the middle of the landing to the ballroom.*

Seedy pressed the lower button, there was the slightest of jerks, and we began our descent. When we reached the ground floor there was the now familiar small bump and I opened the door.

Again, Seedy gasped. I headed toward the green leather topped desk to start our search for the original prospectus. It wasn't hard to find, sitting front and center on Clayton's massive desk, a space so immaculately sparse and meticulously organized that it would have been impossible not to see the folder clearly marked, "Investor Prospectus." Seedy slipped into the big black leather desk chair and opened the folder.

Looking up at me, she asked with a laugh, "Don't you hate it when your feet don't touch the floor?"

It was one of our pet peeves, and we both always commented when it happened. I could only assume that Mr. Foster's chair was adjusted to his height. And I knew that to be much taller than the five-foot three-inch height that Seedy and I shared. As Seedy opened the file and began to study its contents, I noticed the only other thing on Clayton Foster's desk top, a manuscript. I picked it up, pulled open the cover and looked at the title page. *Women of Distinction.* It had no author's name below the title. That was odd. I thumbed to the synopsis page. I scanned it, then closed the manuscript and pitched it back on the desktop.

I glanced around the cavernous room in awe. I walked across the way to the seating area surrounding the huge fireplace. Even standing right behind one of the six Davenports, I still had a hard time grasping the immense proportions of the space. Beside the fireplace, on the wall closest to the bank of windows, hung a portrait of a much younger RC. The artist's style as well as the stunning realism led me to assume it was by the same artist that had painted the portraits of both Theodora and Reginald Montgrieve.

But instead of facing the artist like the two portraits with which I was already familiar, in this one RC was slightly turned and looking upward as though looking at something in the room. I followed his gaze which led to a small oil of some spring landscape. I thought maybe it was a painting by one of the old masters and priceless. But before I could walk over to look for the artist's signature on the canvas, my attention was snagged by the wall on the opposite side of the fireplace. It was blank and stood out like a sore thumb, as they say.

Except for the blank wall, the entire space was symmetrical. The focal point was the fireplace, anchoring the area. It was flanked by six matching sofas, two on each of the three open sides of the rug, all encircling the fireplace. Six matching craftsman tables were in front of the sofas, carefully centered in front of each. As my eye moved up, there was the portrait of RC. Above the fireplace, the small oil he seemed to be gazing at was neither to scale with the rest of the room, nor did it match the room's very masculine decor. And to top it all off, on the other side of the fireplace was that totally blank wall.

I walked over to get a closer look at the small oil painting. The painter's scrawled signature was not one I recognized. I looked more closely at the blank wall. High up was a nail. And as I moved around and caught it just right with the light, I could see that the wallpaper was slightly discolored. There had been a picture here. And judging from the size of the vague outline, it was the same size as RC's portrait.

"I've got it, I think," Seedy called out.

I turned to her as she was closing the file.

"Mr. Foster was one well-prepared man," she mused. "There are detailed notes on every collection of numbers in the report. All I'll need to do is draw their attention to the particular areas and read his notes." She stood up. "Are you ready to go?"

"Not really," I said warily. "But I don't think we have a choice."

Seedy and I moved to the elevator without giving the incredible room a backward glance.

# 8

When Seedy and I arrived at the studio offices, Edwina saw us come through the glass doors. Clearly, Samuel had called ahead and apprised her of the situation since she jumped out of her chair and ran to meet us. As Edwina drew near, I could see her eyes were swollen and rimmed with red, betraying that she'd been crying. I had only seen Edwina a few times and she was always in the background. For her to run to me, throw her arms around me, and sob into my shoulder was entirely unexpected.

"Oh, Miss Desmond, it is such a travesty. Clayton was such a wonderful man. I don't know how Mr. Crawford will go on without him."

I patted her back. "Mr. Crawford is indeed mourning his loss greatly. But I'm sure he will bounce back quickly and be as right as rain," I tried to say with encouragement.

Edwina pulled away from me and looked at me, confused.

"I don't know how you can say that," she said, leaving me bewildered. She let me go and moved back towards her desk.

"Edwina, where are these meetings usually conducted?" I asked.

She changed directions and moved towards a door. When she opened it, I could see a heavy walnut conference table surrounded by ten leather executive chairs, with an easel at the far corner of the table. It looked as if Edwina—or possibly Mr. Foster—already had the presentation ready. Four portfolios were lying on the table, three along one side and one at the head.

"This is where the gentlemen will sit," Edwina said, motioning to the three chairs. "Mr. Crawford's place is always at the head, and Clayton's place is next to Mr. Crawford, of course, next to the presentation cards," Edwina explained. "Mr. Crawford greets his investors only as a group once the meeting is ready to start. Why don't I show you to Mr. Crawford's office? You can wait there until all three investors arrive, and then you may convene the meeting."

She led us out of the room, closing the door behind her. Crossing the hall, she opened the door to a huge office with windows looking out onto Colossal Studio's immense backlot. Backlots primarily housed exterior building sets— dusty western towns, small modern villages and vast cityscapes. It wasn't like looking out at a mountain range or the ocean, but it was a swell view none the less.

"Could I get you some coffee while you wait?" Edwina offered.

We both shook our heads and Edwina departed, closing the door behind her. As I strode around the room looking at pictures of famous people and various awards, I heard a tone coming from RC's desk. I looked over. The yellow light on the interoffice communications system was lit up. Seedy noticed too.

"What does that mean?" she asked, pointing at the light.

"It means that we can hear them, but they can't hear us."

No sooner had the words left my mouth than I could hear Edwina welcoming the first of RC's investors.

"That is Ezra Blum of Blum Brothers Jewelers of New York

City," I informed Seedy. "They designed the new diamond and pearl mounting for the Duke's ruby. The Duke must have introduced them to RC."

I heard the clink of ice against glass and added, "Edwina must be fixing him a drink."

As another male voice joined the party, I explained, "That is our thoroughbred horse breeder, Grady Chesterfield."

Again came the clinking of ice going into a glass. And finally, voice number three joined the fray.

"How appropriate," I chuckled. "First comes the horse breeder, and bringing up the rear is the horse's ass, Mr. Raymond Housley Overholser. Tex, as he calls himself."

"Mister way-too-many-yellow-roses?" Seedy inquired.

"The very one," I said with a sneer.

There were the muffled noises of people moving around, the sound of chairs scuffing the floor, and then the yellow light went out. Silence filled RC's office.

"Dang! One of my grandfather's favorite sayings is, 'I'm as nervous as a long-tailed cat in a room full of rockin' chairs.' Right this minute I am too. Seedy, I've got butterflies."

"You are Theodora Desmond, world-renowned seductress of the silver screen. And just like old Samson, you can lead these men to their doom," she said in her most positive and uplifting timbre.

"To their doom?"

"That did sound a great deal more ominous out loud than it did in my head," she said with a chuckle. Just look at it as a role, another part to play. Theodora Desmond —siren businesswoman." She shrugged, and we both laughed.

After a long few minutes, Edwina stuck her head in the door.

"They are all in the conference room and waiting on you. I did not tell the gentlemen that they would not be meeting with RC, and I don't think any of them even know Clayton."

She looked from me to Seedy.

"It's show time! Let's get those smiles in place," I said to Seedy, doing my best imitation of Father. And with me in the lead, we headed across the hall.

I had a broad smile on my face as I confidently stepped quickly into the room with Seedy behind me. At least I hoped I looked confident, after taking in the pained expression on Edwina's face as she closed the door behind us.

"Gentlemen, I sincerely hope today finds you well." The smile now felt as if it were plastered on my face. "Grady, how are you today?" I put out my hand to shake his. I had already determined I would use their first names.

"I am doing quite well, Miss Desmond. Thank you for asking."

"Oh, please call me Theo," I said, shaking his hand, but not before turning my palm up. He immediately turned it back even. Fifty-Fifty, I knew the score and moved on.

"Ezra, I trust you are doing well also. I have to say, we got so caught up in our shoptalk last night at the party, it completely slipped my mind to tell you what a superb job your family's company did on the choker that now holds the Rose of Kintyre."

Ezra's face lit up radiant with pride. "That is true praise indeed," he responded, "coming from a lady who is celebrated for her own jewel collection. Thank you, Theo." This time, he thrust out his hand first. I clasped it and turned mine so that it was on top. He thought nothing of it and shook.

In my best Texas twang, I greeted the last of the three.

"Well, Tex, I have to thank you. Four dozen yellow roses are pretty damn impressive!"

I thrust out my hand, and just as he started to take it, I drew it away.

"Now before I let you get hold of my hand again, Tex, I

have to make sure I'm not going to get caught up in another one of your fisherman stories about who has the biggest fish."

Chesterfield snorted, and Tex tried to laugh it off. But I could tell my comment hadn't set well with him. I clasped his still outstretched hand and gave it a quick, very firm handshake.

"I was not aware that actresses attended financial meetings of the investors," Tex drawled.

"They do if they are conducting that meeting, Tex."

Tex looked aghast and began to voice his disbelief and displeasure. After the Texas oilman muttered a few complaints, Chesterfield joined in, but I was determined to forge ahead. I held up a hand.

"RC has had a death in his family. He values your time, so rather than try to reschedule and cause any of you to incur extra traveling expenses and the loss of more time from your regular schedule, he asked me to conduct the meeting. I have to say, gentlemen, that I'm only here to be the pretty face of business. Miss Cecilia Schofield is the brains behind the figures. Miss Schofield." I gestured to Seedy.

Cecilia stood and moved to the chart.

"If you will open your prospectus, gentlemen, and turn to page one, we will begin with the allocation of funds and finish with projected profits."

"I don't know what RC's playing at here," Tex blustered, "sending a woman whose sole purpose in life is to play 'make-believe' in here to tell us how our money is going to be used. Suddenly I don't feel so good about my investment."

"I have to agree with Mr. Overholser here, Miss Desmond," Chesterfield chimed in. "I had no idea that RC Crawford relied on a woman to handle money and profits." With that, he sat back in his chair and crossed his arms in a huff.

Ezra, to his credit, said nothing.

They had no idea I was not a woman, but still I was

seething at their reaction. I could hardly believe their arrogance. How in the world, I wondered, must Seedy feel at this moment? I knew that she and I both were fighting to look stoic.

Tex rose from his chair, commanding, "You tell RC I'll give him seventy-two hours to show up and conduct this meeting properly, or I'm pulling out." Chesterfield was moving to his feet and agreeing as well. Although he seemed to be reluctant, Ezra slowly did the same. Overholser and Chesterfield immediately stormed from the room while Ezra tarried, as if he had something to say, but then he changed his mind and followed the other two out. Seedy and I were left standing alone. Edwina stepped into the room.

"That went better than I expected. At least there wasn't any cursing," she said, and smiled faintly.

I walked back to the reception area, found the bar, and silently made three Gibsons. I handed one to each of the two ladies and kept the third for myself, finally saying, "Ladies, we need a plan."

The three of us drank our Gibsons and paced the floor for nearly two full hours, trying to come up with a solution. Maybe RC would be ready to conduct the meeting in three days but perhaps not. In either case, we'd still have the problem of the presentation. Even if RC was back, Mr. Foster would not be returning.

"If RC can conduct the meeting, I could coach Mr. Densmore to deliver the presentation," Seedy proposed excitedly.

"That could work if we knew for sure that RC could moderate. But at this point, there is no way of knowing that. I think we need a contingency plan."

"A solid contingency plan," threw in Edwina.

And we paced some more.

"Too bad we can't find a few strong wealthy women to

invest. They would love that a woman was in charge and conducting the meetings," quipped Edwina.

"You have a contradiction in terms there, my dear Edwina." Seedy sounded a little tipsy. "There are strong women for sure. But I don't know of any strong and wealthy women willing to take on men like Tex and Chesterfield. Any woman like that would be considered a demon from hell in today's society."

We all broke into laughter, so much so that a tear was making its way down Edwina's cheek. I had just started to take a sip of my cocktail when it came to me.

Suddenly, I remembered that I actually did know a woman who had once been described as the Demon from Hell. "Oh, My God!" I exclaimed.

Edwina and Seedy immediately sobered.

"Seedy, where do you think Georgie would be right now?"

"Georgie? You are not possibly thinking of sending Georgie in to take RC's place."

I snorted, nearly spraying my two companions with gin, picturing Georgie standing in front of those three men with his hip cocked out and his hand perched on it.

"No, I need to get someone's telephone number from him."

"Whose number?" she asked, suddenly looking more interested.

"The Demon from Hell!"

# 9

I reached Georgie by telephone at the Drakestone Hotel.
Catering to a homosexual clientele, the Drakestone has a
nefarious reputation. Fifty years ago, it was a prominent
establishment with wealthy patrons; but now, although still
always very clean, it looks old and tattered. Its proprietress is
a female impressionist who goes by the name of Madam
Rochelle. The Drakestone houses a speak-easy whispered as
a place where female impressionists perform, although I have
never been quite sure what they perform. While I have been
to the Drakestone several times, I've never been to the speak-
easy.

When I initially met Georgie, he had a dressmaking studio
in one of the Drakestone's old ballrooms. He moved it
temporarily into the ballroom at my house during the
Montgrieve murder investigation but had subsequently
moved it back to the Drakestone after being exonerated in the
murder of silent movie star Reginald Montgrieve.
Montgrieve, as it turned out, was not dead at all.

I told Georgie I needed to contact one of his past clients. He
asked who, and when I replied Florence McCarney, I heard an
audible gasp on the telephone.

"Why in the world would you want to talk to the demon

from hell?" he asked.

"Precisely because that is what she is."

He asked me no further questions and gave me the woman's telephone number in San Francisco.

Florence McCarney is the wife of Aloysius McCarney, owner of the Happy Scotsman gold mine. I met the woman and her husband while Georgie operated his studio from my ballroom. He had been commissioned by the McCarneys to design a wedding dress for their daughter, Estelle. All three members of the McCarney family had attended the fitting. I entertained Florence and Aloysius while Georgie worked with Estelle. Mrs. Florence McCarney, to put it mildly, is a very domineering woman. Yet for reasons unbeknownst to me, the two of us hit it off from the start. She claimed that she and her husband were great fans. And to be quite honest, even if her husband were not a fan, he would never have had the courage to disagree with her.

That afternoon, Florence told me the story of the Happy Scotsman gold mine, and how she met her husband when he came to California from Scotland to seek his fortune. She had hated living around the rough men in the prospector's camp. She said most of the prospectors drank too much and bathed only on special occasions. And from her nose's point of view, those special occasions where way too few and far between. She insisted her husband work a new claim, well off the beaten path, and far away from the other prospectors; subsequently, far from any areas where miners were having any success finding gold. But Aloysius mined his new claim diligently.

One autumn day, he was almost buried alive when his mind shaft collapsed. Florence dug him out with her bare hands. Once he was safe, she forbade him to ever return to the mine. She decided herself, that they would move back to San Francisco where he would seek a job as a shop's clerk.

# All That Glitters

The next morning, while Florence was still sleeping, Aloysius snuck out of the house and stole back into the mine. Crawling back into his now deepened mind shaft, he discovered that the collapse had opened a gold vein. That vein eventually became one of the richest claims in California history, the Happy Scotsman Mine.

Aloysius may own one of the richest gold mines in California history, but it is Florence who runs the business. Workers cower in her wake. She was and is a force to be reckoned with, and in my current predicament I needed that reckoning force. I placed the telephone call to Florence.

As a rule, I would have had Seedy call the McCarney's residence and had her request to speak with Mrs. McCarney. However, Seedy had asked me if she might take the evening off. In the nearly ten months we had been at this—this masquerade? I wasn't even sure what to call what we were doing anymore. During that entire time, she had never asked for any time away. Legitimately, she had Sundays off like everyone else, but she never took them.

As it turned out, while she and Mr. Densmore had been isolated in RC's parlor, she'd confessed to the charade that we perpetrated to secure Georgie's release from jail. They'd had a great laugh. After talking some more and armed with the knowledge that Seedy was neither married, committed to another, nor grieving over a lost love, Mr. Densmore had taken the initiative to ask her out on a date for this very evening.

That left me to place the call to the McCarney's residence myself. To maintain proper propriety, I impersonated Seedy when talking to the McCarney's butler. As luck would have it, Mrs. McCarney was indeed at home when I rang, and she accepted my call.

"Hello?" She was imperious as she answered the telephone, but I could hear the intrigue in her voice.

"Good evening, Mrs. McCarney. I hope my call doesn't come during your dinner hour?"

"No, no, Miss Desmond. We are late diners."

"That is good then. As I know your time is precious and that you are a very frank woman yourself, I will omit any further pleasantries and get directly to the purpose of my telephone call, if that is all right with you?"

Her voice brightened.

"That would be more than acceptable, my dear."

I went on to explain the situation in detail, telling Mrs. McCarney I was calling to beseech her wisdom and guidance.

"That man is a rogue!" she exclaimed.

I agreed with her. Then I waited while the telephone remained silent for a long pause. I knew the line was not dead because I could hear her breathing, so I waited, trying my best to be patient.

When she spoke, she was all business. She began by barking out orders, and I did my best to take notes. You could tell she was a woman very much accustomed to being in control and being obeyed.

"Get in touch with Mr. Crawford's secretary. Tell her you'll need Mr. Crawford's dossiers on all three of these investors. We need to know everything there is to know about our adversaries. It's a great deal easier to obtain what we want, if we know what they want. And more importantly, what frightens them."

I felt a knot form in my stomach. Without a doubt, I now knew why this woman was so formidable.

"Do you think Mr. Crawford will have such files?"

"My dear, of course he will. One doesn't get to the top of any industry without knowing the golden rule."

"Do unto others…?"

She cut me off.

"Lord no, child!" she laughed. "Know thine enemy!" she

said, with great aplomb. "I will take my private rail car to Los Angles first thing tomorrow. I should arrive late afternoon. Would you please have those dossiers sent over to the new Beverly Wilshire Hotel? I've been looking for a reason to stay there since they opened. Seems I've found a good one. Are you available for a dinner tomorrow night?"

"Yes, Ma'am, I am. However, I don't want to waste your time at all. I haven't spoken with Mr. Crawford as of yet. I have no idea if he will be available to conduct the second meeting himself or not."

"Nonsense! It's been my experience that those who are stricken severely with grief do not miraculously recover overnight. It is a process that takes time. Sometimes a great deal of time. But be that as it may, being prepared for all outcomes is by far the best strategy. I will meet you tomorrow night at eight-thirty at the Brown Derby on Wilshire. It is one of my Aloysius's favorite places to dine."

Then abruptly switching topics, she asked, "Do you own any jewelry that was designed by Blum Brothers Jewelers?"

"No, Ma'am, I don't," I replied, reluctantly. "I often use a local designer. And I also have several pieces by Cartier, Tiffany, Harry Winston, and Coco Chanel, but not any by Blum Brothers." I was hoping that was the truth. Honestly, I wasn't sure where Molly had bought most of her jewelry. "I was, however, fortunate enough once to wear the Rose of Kintyre, which belongs to the Duke of Kintyre and Lorne. Blum Brothers designed the new diamond and pearl choker that now anchors the ancient ruby."

"Is the Duke still in town?" she countered. "If so, contact him and inquire as to whether or not he would permit you to wear it for this meeting."

I must have stammered in my reply, stunned at her thinking me so brazen as to merely telephone the Duke and ask to wear his wife's necklace, because she instantly barked back, "Good God girl, this is no time to stand on ceremony."

At that, I jumped. "I will telephone him immediately," I assured her.

"Then I think we have conducted our business thus far. I will see you tomorrow at eight-thirty for dinner. Oh, and Miss Desmond?"

"Yes, Ma'am?"

"Eight-thirty means eight-thirty. It does not mean the fashionably late time of eight-forty."

She hung up before I had a chance to respond.

# 10

When my conversation with Florence McCarney abruptly ended, I immediately telephoned the Beverly Hills Hotel, where the Duke and Viscount were staying.

"Good Evening, Beverly Hills Hotel, Mr. Bell speaking. How may I assist you this evening?"

I used my best impression of Seedy.

"Good evening, this is Miss Cecilia Schofield, calling on behalf of Miss Theodora Desmond. Please connect me with the Duke of Kintyre and Lorne's bungalow. "

"Please tell Miss Desmond that we regret to inform her that the Duke, as well as the Viscount, has checked out."

I found this information not only to be a great surprise but also a bit disconcerting.

"I wasn't aware that the Duke and Viscount were leaving. Have they gone home to Europe?"

Mr. Bell's voice took on a curt air. "I sincerely doubt that a Duke or a Viscount would consult anyone other than their own personal secretaries as to their traveling plans."

I had forgotten that I was impersonating Seedy.

"Oh, Mr. Bell, I'm so sorry. Please forgive my impertinence. I was merely thinking out loud. Would you know if they left any forwarding information? Perhaps I might be able to intercept them during their travels. Miss Desmond wishes very much to speak with the Duke."

Mr. Bell gave a snort and a slight laugh. I assumed he had forgiven me for overstepping my station, especially since his own station was certainly no higher, and maybe less so, than Seedy's.

"The Duke and Viscount have taken a house in Beverly Hills. The Duchess arrived two days ago. Seems living at a hotel did not agree with her; therefore, the Duke rented an estate." Although still fairly pleasant, his tone had taken on the slightest hint of bitterness. "They have left an address and a telephone number." He gave those to me, and I bid him a pleasant good evening.

So, the Duchess of Kintyre and Lorne had come to Hollywood. Since the necklace rightfully belonged to her, I decided I should probably ask her if I could borrow it. Besides, Charlie had talked so highly of his mother that I sincerely wanted to meet her. He adored his mother, who always insisted on calling him "Charles." He in turn described her as charming and gracious. I wanted to see for myself if she was truly as wonderful as he painted her, or if he only saw his mother through rose tinted glasses.

I asked the operator to connect me to their number. One more time, I impersonated Seedy. I asked for the Duke, since I had yet to be introduced to the Duchess.

"Hello, my dear. So good to hear from you. Have you news as to RC's condition?" His concern was sincere.

"No, Your Grace. I'm afraid I don't know anything as of yet."

"Then, to what do I owe the pleasure of your ring up?"

"I have heard that the Duchess has joined you."

"Yes, she has." He sounded delighted.

"I was hoping to welcome her to Hollywood. But not wanting to come off as one of those brash Americans, I thought it best to speak with you first and arrange an introduction.

He laughed.

"Oh, my dear, I do so appreciate your efforts toward European propriety. I will be happy to make the proper introductions."

"That would be wonderful. I know this is exceedingly short notice, but would the two of you be available for a luncheon tomorrow?"

"Not short notice at all. I would love to introduce the Duchess to someone who can help her meet other members of Hollywood society."

"Wonderful! Shall we say one o'clock at the Coconut Grove Restaurant at the Ambassador Hotel?" Like Mrs. McCarney and the new Beverly Wilshire Hotel, I had been dying to find a reasonable excuse to visit the opulent nightclub and eatery.

"That will be perfect, my dear. We will see you there tomorrow at one o'clock."

We ended our call, and I moved to the next task on the list of instructions Florence had given me. I called Edwina at her home.

It would seem that RC did indeed have dossiers on all three men, and Edwina said she would see that they were couriered to Mrs. McCarney at the Beverly Wilshire the next day.

With Mrs. McCarney's orders completed, I had Wallace arrange for Randel to bring my automobile around. I rang upstairs and spoke with Claudette, informing her of my plans for the following day. I told her to get in touch with Georgie to make sure I had something appropriate to wear for lunch with a Duchess.

I then hopped up from behind the desk, wincing from my throbbing feet. I'd been in these shoes far too long. But no matter, I snatched up my fox, gloves, and handbag from the wingback chair by the desk and made my way toward the door. I was about to be an uninvited, unannounced guest at the home of RC Crawford. That was never a particularly good idea.

# 11

The sun was nearly down, and the sky had become a velvety aubergine when we arrived at RC's front gate. Randel started to crank his window down to speak with the guard, but I told him to pull forward. I would talk to Curtis. I knew Randel didn't consider this proper behavior, but he didn't question me. The guard approached and started to walk around the English drive automobile to the driver's side. I cranked my window down quickly.

"Good evening Curtis. " Looking surprised, he tipped his hat to me and changed directions immediately.

"Good evening, Miss Desmond. This has been a dark day indeed, hasn't it, Ma'am?"

I nodded. "It has indeed. I know that I have no appointment, nor did I call before I came, but I was hoping Mr. Crawford might agree to see me. Curtis, I wondered if you might use your influence with Samuel to get him to at least inquire of Mr. Crawford as to his availability."

Curtis gave a quick bark of laughter. "Alas, Miss, I have no influence with old Samuel, but I will be more than happy to ring up to the house and speak with him on your behalf." He smiled.

"I would be so appreciative, kind sir."

Again, he tipped his hat and excused himself as he walked back to the guard house to make the telephone call.

He was only gone for a few moments before returning.

"Ma'am, Samuel says that Mr. Crawford is in no condition to receive guests, but if you would like to speak with him, he would be more than happy to answer any questions he could."

I nodded in the affirmative, and he moved back towards the gatehouse. In moments the gates were swinging open, and Randel drove through. When we reached the house, Randel opened my door and helped me out.

The estate was just as well-lit as it had been the night before at the party. Colored lights twinkled from the tower balcony some four stories above. From the front lawn, the sound of splashing water came from the swimming pool-sized fountain that shot a plume of water some twenty feet into the air before gravity caused it to crash back down to the glistening pool below. But despite the festive sights and sounds, there was a somber pall to the place. I walked alone up the sidewalk and towards the house.

Just before I reached the massive doors, the one on the right began to swing inward. Mary was pulling the big door open, and I could see Samuel waiting for me, his back erect and hands crossed in front of him. He stood in front of the ornately carved mahogany table in the center of the room. Although impeccably dressed, he looked haggard and beyond weary. His face seemed to be struggling to create its usual pleasant and congenial demeanor, but it was not being successful. I walked through the open door.

"Good evening Mary," I said as I passed her.

"Good evening, Miss," she replied, with a curtsy.

I moved in a direct path towards Samuel. Now that I was here, I wasn't sure what to say or do next. As I approached, Samuel extended his hand toward the parlor.

# All That Glitters

"Shall we speak in private, Ma'am?"

I nodded my consent, shifted directions, and followed him. Once we were secure within the parlor, he gestured for me to sit. I declined, for two reasons. I knew Samuel would not sit in my presence, and also, I was simply too nervous. I preferred to pace no matter how much my shoes pinched.

"Could I offer you something to drink?" He pointed to a cart where several cut crystal decanters held liquors of various shades, accompanied by a matching crystal ice bucket with tongs, and again matching rocks glasses.

"No, I don't think so. I'd better keep my wits about me."

He gave a dry laugh and nodded his agreement.

"Samuel, could you please explain to me what is going on? I did as we discussed this morning. I tried to conduct the meeting with the investors, but that ended in what I would classify as a disaster. I have no information as to what happened *here* after I left. I am completely unclear how to proceed in regard to the investors, Mr. Crawford's well-being, and the murder of Mr. Foster."

Samuel was silent for a long moment. When he first began to speak, it was if he were trying to organize as well as edit his thoughts.

"I think I should start, Ma'am, with the events that took place after your departure. The police interviewed the entire staff, gardeners included. I requested they interview me first, so I could watch over the proceedings as well as the processing of the crime scene on Mr. Crawford's behalf. Detective O'Flaherty thought it odd for some reason, but Mr. Wainwright assured him I would not obstruct their investigations.

"In fairly short order, the police had covered almost every surface in Mr. Crawford's study with black powder, saying they were dusting for fingerprints. They confiscated one of Mr. Crawford's antique blades, the one used to stab Mr.

Foster. They also removed Mr. Foster's body, still seated in Mr. Crawford's throne. It was disgraceful." He pulled a face of disgust.

"At first, the police looked toward Mr. Crawford as the murderer," he continued. "But his whereabouts could be accounted for all through the evening, and most of the early morning hours as well. The last of the party guests didn't leave until almost three-thirty in the morning. After that, I myself helped Mr. Crawford prepare for bed."

With a sigh, Samuel explained, "Neither Detective O'Flaherty nor Mr. Wainwright could find a motive for Mr. Crawford to have killed his lawyer and personal secretary of over twenty years. Before they left, Mr. Wainwright told me that the police thought Mr. Foster had been murdered around midnight. If that's the case, it could have been any one of hundreds of people. At midnight, the house was packed."

"I would have to agree with you." We had both started to pace in opposite directions. "Tell me about RC. How is he?"

"He slept off the effects of the laudanum around one-thirty this afternoon. He contacted his brother and made arrangements to use his brother's home in San Francisco. He had his private rail car readied, and he left shortly after speaking with the police."

"He what?" I bellowed. "Well then, I guess the investor meeting is inconsequential, and I should wash my hands of it."

"No, Ma'am. On the contrary." Samuel spoke without getting excited or raising his voice. "I was to call you first thing in the morning to tell you that all Mr. Crawford's resources are at your disposal. He needs you to make sure the investors are sated, if not happy. He has made his entire staff, his house, and his automobiles available for you to use however you see fit."

I started to speak, but Samuel raised his hand.

"He told me that he owes you an explanation, and he assured me that upon his return you would have it. The most important thing he wanted me to stress to you is, *above all,* discretion is paramount."

"What in the devil does he mean by discretion? You told me that this morning as well." I shook my head.

Even as I said the words, I was taking in Samuel's countenance.

"Samuel, what am I supposed to be discreet about?" I was sure he knew the answer to my question, but I could also tell by the determination in his eyes that he would never tell me without RC's explicit permission. "Never mind. I know you know, but I also know you are devoutly loyal. I just hope I figure out what it is on my own before I accidentally divulge something I should not."

It would seem that Mrs. McCarney had been right about being prepared. I walked over to the decanter, poured myself a Scotch with no ice and swallowed it down in one gulp. I picked up my fur, gloves, and handbag and departed.

As Randel drove me home, I was lost in thought, utterly baffled as to why, on God's green earth, RC would place so much trust in me. I made up my mind to telephone my half-sister, Molly, in Texas. I needed to ask her if RC had ever placed this type of burdensome responsibility on her.

# 12

By the time I returned home that evening, it was fast approaching eleven o'clock. I picked up the telephone to call Molly, then remembered it was nearly one in the morning in Texas. So, I decided to wait until morning to call.

Morning, however, also brought clearer thinking. As I awoke, having slept fitfully, I instinctively knew that RC would never have entrusted his studio to her control, so I decided not to call. Instead, I put on my robe, brushed my teeth, sat in my proper chair, and waited for Claudette and Seedy to burst through the doors as usual. But on this particular morning, the door opened gently, and both ladies entered slowly, deeply engrossed in a hushed conversation peppered with stifled giggling. Without a doubt I knew the topic of their conversation. It was Mr. Densmore.

"Oh, no you don't, ladies," I warned. "Come on, spill. I want to hear all about it."

"We don't have any time for that conversation now," Seedy chided. "We have to get down to business."

"My business is no fun at all, and yours is. I'm opting for fun first," I laughed, motioning them to hurry and sit.

As Claudette poured the coffee, Seedy giggled and started in.

"You know, Willard and I went to see *Samson and Delilah*."

"Oh, Willard is it?" I asked. "Already on a first name basis? And you saw *Samson and Delilah*, did you? I hear the leading lady is awe-inspiringly beautiful as well as being astonishingly talented."

"Oh, quit fishing for complements, Eddie," Seedy replied. "And yes, we are on a first name basis."

"Does he call you Cecelia or Seedy?'

"What do you think?" she grinned and blushed.

Claudette and I both giggled.

"I was glad we were going to see a picture I had already seen," Seedy added, "just in case."

"Just in case there was necking going on while the lights were down," I teased. At once Seedy turned beet red, and I knew I had hit the nail on the head. "So, was there?"

"No," she said sounding almost disappointed. "Willard had never seen a talkie before, so he was totally mesmerized."

"Oh, like you've seen so many," Claudette cooed in her lush French-accented English.

"I've seen two. *Samson and Delilah* and *The Jazz Singer*," Seedy said, in justification.

"Oh, so worldly," Claudette countered, unable to hide her smile.

Seedy went on to tell us about their dinner and the long walk in the park afterward, holding hands. Mr. Densmore had offered to hire a taxi to bring her home since he had no car, but Seedy had already made arrangements with Randel to pick her up at ten o'clock, right after he had dropped me off at RC's.

The telephone rang, and Claudette hurried to answer it with her standard, "Hello, Desmond residence."

She listened for a moment, said, "Let me give you to her secretary," then handed the telephone to Seedy.

"This is Cecelia Schofield, Miss Desmond's secretary."

Seedy listened quietly to the person on the other end of the line, then replied, "I'm afraid ten o'clock will not work. However, she could see you at eleven or eleven-thirty." Again, she listened before saying, "Then Miss Desmond will see you at eleven." Seedy hung up.

"That's interesting. It seems the studio's attorney, Mr. Crenshaw, needs to meet with you this morning."

"The studio's attorney? I thought Clayton Foster was the attorney for the studio," Claudette probed, looking puzzled.

"Yesterday Seedy and I talked with Edwina, Mr. Crawford's secretary. She told us that since the studio has grown so, it now has an entire team of attorneys. Mr. Foster, it seems, was more a supervisor, most of the time putting his seal of approval on big studio policy changes or special interest connections, whatever that means. I wonder why he needs to talk to me. Whatever it is," I remarked, "I hope he'll be brief. I have a luncheon at the Coconut Grove at one o'clock with the Duke and Duchess."

"I don't have any lunch on your schedule," Seedy interrupted. "Our Duke? And his wife, the Duchess?"

"I made the appointment last evening while you were out. And of course, it's 'our' Duke. I don't know any other Dukes. The Duchess arrived just two days ago, and I want to meet her. Besides, Mrs. McCarney wants me to borrow the Rose of Kintyre choker. Oh, and by the way, I have dinner with her — Mrs. McCarney, that is — this evening at eight-thirty at the Brown Derby."

"I take one evening off, in almost a year..." she whined, rolling her eyes.

"It just goes to show how lost I'd be without you," I countered and gave her an exaggerated smile, then rolled my eyes right back at her. I quickly related my telephone call with Florence McCarney, including all about her version of the Golden Rule and her views on being fashionably late. I looked at the clock.

"I'll tell you all about it later, but right now I suppose I'd better get ready for Mr. Crenshaw's visit."

Seedy pulled out my calendar and had everything scheduled in a flash. Then she whipped out her pad and started reading down her list.

"The new electric gates are being installed tomorrow. The installation will take the better part of the day. Please be conscious of that with your comings and goings tomorrow. Thankfully we've already had the electricians out to run the electrical lines. I telephoned down to Mr. Truman to remind him that the electric gate opener company would be here tomorrow, and he requested a meeting with you. I was going to schedule him for this afternoon, but it sounds like you already have a full schedule now."

"I'll have to meet with him tomorrow. The following day is the investor meeting, and I'll need to be fully focused on that."

I set my cup and saucer on the silver tray. Claudette was already in motion towards the bathroom, and in seconds I could hear the water running in the shower.

When I exited the bath twenty minutes later, two separate outfits were lying on the bed. As I looked at the two ensembles, it appeared that I had yet another new business suit. This one was a chocolate brown worsted wool with a tiny robin's egg blue stripe running crisply through it. The jacket lapels were embroidered in a fleur-de-lis pattern of the same shade of blue. The suit was paired with a barely-blue silk blouse. Sitting on the floor in front of the ensemble were robin's egg blue shoes with a t-strap and five-inch heel.

"W-e-l-l," I said, lightly stroking the buttery soft wool. "It looks like I may be 'all business,' but not so much so that I'm reduced to wearing sensible brown shoes."

"That's for your meeting with Mr. Crenshaw."

Next to the business suit lay an ecru drop-waist dress with an intricate lace bodice, a pleated satin skirt, and a seed pearl-covered sash that melded the two together. There was a matching skull style hat with a small veil and seed pearls accenting the webbing. Again, five-inch heels were the shoes of choice.

"Ditch the hat and find me a headband instead," I suggested. "If I'm having lunch with someone I've never met, I don't want to spend the entire meal trying to see around those dang tiny pearls."

Claudette nodded her approval.

In just over forty-minutes, I was finally ready. I wore the enormous sapphire and diamond ring that had been patterned after Evalyn Walsh McLean's necklace, the one bearing the infamous Hope diamond. A three-strand choker of pearls circled my neck, and clipped to it was a removable pendant, one of the jewels that I had inherited from Reggie. The thirty-three karat emerald-cut aquamarine twinkled boldly from its place of pride at the hollow of my throat.

There was a knock at the door. Seedy popped into the room. "Golly, you look nice today. It's eleven o'clock, and Mr. Crenshaw has arrived. I had Wallace put him in the long gallery."

"My guess is Mr. Crenshaw is more like Mrs. McCarney than he is the typical Hollywood starlet," I said, as Claudette slipped my foot into the soft leather shoe.

"How's that?" Seedy asked.

"Eleven means eleven, not the fashionably late of eleven-ten," I chuckled.

"Judging from his rather bookish look, I would have to say, yes, you are correct."

Claudette finished fastening the strap on my shoe. I stood, straightening and smoothing my dress.

"Then there is nothing for it. Let's go hear what the man

has to say." And I marched out the door with Seedy at my side.

When we reached the long gallery, Wallace was in his position outside the door. As I approached, he opened the door and let it swing open into the room. I passed in, followed by Seedy. The man in the room stood as we entered; and Wallace reached in, clasped the doorknob, and closed the door as he left. Seedy had been spot on when she characterized him as "bookish." The man before me was of average height and rail thin. His suit, although of high quality, was ill-fitting. He had begun balding on top, his face was pinched, and his lips puckered like he had just bitten into a lemon. He wore thick-lensed wire-rimmed spectacles that magnified his bleary blue eyes to nearly the same size as that of a twenty-dollar gold piece. When he looked at me, I was reminded of one of those bug-eyed fish.

"Good day, Miss Desmond. I am Mortimer Crenshaw." He extended his hand as I approached.

"Good day, Mr. Crenshaw." I slid my palm into his clammy hand. He smiled up at me, and for a brief moment, I thought he might curtsy.

"Please, allow me to introduce my secretary, Miss Cecilia Schofield," I said as I gestured to Seedy. He bobbed his head, as did she. "To what do I owe the pleasure of your visit today, Mr. Crenshaw?"

"I am here today at the behest of Mr. Crawford. I will need your signature of acceptance on these documents," he announced, reaching for a black leather portfolio that lay on the sofa. "Shall we?" He gestured to the card table, and we walked toward the elegant knotty alder table with its inlaid marquetry top as he sorted through the papers. He pulled out a large set of documents and divided them into two stacks, the first an imposing stack of pages, the second only a single sheet, the signatory page.

"Exactly what are these documents you need me to sign?"

The man looked up at me in disbelief.

"Why, Miss Desmond, it is the temporary power of attorney conferring complete control of Colossal Studios and unrestricted access to Mr. Crawford's home to use as you see fit. You mean, Ma'am, you didn't know?"

Suddenly I was feeling faint. Without ceremony, and without offering one to anyone else, I pulled out one of the four chairs surrounding the gaming table and sat.

"I'm not sure I understand."

"Samuel, Mr. Crawford's manservant, told me that he had informed you."

I was pretty dang sure Samuel would take a dim view of being called a "manservant."

"Samuel did inform me that Mr. Crawford was giving me access to everything. However, it was not my understanding that 'access' meant putting me in charge of the entire studio."

"Miss Desmond, those are his very instructions. That you are to become acting studio head in Mr. Crawford's absence."

"Why?" I asked bewildered.

"Ma'am, I certainly have no idea as to why, but if I could just get your signature," he said, holding out his pen, "then the power will be transferred to you, and you can inquire for yourself."

I looked up at Seedy, finding her mouth was slightly agape. When she noticed me looking, she quickly shut it and gave me a baffled look.

When I hesitated to sign, Mr. Crenshaw shook the pen at me, "Ma'am this gives you the ability, among other things, to agree to reimburse the investors, if the situation should arise."

That was really the first thing Mr. Crenshaw had said that made sense. Shaking my head in confusion, I signed the papers. Immediately Mr. Crenshaw began to put the now signed documents back into his portfolio. He fastened the clasp, looked up, and gave his ill-fitting suit a brush, a motion that indicated he was finished with his business.

Mr. Crenshaw then fished in his pants pocket and pulled out a ring with three keys. He held them out and I took them. "As the new Chief Executive Officer," he said officiously, "here are your keys. One is to your office building at the Studio, one is to your private office within that building, and the last is the key to Mr. Crawford's home. I seriously doubt you will ever be in need of any of the keys since it is likely you will always be preceded to any of those locations by a member of your staff. If you need nothing further of me, I will bid you good day."

He moved toward the door as I just sat there, my elbow on the table and a set of keys dangling from my index finger.

"Oh, I almost forgot," he said, turning back to me. "Mr. Crawford has sent his Rolls-Royce over. He said that it's well known at all of the studio gates and by his gatekeeper. He suggests that you use it. He knew you would prefer your own chauffeur, so he has taken his personal driver with him."

He opened the door, passed through, and was gone.

The entire surreal encounter had taken nearly a full hour. I was due to be at the Coconut Grove at one o'clock, so I was going to have to hurry, especially since I needed to change clothes before leaving for the restaurant. With my new keys now clinched in my fist, I literally ran back to my bedroom, Seedy following closely behind. I was out of one dress and into the other in no time flat. After retouching my makeup, Claudette flew into the closet, returning with the headband I had requested. It was a complicated web of seed pearls with a large bronze topaz glittering at its center. I was also going to wear a new necklace I'd had designed by the same jeweler who designed the sapphire and diamond ring. It was a laurel wreath made of platinum and paved in diamonds. Set slightly off-center was a nearly forty karat canary yellow diamond. It had only fourteen facets, but it sparkled with a brilliant, almost sunshine-like radiance. When the jeweler had described what he wanted to create, I thought it sounded absolutely stunning, and he had not disappointed. My ears sported the topaz earrings that I had worn with the hijab made from a bedside tablecloth. The big difference this time was that both studs were visible. I dropped the ring of keys into the largest cream-colored leather clutch I'd ever seen.

"Wow! This thing is huge," I complained to Claudette.

"Georgie says handbags are much larger this season. He thinks it's because so many women have become 'working girls' and they need more space to carry things like money purses, brushes, lipsticks, compacts, and keys."

I tucked the large purse under my arm and shot out the door. I was supposed to meet the Duke and Duchess in a little over twenty minutes. At the bottom of the stairs, Wallace was waiting to assist me off the last step and usher me out the door.

As Wallace opened the front door, I saw Randel standing beside the open door of RC's Rolls-Royce. I hadn't planned to use it, but there was no time to switch. The sleek, low slung automobile was an eye-catching black and white, its interior all handcrafted burgundy leather and burl wood. I slipped into the seat to the smell of rich leather with a faint hint of cigar smoke.

As Randel closed the door, I suddenly felt cocooned in luxury. I took in my surroundings. The thick, hand-tooled leather of the privacy shield shut out the view forward. Between the two facing seats, a burl wood console housed a wet bar, fully stocked with a variety of liquors, all in Waterford decanters. The matching cut crystal glasses and ice bucket were nestled in their individual velvet-lined compartments, insuring no rattles when the car was in motion. I breathed in a long deep breath, held it for a moment, and exhaled it with a contented sigh.

As we pulled away from the house, I let all the events of the day thus far, flee from my mind as the blissfully smooth ride of the Rolls-Royce Phantom lulled me into a peaceful calm. By the time we pulled into the circle drive of the Ambassador Hotel, I felt renewed. I couldn't wait to give the food at the celebrated Grill of the Coconut Grove Nightclub a try. Little did I know that this was indeed the calm before the storm.

# 13

The door to my cozy cocoon opened, rousing me from my reverie as the hotel valet's hand slipped in to assist me. Exiting the Rolls proved much easier than my own Daimler. The door opened from the rear like my roadster, giving me more access.    And the Rolls rode closer to the ground, eliminating the high step off the running board, perfect for someone my height, not to mention in a dress and five-inch heels.

With the privacy shield up for the entire ride, I hadn't noticed that the Rolls was preceded by one of the studio's limousines. I only recognized it because I had borrowed it just two nights before to ferry my staff back and forth to the movie premiere.  As it pulled away, having relinquished its passengers, on the sidewalk in front of me stood the Duke. Next to him was a beautiful woman I took to be his wife, though quite unlike the Duchess I had created in my imagination. I'd envisioned a tall, gangling woman with that very British pinched face, bad teeth, and a pointed nose that, no matter how she looked at you, one always felt as if she were looking down her nose. This lady was nothing like that. Perhaps my height, she too wore five-inch heels.  She was bedecked in a lavender raw silk sheath that dropped to just below her knees. Over that was a sheer full-length jacket of lavender organza, the sleeves ending in a satin cuff with jewel buttons. And, of course, she wore lavender kid leather t-straps with five-inch heels. The look screamed Coco Chanel. But I then had to smile as I corrected myself because her hat was most definitely British, its brim as broad as a Mexican sombrero and swathed in lavender organza. Tucked under her arm was a handbag every bit as large as the one I was carrying. The Duke waved when he recognized me, then looked puzzled as Randel pulled away from the curb after leaving only me.

"How wonderful to see you, my dear," he called. As I walked towards the couple, he added, "Isn't RC with you?"

"No," I answered, looking baffled at the question.

"Isn't that his car?"

"Yes, it is," I said, as I reached the couple. "But that is a long story and one best told in a more private surrounding, not standing in a portico."

The Duke nodded his understanding. "My dear," he spoke to the Duchess, "I would like to introduce Miss Theodora Desmond. Theodora, this is my wife, Lady Elizabeth Pennington, Duchess of Kintyre and Lorne."

We each nodded to the other, then I reached out, and the Duchess clasped my hand. We exchanged that European kiss just above each cheek, a custom I was beginning to enjoy.

"I have a table reserved for us. Shall we go in?" I asked, with a slight gesture towards the door.

The doorman held the door for all three of us as I led the way. Before we could reach the concierge desk just to the right of the entrance, a young man in a navy pin-stripe suit jumped up and rushed around the counter to greet us.

"Good afternoon, Miss Desmond. Good afternoon, Duke, and to you as well, Ma'am," nodding toward the Duchess. Turning his attention back to me, he gushed, "I am told you will be dining with us this afternoon. We are so excited to have you back. It's been several months since I've seen you, Miss Desmond."

I knew it had been almost a year at least since Theodora had been to the Coconut Grove because I assumed the identity that long ago, and I had never been here. I had merely wanted to see the inside when I suggested the venue. The Moroccan themed oasis filled the entire first floor of the Ambassador Hotel's interior courtyard, towering man-made palm groves and Persian tiled archways soaring to the nearly four-story ceiling. It was one of THE places to see and be seen. Noted for its famous clientele and floor shows filled with beautiful showgirls, the Coconut Grove featured some of the country's most popular musicians to draw people to its giant dance floor. As though that were not enough, the Coconut Grove offered the finest cuisine, held in the highest repute by food connoisseurs around the globe.

The concierge gave a half bow as he motioned in the direction in which we were to follow, offering, "I will be happy to escort you back to the *maître d'hôtel.*" People catering to the needs and wants of the wealthy and famous — like hotels, nightclubs, and restaurants — were often evaluated based on the people with whom they were seen. Being the person who provided for the desires of the aristocracy came with its own kind of prestige. And so, it was, with that, our party was handed off twice before arriving at our table.

We had been seated, received our cocktails and were enjoying a delightful conversation when I looked up to see Charlie, the Viscount, striding across the room aiming directly for our table. His face did not bear its usual congenial visage. In fact, his eyes looked worried, and his color was a bit pale. When he reached the table, his mother the Duchess spoke first.

"Charles, darling, how wonderful to see you." Her words were polite and loving, but her face bore a look of consternation. A mother could always sense when something wasn't quite right.

"Good day, Mum," he said, as he leaned in and gave her a quick peck on the cheek. "Father," he nodded to the man now standing across the table from him. The Duke nodded back, then both men sat down at the table.

Both the Duchess and I were taken aback, to say the least, that a man of the Viscount's breeding would sit at a table without being expressly invited. Charlie looked directly at me, then reached over to grasp my hand. That hand, however, was currently encircling the long crystal stem of the glass holding my extra dry Beefeater's Gibson. Jostling the glass, it sent a small wave of my drink over the edge and down the side of the glass, causing a dark stain to spread across the white linen tablecloth. Charlie didn't even bother to offer an apology. He stared pleadingly into my eyes.

"The police have arrested Regina for the murder of Clayton Foster," he blurted out in hushed tones.

"They've what?" I almost bellowed, then looked around to make sure I hadn't drawn unwanted attention.

"They found one of her fingerprints in RC's office close to the body."

"That doesn't mean a thing. Most likely half of Hollywood's fingerprints are in that office. RC conducts business meetings there all the time."

"Yes," he replied hesitantly, "but hers was on the desk, and it was in Mr. Foster's blood." His eyes were pleading now.

"When Hugo, Samuel and I were looking at the body yesterday…"

Before I could finish, the Duchess gasped, put her hand to her mouth and looked horrified. "You saw the dead man after he had been stabbed."

I thought that her comment had been rather silly. *If I had seen Mr. Foster's body before he had been stabbed; he would not have been dead.* Then I noticed the etched frown lines of dismay on her face, and with her next statement I immediately felt like a complete cad for my tactless cynical thought.

"Oh, my dear girl," she said. "During the great war, I saw many deaths. No matter how often you witness it, death never gets easier. I am so sorry you happened upon that poor man unawares."

I had to smile at her, grateful for her concern.

"Please don't be horrified, Lady Pennington. I didn't just happen upon the body. I was one of three, at the time, that went to view the scene, to better discern how this extremely disturbing tragedy could have occurred." Again, I smiled at her.

Charlie looked to his mother, while still holding my hand. "Theo has already solved one murder case, Mum. That is why I've come to her. I need her to prove Regina's innocence."

"Charlie. Hugo and I deduced the circumstances surrounding the Reginald Montgrieve case quite by accident," I added.

"Please, Theo, she needs your help," Charlie begged. "I need your help."

I nodded my head, but I had no clue where to start.

"Thank you, Theo," and he wrapped both his hands around mine. He pressed his lips to my hand with a soft, lingering kiss of gratitude. "I have all the faith in the world in you." When he looked back up at me, those fairytale-prince blue-gray eyes were clouded with tears. "She is everything to me, you know. I love her so much."

He let go of my hand and silently rose. He nodded to his father, and then kissed his now stunned mother on each cheek once more before he departed. The rest of our luncheon may have looked to the other diners like three long-time companions sharing a meal in amiable silence. But in reality, each member of our little party was quietly lost in their own thoughts. I could tell that Lady Pennington was beside herself with her son's declaration of love for Regina Banks, and the Duke and Duchess kept sharing furtive glances all through lunch. It was clear that Regina's reputation as a black widow was not unknown to them before Charlie's pronouncement of love. And now that Regina had been openly accused of murder, I would not have wanted to be in their shoes. But as for my shoes, currently with their five-inch heels, a promise was a promise. And if Regina Banks was innocent, I would do everything within my power to exonerate her. So much for enjoying lunch at the Coconut Grove.

# 14

Once swaddled back in the confines of RC's Rolls-Royce, my mind raced. It wasn't until we were nearly back at the house that I remembered the real reason for my luncheon with the Duke and Duchess. I had forgotten to ask to borrow the Duchess's ruby necklace. When we stopped at the gates, I watched as Mr. Truman unlocked each side and pushed them open. Tomorrow the new electric openers would be installed, and his work would become so much easier. When they were both fully opened, the auto bumped slightly as it crossed the threshold and glided its way to the front steps. Randel opened the door and reached in to help me out.

"Georgie wanted me to let you know that he would be up to help you dress for the evening," he said with a rare grin.

"Oh? And to what do I owe the pleasure?" I smiled back.

Randel openly laughed, "He feels you are marching into battle tonight. He says you'll need to pull out all the stops."

I looked a little puzzled.

"He's afraid of her...Mrs. McCarney, that is."

"I should have guessed from his description. 'The Demon from Hell' indeed!"

Again, Randell laughed. "He means well, Ma'am."

Still smiling, I climbed the stairs.

# All That Glitters

I had barely reached my bedroom and gotten my shoes off my aching feet before the doors swung open. In came my own personal "not so holy trinity," Seedy, Claudette and Georgie, the last carrying a clothing bag. Before I could utter a hello, Georgie stepped in front of the other two and stood with his feet planted entirely in the room ready to dress me for the evening. He immediately started spouting out commands.

"Wait!" I held my hand up signaling him to stop.

"Before we move on to my next engagement, I have some news." Instantly, you could hear a pin drop. "Regina Banks has been arrested for the murder of Clayton Foster." All three looked stunned.

The first to recover her composure, Claudette protested, "If the police have arrested her for murdering Clayton Foster, they have arrested the wrong person." Then abruptly she returned to her preparations for getting me dressed.

"Why would you say that?" I asked.

"Two simple reasons. He was not rich. And she was not married to him. If it would have been one of her dead husbands, I would have readily agreed."

"Yep! I'd say the same thang," drawled Georgie.

"I don't much care for the woman," Seedy said from her chair nearest the door, "but I cannot see her as a murderess. What makes them think she did it?"

"They found a bloody fingerprint. That fingerprint was Regina's. The blood was Mr. Foster's," I explained. "But honestly, as I've thought about it, it only means that she was in the room after he was murdered."

"In the room after he was murdered and...didn't tell anyone." Seedy corrected. "That, however, doesn't interest me as much as your other news. Have you figured out yet why RC has made you the Chief Executive Officer of Colossal Studios?"

Immediately, they all started speaking at once, the room filled with the brouhaha of competing voices. I'd hoped that bit of news would stay hushed for just a little longer.

I shushed them and tried to regain control of the conversation. "I have no earthly idea why he did, and I didn't want to be head of the studio. My best guess? It has something to do with the investors meeting. That's the best explanation I have right now, so perhaps it's best that we just focus on getting me dressed for the evening."

Just over an hour later, Claudette and Georgie were putting the finishing touches on this evening's ensemble, an off the shoulder black lace dress, the bodice peppered intermittently with sparkling black glass beads that gave the gown a subtle coruscation when the light caught it. Although it was tea length, I thought its impact made it marvelous as an evening dress.

"And the icing on the cake for this stunning creation is a cloud, a shimmering dark cloud," Georgie whispered, slipping a nest of black organza over my bare shoulders. "And you know what every dark cloud has at its heart? A silver lining."

Claudette produced a diamond broach the size of my fist. An oval ten karat diamond was mounted in the center, surrounded with swirls of platinum spiraling out in a pinwheel. Each tendril of the pinwheel was dotted with smaller (but still substantial) diamonds. And hanging below the broach was another removable clip pendant that looked very much like two shoelaces, one crossed over the other. In this case, however, the shoelaces were two strands of diamonds, ending with two large teardrop diamonds serving as the aglets. The diamond drops were matching except for size, with the larger one hanging just below its sister. The jeweler who designed the piece had surmised that those two stones had once been one large diamond before being cleaved, cut, and polished. He had called them brother and sister. It made me think of Molly, and I felt the name so appropriate that the jeweler officially named them the brother and sister diamonds.

"There you go," Georgie said. "You look beautiful, and you will make a perfect foil for the Demon wearing red."

"You do understand, Georgie, that Mrs. McCarney and I get along rather well. You have to stop being so mean when you talk about her, calling her a demon and saying she'll be in red."

"Oh, she will be dressed in red all right. She always wears some shade of red. And not to speak ill," he said, putting his index finger under his chin with a curtsey like Mary Pickford had done in so many films, "but it is not a flattering color on her. It makes her look like a tempestuous matador." He swished the garment bag like a matador's muleta. "Or maybe a better description would be the bloody enraged bull itself." And then Georgie shifted from matador to the bull using his index fingers as horns and snorting, flaring his nostrils, just before he once again placed one index finger under his chin and curtsied with a sweet smile.

Everyone laughed. I slugged him on the bicep, and he feigned grievous injury, rubbing the spot. "You are incorrigible."

"Earlier today, I called the Brown Derby restaurant to reconfirm tonight's reservation," Seedy interrupted to inform me. "When I gave the hostess the name of the party, she said Mrs. McCarney's secretary had called to cancel. Then, just as I hung up with the Brown Derby's hostess, Mrs. McCarney's secretary telephoned the house to inform you that the location of your meeting had changed. It seems you'll now be dining across the street from the Brown Derby at the Coconut Grove.

"After I disconnected that call," she continued, "I

immediately called the Coconut Grove to verify the new reservations. The concierge confirmed it, but he told me the reservation is for four people, not three."

At that point, Wallace called up to say Randel was at the front door.

On the ride to the Coconut Grove for the second time that day, I wondered who the fourth member of our party might be. I arrived just before eight-thirty and was making my way toward the door when I heard Mrs. McCarney call out to me. Her thunderous distinctive voice could not be mistaken or misunderstood. It was, as always, demanding and succinct.

"Miss Desmond!" she bellowed and waved heartily as she extricated her immense torso from her auto. She shooed away the valet trying to assist her.

In spite of this comedic Charlie Chaplin-like process, I couldn't help but notice she arrived in a Daimler like mine, except for its deep claret color. I was not surprised since it matched her reputation. After all, it's the largest limousine ever built, at least so far. And she was indeed wearing red, just as Georgie had predicted. But she was neither matador nor raging bull. Instead, she reminded me of the legendary phoenix bursting into flames. Over the black and gold brocade fabric of her dress, red, orange and black feathers were interspersed with gold beading. I wondered if they were twenty-four karat gold beads, like the ones Georgie had used on her daughter Estelle's wedding dress. Perched on her head was a stylish black felt hat adorned with more of the vividly flame-colored feathers spewing forth from another cluster of the golden beads.

"Good evening," I called back as I waved.

Climbing out behind her was the much slighter and wirier form of her Scottish-born husband, Aloysius. Once on the curb just outside the large auto, he turned around and stuck his head and arms back inside. Emerging once again, he seemed to be assisting another passenger, a female judging from the gloved hand that now appeared in his.

When the woman stepped out, I recognized her at once from our single brief meeting when she met with Georgie at my house. It was Estelle McCarney, or more accurately now Estelle McCarney Hawthorne. And I was sure I was looking at the fourth in our dinner party. Estelle McCarney Hawthorne was one of those "best of" mixtures of her parents. She had the slight frame of her father, but her chestnut hair, styled into a Marcel wave, complimented her piercing bright green eyes that were so fetchingly like her mother's. And from what I'd heard, she was also possessed of her mother's infallible head for business. That combination of appearance and business acumen made her a formidable woman in her own right.

She was dressed impeccably in a white and gold brocade drop waist dress with a pleated white crepe de chine flounce that was longer in the back than in the front. I believe it's called a mermaid flip. She was wearing white hose along with white kid leather t-strap heels, accented of course with gold beads. She wore a choker of unadorned gold, intricately woven into a mesh that encircled her neck and hung down deeply in the open neckline of her dress. Cresting just above her décolletage, a single champagne pearl the size of a quail's egg swung from the tip of the golden choker.

I waited as the small party joined me at the front doors of the hotel. When all the proper introductions had been made and everyone was sufficiently greeted, we allowed the doorman to usher us inside the Ambassador.

# 15

Mrs. McCarney's secretary had not only changed the reservation, but apparently she also requested a particular table. Rather than the typical square table, we were led to a half moon affair with four chairs on the rounded side. The straight side overlooked a dance floor the size of a train station platform, that allowed floor seating on either side of its expansive polished wooden surface.

As we arrived at our table, the maître d' motioned for Mrs. McCarney to take the end seat facing the dancing and floor show, pulling out her chair. However, she insisted that her husband take the seat with the best view, and then sat next to him. Estelle took the chair next to her, leaving me pretty much with my back to most of the dance floor.

Once we all jostled around and were seated, Aloysius' attention seemed to drift away from our dinner party entirely as he began to watch people coming and going. He was mesmerized by the crowd. Mrs. McCarney noticed me looking at the man, now altogether oblivious to all three of his dinner companions.

"He has always loved watching people. When we first met, it drove me to distraction. He would take me to the weekly socials held by miner's wives at the tent town every

# All That Glitters

Saturday evening. Instead of focusing his attention on me, his sweetheart, he would be watching all the people around us. I learned that when he was in public, he simply got lost in his observations and his thoughts." She spoke as if he wasn't sitting right next to her, and he never reacted one way or another to her comments. It would seem the two ladies were both accustomed to his eccentricities, for they carried on as if he simply weren't there.

The Coconut Grove at night was a far cry from the Coconut Grove at lunch. The band was playing softly in the background. It was still considered early in the evening but come ten o'clock the band would get much louder, the singers would appear, and the dance floor would be packed. But even at this hour, lights in the man-made palm trees shot beams towards the ceiling as well as lighting the tables below. The vast room thrummed with conversations, as hundreds of people shared cocktails, food, and laughter. Our waiter arrived. The first thing I did was ask his name. The McCarney women looked at me as if I were insane. Phillip took our order and promised to return quickly with our drinks.

The waiter nodded, but before he could depart, I said. "Thank you, Phillip."

This time not only did the McCarney ladies look puzzled, so did Phillip. I didn't mind the looks because I understood the power of knowing the names of those often considered invisible. When Phillip returned, he placed a Beefeater's Gibson in front of me. The martini glass was large, and it had not one but two skewers of onions floating in the liquid.

*Two skewers of onions would be great. I wouldn't be kissing anyone tonight.*

I smiled and popped one of the skewers of onions in my mouth. The taste suddenly made me think of Reginald Montgrieve. My body involuntarily shivered as I remembered the taste of gin, onions, and stale cigarettes on his lips the night he forced his lips to mine. I decided, however, I would not let that memory spoil the delightfully strong cocktail.

With the arrival of our drinks, the three of us began to chat. Within just a few sips Estelle's tongue seemed to cut loose. The story she began to share with us, though not pertinent to why we were meeting, was nonetheless amazing and enlightening. I guessed this was what was known as *girl talk*.

It seemed the newly married Mrs. Hawthorn had been summoned by her then future mother-in-law just after the engagement was announced. The elder Mrs. Hawthorn, known to her social circle as Gwennie, had asked Estelle to her offices, which were housed within her husband's company building in Manhattan.

Arriving at Gwennie's office on the twenty-fourth floor of the twenty-five-story building, Estelle had found the entire floor dedicated to the woman's personal offices, passing an entire room of typists, several secretaries, and Mrs. Hawthorn's personal secretary, before she was shown into Gwennie's corner office, beautifully appointed in the French style of Louis the fourteenth and overlooking Central Park. She found Gwennie standing at the windows gazing out onto the park. Rather than offering Estelle a seat, Gwennie had simply walked over, put out her arms and embraced her, giving her a sincere, genuine hug.

"How are you, my dear? I trust you had a pleasant trip across the country?" Gwennie had asked.

"I am very well, and I did have a very satisfactory trip, Ma'am. And you? How are you?"

"Please, you must call me Gwennie. And, as to how I'm doing? I couldn't be better." Gwennie then stepped away and moved to her desk. She pushed the large toggle on the box on her desk, announcing, "Greta, please come in."

A tinny, disembodied voice replied through the box, "Yes, Ma'am." And in the blink of an eye, the door opened and Gwennie's personal secretary had slipped quietly into the room.

"Greta, would you please take Miss McCarney's coat and handbag."

"Yes, Ma'am." Greta helped Estelle remove her coat, then took both her jacket and her purse to a hat stand in the corner of the room, where she neatly hung them. Turning back to Mrs. Hawthorn, she inquired, "Will that be all, Ma'am?

"Yes, Greta, you may go. Oh, and Greta, please call the elevator for me." Greta nodded to her employer, and as quietly as she had slipped in, she slipped out again.

"There are so many wonderful things to do here in New York City, that is if you ever get tired of shopping," Gwennie said smiling. "So, I won't keep you long. I just wanted to show you something."

Gwennie then moved with a quick, purposeful gate through the office door, a perplexed Estelle following hurriedly behind her. Typewriters clacked, telephones rang, and the low buzzing of workers' voices filled the air as Gwennie led her across the open floor towards the door of the now waiting elevator with its uniformed attendant. The man tipped his hat and greeted Gwennie.

"Gus, take us up to twenty-five."

"Yes, Ma'am." He waited just outside the car while the two ladies boarded the elevator, then stepped in behind them, inserted his key and turned it to 'ON,' pushed the button to close the doors, and moved the lever to the right. There was a slight jolt as the elevator began to rise. In just moments there came a soft ding. Gus slid the lever back to the middle position, then pushed the button to open the door.

The two ladies stepped out of the car and the door closed behind them. The floor below had looked like an elegantly appointed but busy office, but initially there appeared to be no one working on this floor. The walls were paneled in rich dark mahogany. Large windows lined two sides of the room. The expansive floor was black marble shot through with veins of cream. Thick Persian rugs covered the marble, and heavy masculine leather furniture filled the open reception area that took up nearly one-quarter of the entire top floor. A menagerie of exotic taxidermized animals punctuated the masculinity of the space no matter which direction one turned. On the far wall, an ornate mahogany desk was situated between two massive nine-panel doors, once again made of mahogany. Behind the desk sat a well-dressed and very pretty young woman.

Gwennie strode across the room.

"Good day, Mrs. Hawthorn," the young woman said as the two ladies approached.

"Good day to you as well, Eleanor. We are going to be up here a few minutes. Why don't you take your break now," Gwennie said pleasantly to the woman.

"Oh, thank you, Ma'am."

The young woman gathered her purse, slipped on her hat, walked across the room toward the elevators, and exited through a door in the corner marked only with a tiny sign reading "Stairs."

"Follow me," Gwennie said, gesturing with a nod of her head as she moved to the door on the left of the secretary's desk.

As they passed through into the office beyond, Estelle was very nearly overcome with acrophobia. The three exterior walls of the massive space were all glass from floor to ceiling, allowing the cityscape far below to create a spectacular vista. The view, however, gave Estelle the sensation of standing on a rocky outcrop of some soaring mountain peak, looking out as everything dropped away to the world below. She pushed her back hard against the wall next to the door through which she had just passed. For reasons she knew were irrational, her breath grew short, and she couldn't seem to move. Standing in the center of the room, Gwennie looked back at her and smiled. "It does take some getting used to, I have to admit."

"It does indeed."

Seeing that Estelle would not be able to relax, Gwennie led her back out of the office and closed the door, allowing Estelle to breathe a sigh of relief.

"I am truly sorry to have caused you such a fright, my dear. But I needed you to understand what you will be marrying into."

Gathering her wits, Estelle muttered, "Ma'am?" as a puzzled look crossed her face.

"Before you take the vows of marriage to my son, I wanted to make sure you understood what it meant to be a Hawthorn woman. My mother-in-law explained it to me, and I want to explain it to you. The big difference, however, is that my mother-in-law waited until after I had already wed her son. I was just like you, an heiress. Growing up, I'd been trained to run a household, to entertain two guests for tea or two hundred for dinner. I could organize a house party, a garden party, a tennis or croquet sporting party, and in my case even a yachting regatta, thanks to my family's love for sailing.

"But I knew nothing of business in general. I especially had no knowledge of the monstrously overwhelming textile business that was, and is, Hawthorn Textile Industries. I had naïvely married my husband, thinking I knew my role and my place. We'd just returned from our honeymoon of nearly three months in Italy when my mother-in-law, God rest her soul, dropped the same bombshell on me as I'm dropping on you now."

"Bombshell?"

"Tell me, my dear, what's the difference between the twenty-fourth floor and twenty-fifth? Besides the view, that is," she asked with a laugh, waving her hand back towards the office from which they had just made such a hasty retreat.

"The floor below is busy. People are working, and it seems very productive. This one, although beautiful, seems unoccupied, or maybe I should say vacant," Estelle said as she tilted her head.

"These two floors really describe the Hawthorn family. The twenty-fourth floor is the Hawthorn women, and the twenty-fifth is the Hawthorn men. My husband has spent the last two months hunting Moose in Alaska. And my son — your future husband — as you're well aware, has spent the last month in San Francisco. Meanwhile, I've been here running a company. It has always been this way, and must always be this way if our family's fortune and its place in current polite society is to be maintained. You see, the Hawthorn men can squander money almost as fast as the Hawthorn women can earn it."

At that, Estelle's face broke into a wide smile. Unshed tears suddenly threatened to flow. She rushed towards Gwennie, arms outstretched, and embraced her, hugging her tightly.

"I am so relieved!" Estelle exclaimed. "I love Ernie so much. But each day that's passed since I accepted his marriage proposal, I've grown more and more melancholy. I was afraid of the years ahead, being a subservient wife, spending my days doing all those mundane tasks you just listed, the tasks an heiress is trained to perform. Oh, Gwennie, you could not have given me any better news."

According to Estelle, Gwennie then smiled, saying, "I was almost positive you were the right woman for my son, but I wanted to make doubly sure before it was too late. Welcome to the family, darling."

# All That Glitters

As Estelle had woven her mother and I through her tale, all four of us had worked our way through oysters Rockefeller, tomato aspic, prime rib of beef with a horseradish sauce, creamed spinach, and new potatoes. Estelle and I had passed on dessert, but both Florence and Aloysius ordered strawberry rhubarb pie à la mode. Estelle and I opted for champagne instead. While we had dined and Estelle had regaled us with her narrative of Gwennie Hawthorn, the crowd at the Coconut Grove had swelled. Estelle drew her story to a close by telling us that Gwennie had also told her that once the romance faded — and she assured her it would — that it would be perfectly acceptable to take a lover.

When she reported that Gwennie confided she herself had chosen several lovers over the years, I gasped and Mrs. McCarney blushed. "Nonsense!" Florence blustered. "The vows say for better or worse. That is simply the worse part."

"Oh, mother, don't be so pious. After all, this is the nineteen twenties," Estelle said haughtily.

"I do not care if it's the year two thousand. That is not a proper conversation for a lady to have anywhere. Especially not at the dinner table in mixed company. And moreover, it most certainly is not a proper way for a married woman to behave. Ever!"

"As you wish, mother," Estelle said, sounding suitably cowed, then gave me a wink from behind her raised champagne flute.

I winked back conspiratorially. The dessert plates were whisked away. And the McCarney's were served coffee. Estelle and I had another glass of champagne as Florence sipped her coffee, then looked up. I could tell from her expression that it was finally time to talk business.

"I have read the dossiers on our three gentlemen," Florence began. "Quite frankly, I'm not sure why you had any problem with young Blum. I've met his mother on several occasions. She rules the roost in that household. That's why I find it odd that he would have any issue talking business with a woman. The other two, however, are a different story. That being said, let me point out that Chesterfield is reliant on wealthy horsemen, and a fair number of those are actually women. Some buy and sell horses themselves, while others hide behind the coattails of their husbands." Judging from the look on her face and the condescending inflection in her voice, the latter group of women raised her ire. "I have contacted three ladies whose husbands are among his top clients. They have used their considerable leverage with those husbands to ensure we achieve our desired outcome."

"That brings us to Mr. Housley Overholser," Estelle said, taking over. "He is quite the enterprising businessman."

"Enterprising most certainly, but not what one would call scrupulous, by any means," interjected Mrs. McCarney.

"He likes everyone to think his money comes from oil," Estelle continued. "In truth, a fair amount of it does. But the bulk of his wealth comes from, let's say, the ancillary services he provides. He seems to drill for oil in remote areas in the state of Texas. Wherever he drills, he creates a boomtown in the middle of nowhere. And of course, he owns the general stores, the speakeasies, and the hotels. Two of his most profitable ventures include bootlegging and brothels. Furthermore, it appears he's expanded the operations of his bootlegging and brothel trade throughout the entire state. We think," Estelle added, pointing to her mother, "he feels investing heavily in the entertainment industry will allow him to legitimize his wealth and improve his social standing."

"And that's poppycock! You can't make a silk purse out of a sow's ear! And that man is a sow's ear if ever I saw one," Mrs. McCarney finished with a harrumph.

I was laughing, looking at Mrs. McCarney, when I felt a

light warm touch on my shoulder.

"Good evening, Miss Desmond. I hope I'm not intruding, but I saw you as I came in and wanted to be sure to speak," I heard beside me.

I knew that voice even before looking up. It was Hugo.

"Good evening, Mr. Wainwright." My gaze locked on to those breathtaking, heart-stopping blue eyes. He smiled.

"Allow me to introduce my dinner companions," I said. "This is Mr. And Mrs. Aloysius McCarney and their lovely daughter, Mrs. Estelle McCarney Hawthorn.

"How do you do, Mr. and Mrs. McCarney, Mrs. Hawthorn," he said, nodding first to the couple and then to Estelle.

"Oh, Mr. Wainwright, you must call me Estee. May I call you Hugo?" Estelle asked, smiling up at him.

It seemed to me that Mrs. Hawthorn might be considering taking a lover even before the romance *had* faded, if her batting eyelashes and flirtatious tone that had suddenly acquired a giggle was any indication.

"Most certainly, you may call me Hugo… Estee. I was just reading an article today about Buzzy Hawthorn, the big game hunter. Is that by chance your husband?"

"No, dear Hugo. That would be my father-in-law. He is somewhere in Asia stalking a Bengal Tiger even now. He wants to add one to his collection before the year is out. My husband is Earnest Hawthorn. He is currently in Pamplona, Spain, for the running of the bulls."

The conversation between Estee and Hugo might have gotten a great deal more heated, but at that moment a pretty young blonde woman walked up next to Hugo. I had met her at the studio's reading of our newest script, and RC hoped she would become Colossal Studio's newest ingénue.

Hugo did the honors. "Please allow me to introduce my dinner companion this evening, Zelda Kravitz. Zelda, this is

Mrs. Estelle McCarney Hawthorn, Mr. and Mrs. Aloysius McCarney, and I believe you have already met Miss Theodora Desmond."

"Good evening, everyone. It is so nice to meet you."

Whatever it was she was about to say next, she was cut short by one of the Coconut Grove photographers.

"Mr. Wainwright, could I get a photograph?"

"Certainly," Hugo said as he put his arm around Zelda's waist, and the two of them smiled.

The photographer frowned but took the picture. "If you don't mind," he asked sheepishly, "I was hoping to get a shot of you and Miss Desmond together."

Hugo and I both agreed. I stood up and moved in next to Hugo. We both smiled, and the photographer happily took the shot. After my eyes adjusted from the flash, I started to take my seat, but he quickly added, "Any way I could get one of you saying the line about the stars?"

"What you're really asking for is a picture of them kissing." Florence McCarney interjected.

"Well, yeah, I guess I am."

"I don't think that's such a good idea." Hugo was shaking his head and waving his hand at the photographer.

"Let him have his picture, you two. It's great publicity," Florence assured.

I turned to Hugo. His eyes were no longer smiling. But I smiled up at him.

"I will love you until the stars grow cold," I whispered placing both my hands on his cheeks. I tip-toed up to kiss him, our lips met but the passion that had been there each time before was gone. The flashed popped, and it was over.

"Thanks!" the photographer said, nodding and moving away back into the crowd.

"Well, it seems we'll be doing that forever," I said dismissively.

"I certainly hope not, and if there is a next time, you might skip the onions." Hugo's tone was flat. "Now, if you will please excuse us. Miss Kravitz mentioned earlier that she was feeling a bit peckish." Hugo and Zelda walked away arm in arm.

I tried to turn my mind back to business, but Hugo's coldness had cut deep. I assumed he was just giving me a taste of my own medicine and I resigned myself to it. I had gotten my just desserts. When I returned to the conversation, Florence had pulled from her handbag a piece of paper and was sliding it toward me.

"These are the names of the men who can control Chesterfield. Simply be bold with Blum. And as for Housley Overholser, I am not sure how to use the information we have." She then produced three large brown envelopes, I wasn't sure from where. I was absolutely certain, however, they contained the dossiers of the three investors she'd just mentioned.

"I know you don't have any Blum Brothers jewelry," she continued, "but instead wear any and all jewels that scream 'I'm rich!' Now I'm going to take my husband out on the dance floor before he either breaks his neck from craning it around so much or dislodges a hip from falling off that chair. I'll see you the day after tomorrow at the investors' meeting."

"You plan on attending?" I asked surprised.

"Of course, I am. I would not miss this for the world." And with that, she and Aloysius were up and making their way to the dance floor.

"You know Theodora," Estelle whispered, leaning close, "I think I would love to dance as well. Too bad one of us isn't a man. We could dance together. I think instead I'll just move around the room and look available."

I laughed. Mrs. Hawthorn seemed to have warmed to her mother-in-law's notions of marital infidelity. And I wondered if even now she was open to much more than being available to dance. After she left the table, I signaled Phillip.

"Yes, Miss Desmond, how can I be of service to you?"

"Please bring me the bill."

"Miss Desmond, your secretary telephoned earlier and spoke with the manager. She said that you would be billing this to the studio's company account."

"My secretary? Cecilia Schofield?" I couldn't imagine Seedy having made a telephone call like that.

"Ma'am, I don't know, but I would be happy to get the manager for you if you like."

"Please do, Phillip."

He was back in a moment with a well-dressed man who appeared to be in his early fifties. "How can I assist you, Miss Desmond?" he asked, his voice totally devoid of any expression. To call him monotone would be an understatement.

"When my secretary telephoned, did she identify herself?" I inquired.

"No, Miss Desmond. But she didn't need to. I would recognize her voice anywhere."

I know I looked even more puzzled, wondering why he would recognize my secretary's voice.

"Your secretary may be new to you Ma'am." He continued, smiling and shaking his head from side to side. "But Edwina has been Mr. Crawford's secretary for years. And Mr. Crawford has used the Coconut Grove to entertain his guests, both business and personal, for a very long time."

"Edwina Sullivan?"

"I'm not sure of her surname, but it was certainly Edwina from Mr. Rodrick Crawford's office. She said you had recently taken over as head of the studio and that it might slip your mind to bill dinner to the studio's account."

"Thank you. Yes, it had slipped my mind. I'm sorry, but I

didn't catch your name."

"That is because I didn't give it, Ma'am. It is Felix."

"Thank you, Felix. I greatly appreciate both you and Phillip for keeping me on track. Oh, and Felix, could we please keep the fact that I'm the new studio head quiet? Please."

"Ma'am, you can rest assured that Phillip and I will remain a pinnacle of discretion. However, if you wanted the news to be held in secret, I'm afraid it is already too late for that." My brow furrowed. "The announcement appeared in the business section of this evening's newspaper."

Suddenly I felt numb. "Well thank you, anyway." I wasn't sure what else to say.

The two men departed, and I fumbled for my purse. I folded the three large envelopes in half and shoved them into my new mammoth handbag, all the while thanking Georgie for being so fashionable and all the world's working girls for needing larger purses. I prepared to leave the Coconut Grove and hurry back to the house that had become my sanctuary. However, my mind was reeling as I rose, and I absentmindedly found my feet carrying me towards the bar. The club had several bar areas, but the one I was in route to was two floors up. It jutted out over the main room like an enormous Romeo and Juliet balcony. As I took the grand staircase up, I was lost in thought.

*"Who would have contacted the newspapers and why?"*

# 16

Reaching the bar, I slid onto a stool. I noticed it was upholstered in a tropical floral print. Noticing the print, I sincerely hoped that while sitting here there wouldn't be another murder. The last time I had admired an upholstery fabric flashed into my mind—the print had become part of my next day's dress-well ensemble for a murder interrogation. Gathering my thoughts, I returned my focus to the present.

My seat at the bar afforded me a view out over the palm trees, down to the dance floor and across to the far side of the club. I started to order another Beefeater Gibson but thought better of it.

"Give me a glass of champagne, please."

When the bartender returned, he placed a cocktail napkin in front of me and set the tall crystal flute with its bubbling golden nectar on top of it.

"Enjoy," he said in heavily accented English.

"French or French Canadian?" I smile brightly at him as I made my query.

"I am French, Mademoiselle."

"I have someone very dear to me who is French as well."

"I miss my home so much. Sometimes, I get so homesick to

hear my native tongue that I want to kick myself for ever coming to America. But the very next day, the sun is shining, and there are so many wonderful things that surround me, I know exactly why I came."

"And what's your name?"

"My name is Jean-Luc, mademoiselle."

"My name..." I began, but he held up his hand, stopping my words.

"Please, Miss Desmond, I know who you are. I don't think there is any man in this country that doesn't. I loved your new movie too. It is certainly an interesting take on the Bible story, is it not?"

"That it is. It is a fascinating take," I said with a laugh.

"Ah, well, I know your job is to sell movie tickets. No man would pine for a hard-hearted spiteful seductress. And although I don't pretend to know a woman's mind, I doubt that women would run screaming after a man with gouged out eyes." He chuckled.

"I see, my dear Jean-Luc, you very much understand the entertainment industry."

He gave me a wink and went to attend to the only other person at the bar. I turned to look out across the club. The band was playing the Charleston, and there, in the center of the dance floor were the McCarneys. Aloysius looked light on his feet, as his wiry frame bounced its way through the high-spirited dance. Florence, despite her girth, was equally agile. I smiled. The song ended, and the band segued into a slower number. The lights on the dance floor dimmed, and couples moved in close. I noticed a new couple join the fray, just at the edge of the floor. It was Hugo and Zelda. I winced as he held her close. He was a good dancer. My eyes were fixed on them. I knew the feeling in my chest was jealousy, but I couldn't seem to shake it.

*"This is how it has to be,"* I kept telling myself over and over

again, but the tightness would not relinquish its hold.

I was so caught up in my thoughts that the sixth sense we all sometimes experience, knowing when someone is in close proximity and looking at us, simply didn't kick in. When I finally registered an intruder within my personal aura, I jumped.

"I'm so sorry. I didn't mean to frighten you, Miss Desmond," a man's deep voice soothed softly.

It was Grady Chesterfield, dressed in a white dinner jacket, black slacks, and a crisply starched white shirt with a red bow tie, and shiny black patent-leather shoes. For a horseman, his stylish mode of dress didn't seem to fit his persona. But he looked damn good in it. He was on a stool one away from mine, seated at an angle. He had one elbow propped on the bar, one leg stretched all the way out and the other leg perched on the rail that encircled the barstool. Even leaning casually, he sat virtually upright. He was tall; I placed him at nearly six-foot-three, or maybe even four. It wasn't because I possessed some keen eye for measurement, allowing me to accurately estimate heights. It was just because my father was six foot four, and I had seen him sit like that many times before. He must have just sat down because there was no drink yet in front of him.

"I saw you sitting alone, and I thought it might be a prime opportunity to talk. Unless you are waiting for someone?" He finished up.

"I am not. Have you ordered a drink yet?"

"No. Is this a good time then?"

"It is as good a time as any. What will you have?"

"I'll take a Scotch on the rocks."

"Single malt or blended?"

He smiled.

"Single malt."

"Jean-Luc," I called out as I signaled holding up a finger.

He looked up. "Would you please bring my guest a Macallan twelve-year-old single malt on the rocks please? And a fresh chilled champagne; this one has gone warm."

"Wow! If I'm going to drink something that fine, bring it to me neat," he called back to Jean-Luc, barely looking over his shoulder.

"Yes, sir."

The drinks were there in moments, each with its own fresh napkin, and my warm champagne whisked away.

"I'd heard that you knew every servant along with every service provider and purveyor in Hollywood by name. And I guess it's true."

"To know someone's name is to honor them. Besides, it seems to get me amazing service."

He laughed. "I'm sure it does. But great service most likely comes naturally to a beautiful woman such as yourself."

"Not everyone who provides me service is a man, if that is what you are implying. So, Mr. Chesterfield, how can I be of service to you this evening?"

"I want to start by congratulating you on your new position as Chief Executive Officer of Colossal Studios."

"Thank you," I said, with a slight nod. I noticed that although it was a stretch for me, I had mimicked his posture unconsciously. It was very un-ladylike, but if he'd noticed, it didn't appear to bother him.

"I have to say," he continued, "that after three significant conversations I had today, RC Crawford knows his business and his people."

"And why do you say that?"

"I am very impressed with how you do business, Miss Desmond. Three men who are essential to my business telephoned me today. Each strongly encouraged me to review the business portfolio you supplied at our brief meeting the other day. And all three also encouraged me to proceed with my original decision to invest in your movies."

I worked hard to maintain my poker face, even though I wasn't at all sure what had happened. It had to have been the work of Florence McCarney, or perhaps even Estelle.

"There was no force in their words," he said, holding up his hand as if to reassure me. "They simply asked me to give you a chance. I had no idea you were so well connected. Most men in your position would have used those connections to create a hangman's noose, and then happily placed it around my neck and perched me on the horse's back. They would even threaten to slap the horse's rump if I didn't fall in line. You did not. And I thank you for that."

Looking a bit more intense, he explained, "However, just so you're aware, it wasn't necessary. I let Overholser get me riled up, and I'm not sure why. I've dealt with many women in my professional career over the years. I had already read through the portfolio which we never allowed you to suitably present. Miss Desmond, I'm a pretty savvy businessman. I know a good investment when I see one. I'm still all in, and my money remains with Colossal Studios."

He shot back the remainder of his twelve-year-old single malt and sat up to his full height. I sat up as well. Demonstrating his ability tending bar, Jean-Luc sprang into action with military-like precision, triggered solely by our posture change. He was back in front of us in an instant.

"Could I offer you another twelve-year-old, Mr. Chesterfield?"

"No, thank you, John Luke," Chesterfield said, his eyes never leaving mine. "I'm afraid if I lost my wits around this woman, she just might chew me up and spit me out. Thank you, so much for your time Miss Desmond." He tipped an imaginary cowboy hat. "I very much admire the way you do business. You are one class act. I will see you Monday afternoon."

He pulled a silver dollar out of his pocket and flipped it on the bar. It made a loud clank and began to spin on edge. As it spun, he turned and strode away with one hand in his trouser pocket.

*"One down and two to go,"* I thought to myself.

"I know you heard that conversation, Jean-Luc," I said, as we both watched Grady Chesterfield walk away. "What does your gut tell you?"

"You really want my opinion?" Jean-Luc asked in amazement.

"Yes, I do." I turned to look him directly in the eye.

"My gut, as you say, tells me he is an honest, upfront businessman. That is the reason he sought you out. He wanted to let you know his position. And whatever it is, it must be important. He did not want to talk about his personal reasons in front of others." There was a long pause as we both now watched Grady Chesterfield reach the top of the stairs and start down. "His actions tonight certainly aren't the actions of a man who would stab you in the back."

"What did you say?" I asked as my mind whirred.

"I said, he didn't act like a man that would stab you in the back?"

*"Stab you in the back."* My mind raced into action. A knife in the back. That was it. I now had the *why*, but what about the *who*?

"Jean-Luc, you are brilliant." I leaned across the bar and gave him a huge hug.

I said a silent prayer to Mrs. McCarney for her invaluable help and vowed to do something special for her. My mood had shifted. There would be no more moping over Hugo Wainwright.

"Jean-Luc, please have the doorman send for my auto, and bring me the tab."

I signed for the bill, left Jean-Luc a ridiculously large tip, and nearly bolted for the front door.

# 17

I was lost in thought as I crossed the hotel lobby. The doorman opened the doors for me, and I shot through. Suddenly flashbulbs began to pop, and reporters started firing off questions left and right. Caught off guard, I staggered backward, putting up my hand to protect my eyes — a cardinal sin for someone in the entertainment business. Seeing my distress, Randel left the Rolls' door open and shot to my side, elbowing two photographers out of the way, knocking one of them to the ground. He quickly grabbed me, shielded me with his body, and hurried me to the open automobile door, covering me from the prying eyes of the press as I got inside before closing the door.

He pulled out of the hotel's drive, and we were safely on the road heading back to the house before Randel looked up at me in the rearview mirror. I was visibly shaken.

"Are you all right, Ma'am?"

I plucked up one of the Waterford glasses, filled it with an amber liquid from the first decanter I could reach in the bar, and shot it back. It burned as it slid down my throat. I shivered.

"Are you all right?" Randel asked again. His voice was filled with concern.

"I am. The photographers just caught me off guard. I'm more angry with myself than shaken."

"I'm sorry, Ma'am. I just assumed you knew that late on Friday and Saturday nights, the press is always at the Coconut Grove. It's a hot spot for celebrities. A lot of the rich and famous simply take a room for the evening. That way, they already have a location for a discreet rendezvous. Of course, the press knows that too. They are always trying to gain access to the upper floors, but the management is good about keeping them out. Occasionally, however, they do get past."

I had regained my composure. "Having grown up in this industry, I guess I should know that. And I'm guessing one of those shots will be in the newspapers tomorrow?"

"Maybe," he offered, "but I doubt it. The photographers don't really have a by-line."

"Good." I pulled the files from my purse and tried to flatten them out, but it was too dark to read them. I breathed a heavy sigh and tried unsuccessfully to stuff them back in my bag.

"This auto has an electric light, just above your head, if you are trying to see something."

I found the tiny switch. Flipping it, the compartment filled with a dim, but sufficient glow.

"Randel, do you like this automobile?"

"I love this motor car, Ma'am. It drives like a dream. And it could almost fly if we needed it to."

"I think I love it too," I mumbled as I opened the first file and began to read.

I had grabbed the dossier on Ezra Blum. Mr. Blum, it seemed, was the fourth of five children. He had two older brothers and one older sister, and there was one younger sister too. All three sons worked in the family jewelry business, whose showroom was in Manhattan. The elder Mr.

Blum had approached RC about investing. According to the file in front of me, normally brother number two, Jacob, would have made the trip to California to investigate the risks and profitability of such a venture. But it would seem that RC himself requested they send the younger Ezra.

There were figures regarding the family's suspected assets, along with information about each and every family member. There were also pictures. One especially caught my eye. It was of Ezra, taken on the streets of what I assumed to be New York City. In the photograph, a slightly younger Ezra was walking down a sidewalk, and he was accompanied by an older gentleman whose arm was around Ezra's shoulders. The two of them were laughing. I thought at first it might have been his father. But on reflection, the man didn't seem that much older than Ezra. It was the only picture of the five in the file with something written on the back. It said, "Both lavender gloves."

I put the photos back in the envelope and with a good deal of effort wedged all three envelopes back in my purse. The light wasn't the best for reading, and I was feeling the effect of the cocktails. All I wanted to do was sleep.

"Before I forget, Randel," I said, "would you please tell Georgie that I need to speak with him tomorrow?"

"Would it be all right if he telephoned your Ma'am? Tomorrow is Sunday and our off day. Usually, it wouldn't be an issue at all, but tomorrow is the monthly performance of the "Ladies Club" at the Drakestone. Georgie helps most of the impressionists with their outfits."

"The Ladies Club?"

"It's what they call themselves. Once a month the Ladies Club gets together and performs at the Drakestone's club. It's very well attended."

"I've heard rumors of shows. What types of acts are actually performed there?"

"They sing, and dance, and do some scenes, mostly comedy. Most of the ladies aren't very good, but everyone gets a good laugh." I noticed him looking hard at me in the mirror. "I didn't mean any disrespect, Ma'am. None of those ladies could ever come close to doing what you do. Living life as a woman would be absolutely impossible for them."

"I'm certainly not offended. I am amazed at myself. But I've come to the conclusion that people see only what they want to see, not necessarily what is really there. Oh well, if he's busy, I guess I have a few things in my closet I could pull out to wear."

There was a loud snort. "Yes, Ma'am, I'm betting you have one or two." I laughed along with him, knowing that Theodora's closet had overflowed into another room down the hall.

"What I meant was that Georgie seems to have a mental inventory of everything I own. I know I'm very spoiled. I simply ask, and it appears. I'm supposed to wear large expensive jewels to the meeting."

"I would say you have that base covered too, Ma'am."

"Yes, but I don't want to look garish. And what color dress would make the jewels look best?"

"Oh, Ma'am, you know the answers to all those questions. Diamonds go with anything, so wear diamonds, and maybe one colored stone. As for the dress color, I'm not a fashion designer or a jeweler, but things that sparkle always look best against black."

I smiled up at Randel. "You and Georgie have a good time tomorrow night. I'll manage."

"Just don't wear that dress with the big white collar, the one you wore that night you got Georgie out of jail. I still laugh when I remember the story Seedy tells about your fight with the detective and how the angrier you got, the more the collar on that dressed bounced."

He was still chuckling when he pulled up to the front gates. It was late, and Mr. Truman had long since gone home. Randell climbed out of the Rolls, went to the gatehouse, used his key to open the door. In seconds the gates were swinging open. I smiled. I loved my new electric gate opener. We pulled through, and Randel once again got out, put his key into a locking switch on a pole beside the driveway that stood far enough inside the estate that the gates could close without hitting the motor car. When we reached the house, Randel helped me from the Rolls.

"Georgie and I would be happy to act as your escorts if you wanted to come tomorrow night," he offered.

"Thank you so much Randel. I honestly would love to come, but Theodora Desmond walks a fine line as it is. I don't want to encourage anyone to think that I might not be as I appear."

"You could always come as the real you," he said. "A man, I mean. I'm sorry," he added quickly. "I've overstepped my place. Please forgive me."

"There is nothing to forgive. Thank you, for your chivalrous offer, and for being my protector tonight. I gave his hand a squeeze and I headed up the steps.

I stopped in the study before retiring, pulled out the three files, and put Blum and Chesterfield to the side. I read through Oberholser's record, but learned nothing more than I already knew. I started a list of items I needed to accomplish tomorrow. Number one was to give Molly a ring. Texas really was a big state, but maybe if she didn't know anything about Overholser directly, she might know someone who did. Number two was to call Edwina. I was hoping she might be able to help with an item I needed. I needed to figure out what to wear on Monday. I was tapping my pencil on the pad of paper, pondering what else should go on my list next, when I noticed three movie scripts stacked on the corner of the desk. I pulled them over to me.

The first I was already familiar with, the script for my next movie, *Raptured Love*. It would introduce Zelda Kravitz to the world. The second script was a western. For some reason, I just couldn't see Theodora, the fashionable socialite temptress, back in the old west.

The third manuscript was entitled *A War Within Him*. I thumbed through it. Obviously RC's copy, the script had notes scribbled everywhere. Inside the front cover was a line written in RC's hard-to-read scrawl. "Should she change her name from Kravitz?" This must be a script that will feature Zelda. RC had written the initials HW next to the role of the leading male. I instantly went through a mental catalog of leading men, but only one had the initials HW. It would appear that RC had planned on pairing Zelda with Hugo.

*What did I think of that?*

I was way too tired and just a bit too tipsy to think about anything. I picked up Hugo and Zelda's new manuscript, along with the western, switched off the light and climbed the stairs to bed.

# 18

I jumped almost frantically as the alarm I had set began peeling precisely at six o'clock. It was the first time I'd set an alarm in almost a year. I rolled over and turned it off, slowly sat up, then nearly jumped out of my skin again. That damnable lifelike portrait of Reggie! The thing had to go, at least from my bedroom, since I couldn't seem to get used to it hanging there.

I hopped out of bed, grabbed my robe and sat down at the dressing table to make my telephone call to Molly. The operator said it could take a while to get the call routed through. She promised to ring me back when she could connect me. I thanked her, hung up, and moved over to the little sitting area where I had left the western script on the art deco coffee table. I opened the cover but found the room still too dark to read. As I started to get up to switch on the lights, the doors flew open and the lights popped on. As usual, Claudette was in the lead with Seedy trailing right behind. Both were still in their night things, which was highly out of the ordinary.

"Why are you both up so early?" I asked.

"It's our day off, and we both have plans later," Seedy explained. "Last night after getting you undressed, Claudette told me you had set the alarm for six, so we thought we'd take advantage of your early rising and get you dressed, fed and informed, not necessarily in that order. And I was pretty sure you'd forget you were meeting Mr. Truman today. Since it's his day off as well, he has to make a special trip just for the meeting."

Claudette set down the tray, filled a cup, and handed me my coffee. I nodded my thanks and sipped the strong hot brew.

"As much as I appreciate both of you getting up so early, even though I understand you have ulterior motives, I cannot believe, Claudette, you woke Seedy at one o'clock in the morning to tell her I was getting up early."

"I didn't have to wake her. She didn't even come in until almost two. That's when I was turning out the light's downstairs, and she gave me such a fright I'm sure I now have a gray hair."

Seedy blushed and made to move along.

"Edwina sent over three scripts from the studio," she said, sidestepping Claudette's comment.

"Wait! Wait! Why were you just getting home at two o'clock in the morning?" I pursed my lips in a smile. "I think, and I'm sure Claudette would agree, it's your turn to spill the beans." I sat back and crossed my arms, waiting for her to talk. Claudette followed suit. Seedy's blush grew even more profound. With her almost porcelain skin, she looked like a bright red beacon.

"Mr. Densmore and I went to dinner and the movies."

"Oh, and where did you have dinner?" I asked.

"We went to the Brown Derby since I knew your dinner plans had changed."

"And what movie did you see?"

Her face went absolutely crimson.

"We never made it to the movie. We talked and talked and

talked some more."

"And?" Claudette questioned.

Seedy's dam finally broke, and for the next ten minutes a torrent of words and emotions flooded forth extolling all of the virtues, and the incredible kissing prowess, of one Mr. Willard Densmore. When she was done, she sighed heavily, then collapsed into her chair where she remained with her eyes lost in a daydream and a goofy smile plastered on her face.

"Well, well, well, Claudette, it would appear that our Miss Schofield here has been thoroughly kissed and is most definitely smitten with Mr. Densmore. Wouldn't you agree?"

"I would indeed."

Seedy cleared her throat and refocused on her original task.

"Edwina sent over three scripts from the studio." She dropped the third on top of the one already on the table and pointed to the one still in my lap. "One, I already know you're familiar with because it's the script you've been running lines from for at least a month. The second is a script RC intends to star Hugo and feature Zelda. The other is a script, a western, she thought you would find interesting. I panicked this morning when I saw they weren't on the desk where I'd left them, but then calmed down when I saw the list you'd started. The western is a script for a movie Mr. Foster had been pushing RC to make. In the back is a sheet of personal notes Mr. Foster wrote for RC. RC already rejected the script and left it on Edwina's desk to file away, but since it just happened last week and had Mr. Foster's notes, she thought you might be interested in seeing it."

"Mr. Foster was suggesting a script to be produced? Don't you find that odd, script suggestions coming from RC's personal secretary and attorney?" I asked, thumbing to the back of the manuscript.

"Yes, I thought it quite odd, and I told Edwina the same. She informed me it was a common practice with Mr. Foster. In fact, it was Mr. Foster who first saw the marketability of Theodora Desmond."

The telephone rang. Claudette started to answer it.

"I'll get it, Claudette," I interrupted. "I'm sure it'll be the operator completing my telephone call to Molly. Would you ladies excuse me for about half an hour?"

While I moved to the ringing telephone, Seedy and Claudette excused themselves.

"Hello."

"I have your call placed. I will put you through."

"Hello, Molly?"

"Eddie?" came her panicked voice. "What's wrong? Is it Pops?"

It had never crossed my mind she would think something was amiss. But it was only the fifth time I had spoken with her since she left.

"Oh, Molly, nothing is wrong," I assured her.

"Thank goodness. When the operator told me the number that was calling, it scared me to death."

"I'm so sorry. I will endeavor to telephone more often; that way you don't think there's been a disaster every time I call."

"I guess that works both ways, little brother. But I'm never certain when to ring. I don't want to catch you when the wrong ears might be tuned to the conversation."

"Understood. However, I'm afraid the reason for the call is not a social one either. I know this is a long shot, but do you know — or know of — a man by the name of Raymond Housley Overholser?

"I only know of him. And that's only recently. His company wants to drill for oil on a small portion of our land. He has been pestering Will to sell him that portion. Will only laughed and told his representative that he would need to talk with the real boss. But it would seem that Mr. Housley Overholser is in Hollywood being courted by the movie producer, RC Crawford."

"I need to bring you up to date. RC was courting him and bagged him actually. There hasn't been much in the news so far, so you may not know, but Clayton Foster, RC's personal secretary, was murdered the night of the *Samson and Delilah* opening."

"Oh my God! Clayton was a wonderful man. When I was just starting out, he took me under his wing and made sure that I knew RC's bark was worse than his bite. I'll say a prayer for him."

"The murder occurred sometime during the after-party at RC's house. As a result, RC went into a deep depression and left for his brother's home in San Francisco near Berkeley School of Law. As if that in itself wasn't strange enough, here's where it gets even more peculiar. In his absence, he made Theodora the Chief Executive Officer of the studio."

"What? Eddie, why in the world would RC have made Theodora head of the studio?"

"Rest assured, I have no idea. Immediately after I took over, there was a meeting with the three investors about Theo's next movie. That's when the issue with Raymond Housley Overholser arose. It seems he doesn't feel a woman has the business sense to run a company."

There was an angry grumble on the other end of the line.

"I have enlisted the aid of a new, but very powerful acquaintance, Mrs. Florence McCarney."

"The mother of Estelle McCarney Hawthorn? I've heard that woman makes men quake in their boots."

"And after having secured her as an ally, I wager those men have good reason to quake. Certain knowledge has come into my possession that indicates that Mr. Housley Overholser is not only in the oil business, but he's also a creator of boomtowns where he owns bars and brothels. He is reputed to be, if not the largest, at least one of the largest bootleggers in the state of Texas. Mrs. McCarney, Mrs. Hawthorn, and I believe he is investing in the entertainment industry in an effort to legitimize his financial holdings. But even knowing all that, he still does not appear to have a weakness we can exploit."

There was a long silence on the other end. When Molly spoke, there was a sound of amazement in her voice.

"Exploit his weakness? Eddie, I think I see why RC made you head of the studio. Something like that would have never crossed my mind."

"Honestly, it was Mrs. McCarney's mind it crossed. But it would seem that a great many captains of industry, no matter their gender, use this technique."

"I'll dig around at this end and see if I can find out anything further for you."

"I'm afraid I don't have much time, Molly. I have a meeting with the three investors tomorrow afternoon at one o'clock."

"He's approached a lot of the ranchers around here. I'll ask around at church this morning, and I'll make some telephone calls this afternoon. I doubt I'll find out anything more than you already know, but I'll do my best."

I thanked Molly for her help and promised to telephone just to catch up soon. I reached over and gave the bell cord three quick tugs. And in moments, Seedy and Claudette were back. This time they were both dressed and ready for the day.

"Was she able to help?" Seedy asked.

"What makes you think I needed her help?"

"Please! You have made only five telephone calls to your sister in the nearly full year you've known of her existence, and I placed the four previous ones for you. This time you placed the call and then ran us out of the room to take it. It has to be something serious."

"It is."

I went on to recount everything that happened last evening. When I was done, Seedy and Claudette both were shaking their heads. At the same time, the grandfather clock in the long gallery struck nine o'clock.

"Oh, Lord, Mr. Truman will be here in an hour — and you are still Eddie," Seedy said, jumping up.

Claudette flew out of her chair and shot to the bathroom to start the shower. I finished my now cold cup of coffee and followed on her heels. I was dressed in a record forty-five minutes. I was back in a silk pajama, this one a Georgie creation. The trousers were pleated silk organza in deep rich jade green, and the halter top was of raw silk in a jade green so pale it was almost white. The neckline dropped dramatically. Georgie had a penchant for dramatically low necklines when it came to designs for me. It was Claudette's opinion it was because he knew that nothing would ever fall out, so it was okay if I could shock viewers with my daring. Pearls hugged my bare skin, and a simple pendant choker, as simple as any of my jewels ever get, nestled in the hollow of my neck. Yet another of Reggie's jewel horde, the chartreuse beryl was an oval faceted stone weighing just shy of forty karats. It sat vertically in its invisible mounting that hung from a chain set with diamonds. Claudette had fastened the clip that held the "brother and sister" diamonds below it. I was a blonde today with a Marcel wave and a headband of seed pearls.

Just before the clock struck ten, Mr. Truman arrived. Seedy placed him in the long gallery right before she and Claudette left for the day. I made my way down to greet him. When I opened the door, the older man jumped to his feet, clutching his hat.

"Good morning, Mr. Truman." I smiled and held out my hand as I crossed the room.

"Good morning, Miss Desmond."

Mr. Truman took my hand and gave it a quick shake. His hand was clammy, which usually indicated to me nerves. I looked over and noticed that either Seedy or Claudette had left a fresh pot of coffee with two cups on the sideboard.

"Would you care for a cup of coffee?" I gestured toward the fresh pot.

"No, Ma'am. It's best that I get right down to business, if you don't mind."

"Certainly, won't you please sit down?"

The man was clutching his hat so tightly he was crushing the brim.

"No, Ma'am. I'll just say my piece and be on my way and leave you to your day of rest."

"All right then. What's on your mind?" I tried to say it brightly, but I was at a total loss as to what could be causing him so much distress.

"Ma'am, you've been awfully good to me. I've enjoyed working here very much. You even used to bring me little treats on Mondays." I started to apologize, but he held up his hand. "I know you've gotten too busy for cookin' anymore, with you making movies and helping the police solve murders and all. But why I'm here, Ma'am, ain't that. I know I'm an old man. And I'm sure you'll be calling me in soon to tell me you don't need my services anymore. But I was hoping that you might see your way clear to giving me a good letter of recommendation, Ma'am. You see, I ain't set up so I can retire. The Missus ain't never worked neither, and she's way too old to start now. So, I'm hoping you'll give me a good reference, so maybe I could get another job."

It seemed he'd said his piece as he visibly relaxed.

"Why on earth do you think I will be dismissing you?"

"You don't need me anymore now that you got that new electric gate opener."

I couldn't believe what I was hearing. I could have kicked myself. I had never even discussed the new gate opener with Mr. Truman. Looking at it from his perspective, if your boss installs a new gate opener, why would your boss still need the old one? I had purchased it solely to make his job and his life a little easier. But instead, ever since Seedy had told him about the installation, he had feared for his job!

"Oh, my dear Mr. Truman." I rushed over to him and put my arm around his shoulder. "I am so sorry I didn't discuss this with you first. You are not losing your job. I purchased the gate opener to make things more convenient for you. I wanted to save you from having to walk over, unlock, open and then close and lock the gates after every car passes through. I just thought it would make it easier on you, especially at those times when reporters and photographers are crowded around the gates. Please, please accept my apology for not talking to you about it. I wrongly assumed you would be as happy about it as I was."

I had both hands on his shoulders now, and I could feel the relief sweep through him. I thought the man might cry, and I felt horrible. But I was relieved to know a problem I didn't even know existed had been successfully resolved.

"Let's get you home to Mrs. Truman so you can tell her. I'm sure she's worried to death."

"That she is Ma'am. And we will both be thanking the good Lord this day, for sure. I'll head on down to the bus stop and let you get back to your day. Thank you, Ma'am."

"The bus?"

"Yes, Ma'am. We don't have a car."

"But this is Sunday." I looked at the clock. It was ten-fifteen. "The buses don't run on their regular schedule today." I tried to picture the Sunday bus schedule in my head. "The next bus won't be at that stop until around noon."

"That's right, Ma'am, but it's a beautiful day. It'll be a pleasant wait."

"Nonsense! Half your day will have been wasted because I failed to talk to the one person that damn gate opener really mattered to. I'll drive you home."

"Oh no, Ma'am, that wouldn't be right."

"Right in whose eyes? It would be a travesty on my part if I didn't drive you home, in my opinion."

"Well, Ma'am, it would surely be appreciated then."

"Let me grab my handbag, and we'll be off."

When we arrived at the garage, Mr. Truman insisted on opening the garage door. He started to open the door that held the Daimler, but I laughed and assured him I didn't have a clue how to drive the big motor car. And I would fear for both our safety.

"You mean… we're going to take your roadster?" His eyes lit up in delight. "Ever since that day you flew out of here to get away from the reporters, I've imagined what it'd be like to ride in it."

"Good Lord, why didn't you say something? I would have been happy to give you a ride."

"Oh, no, Ma'am, it's not my place. But I sure ain't gonna turn it down now!"

I climbed into the sleek red roadster and fired up the engine. I did take the time to open the door and slide in this time, instead of vaulting in, even though it was tempting since I was wearing trousers. Mr. Truman walked over to a box on the wall inside the garage, inserted his key, and I could tell from my vantage point that the front gates were swinging open.

"You can open the gates from here?"

"Yes, Ma'am. There are four locations where you can open and close the gates. The gatehouse, that pole in the front yard, right here, and in the house."

"You see, Mr. Truman, you already know more about the gates than I do. What in the world would I do without you?"

The older gentleman beamed as he climbed into the roadster.

"Hold on to your hat, Mr. Truman. You're going to love this."

We shot down the driveway. I stopped at the pole in the yard.

Would you like to close the gate?"

"You'd better drive up to the gatehouse, Ma'am."

"You think? I wager this motor car is quick enough. I'm game. Are you?" And I gave him a conspiratorial wink.

He hopped sprightly out grinning from ear to ear. He left the roadster's door open, walked to the pole, and inserted his key. He leaned back preparing to make a run for it. He turned the key and pulled it free. Holding his hat on, he tore out for the motor car.

He jumped in, all the while shouting, "Go! Go! Go!" at the top of his lungs.

I punched the throttle as he pulled his door closed. The engine roared and gravel flew as the roadster blasted through the gate's shrinking opening with ease. We both whooped as we sped onto the street. Mr. Truman looked over his shoulder to make sure the gates had closed, then settled in for what might be the ride of his life.

# 19

I arrived back at home nearly three hours after I left. The drive to Mr. Truman's modest home in a quiet, well-kept neighborhood had only taken about twenty minutes. At his behest, I had significantly reduced our speed before reaching his house.

"She'll have a conniption fit," he pleaded, "if we fly up in front of the house, like we're doing now." His words belied his joyous face before I began to let up on the throttle.

My thought was to drop him off in front of his home and be on my way, but so much for best-laid plans. We arrived in his neighborhood just as church was letting out, and the streets and sidewalks were full of people. In this neighborhood of working class and older people, the shiny red roadster with the driver's cockpit on the wrong side drew a great deal of attention. First, passers-by looked at the bright red motor car with curiosity. However, when they recognized who was driving, suddenly everyone who had, seconds before, been walking home from church, now changed direction and were making a beeline towards the auto as I pulled it to a stop in front of the Truman residence. Soon, it seemed like the entire neighborhood had gathered around me. I was besieged to sign autographs almost instantly.

Folks ran to their houses and returned carrying Kodak Brownie cameras. I got requests to pose with entire families. I even had requests from several young men to be allowed to pose for a photograph behind the wheel of the Mercedes. I didn't have the heart to refuse. I lost count of how many people climbed in and out of the roadster.

Mr. Truman had quit holding his hat on his head shortly after we left the house, choosing to keep it safe by holding it in his lap instead. Therefore, when I returned him to Mrs. Truman, the hair on his head was standing straight up. I was glad that I had started keeping a scarf in the glove box to tie my hair down. It wouldn't do for Theodora Desmond to show up somewhere having lost her wig. Before I finally was able to take my leave, I had no less than twenty invitations to Sunday lunch, including one from Mrs. Truman.

Now that I was back at home, I could not keep from smiling. The telephone rang, and I answered it in the study. It was Georgie.

"Randel told me you wanted to talk with me," he began.

"I had wanted to talk with you, Georgie, but I think I can figure it out on my own. Are you having a good time? Will you be performing tonight?"

"We'll put you in the black Chanel," he said as if he hadn't heard me. "I'll be there tomorrow around ten to help you dress."

"I'm afraid I'll need to be dressed and gone long before ten. Claudette can manage dressing me, I'm sure"

"I don't think I like you as studio head," he chuckled, "The hours you have to keep are ungodly. Are you sure you don't need my help? I can be there at whatever time you require."

"Yes, I'm sure. If you are assisting performers, I'm sure it will be a long night for you anyway."

"And to answer your other question, I don't perform. I'm not an illusionist. I just wear a dress for inspiration when I work."

"I wish I could attend tonight just to see what it's like. But you know how it is."

"Come as yourself, Eddie Standish. No one there will have a clue who you are."

"You know, you're right, but I just can't risk it. But thank you so much for the invitation."

"If you change your mind, the floor show starts at eight. Randle and I will both be here. He would enjoy your company because he doesn't enjoy coming to the Ladies Club's shows. He'd much rather go hunting or fishing, be working on automobiles, or playing cards."

I thanked him again and hung up the telephone. Since I had the telephone in hand, I clicked the cradle and had the operator connect me with the home of Mr. George Sullivan. Edwina answered the telephone.

"Good afternoon, Edwina. I'm sorry to bother you at home. Do you have a minute to talk?"

"Certainly, I do, Miss Desmond."

"I was wondering if the studio property department might have another throne similar to the one that was at Mr. Crawford's house. If you would research that first thing tomorrow and get back with me, I'd greatly appreciate it."

"There is no need for me to research it, Ma'am," she giggled.

*Odd reaction*, I thought.

"There is an identical throne. They were created for a movie that Mr. Crawford shelved two years ago because he felt it was ahead of its time, since it really needed spoken dialog, not intertitles. The manuscript is entitled, *The Twin Kings*. The story is about two identical twin brothers who inherit their father's kingdom, and the war between them for control of that kingdom. I will have the throne brought over to Mr. Crawford's office in the morning."

# All That Glitters

"Great! Thank you so much. But have it delivered to Mr. Crawford's house and put it in the study where the other one used to sit. Also, three other things. On the main door to the office, where it has Colossal Studios and then RC Crawford, Chief Executive Officer, in gold letters, do you think there is any way in the world we can get RC's name removed and mine inserted before my one o'clock meeting tomorrow? I would like for you to move heaven and earth to get it done, if at all possible."

"No need to move heaven or earth, Ma'am. My husband, George, did the lettering on that door. He may not have that same style font available, but if that's all right, I can get him to do it this afternoon."

"Oh, I don't want to spoil his Sunday."

"Spoil his Sunday? I've got him ironing clothes. It won't be moving heaven, but I'm sure he'll think it's a Godsend to get out of the ironing." We both giggled at that.

"A couple of other things," I continued. "Please contact Detective O'Flaherty and Mr. Wainwright. Ask them to meet me at RC's house at ten in the morning. Then tell Hugo and Zelda Kravitz to be in my office no later than three o'clock tomorrow."

"Yes, Ma'am. Will that be all?"

"Yes, Edwina, it will. And please thank your laundress for getting that name changed."

Edwina gave a hearty, very un-ladylike snort. "I'll be sure to give her your thanks. Good-bye Ma'am."

It was just after three in the afternoon. I had promised Charlie I would do everything in my power to help Regina, and I hadn't even talked with her yet. I picked up the telephone again and placed a call to detective O'Flaherty to request a visitation with Regina. He wasn't in the office, but the station house telephoned back to say they had contacted him, and he had authorized the visit.

I didn't really want to show up at the police station in the roadster. While I had two limousines at my house, I had no driver. I called Samuel at RC's home. He reminded me that Mr. Crawford had taken his driver with him to San Francisco. Instead, he assured me that the studio driver on notice this Sunday would be at my house within the hour.

I ran upstairs to change before the driver arrived, but then reconsidered. I simply touched up everything as best I could. I'd become practiced at applying lip color, a necessity after my disastrous lipstick debacle in the lady's powder room at RC's house on my first night as Theodora. I also decided to follow Randle's example, so I called the station house to request the same kind of assistance they offered the night Georgie was arrested. They were very agreeable.

The studio driver arrived, but his taxi had to wait at the gate while I first found my key to the electric gate opener, then located the box, which turned out to be in the kitchen. I was grateful Mr. Truman told me there was one in the house, or I would have hiked down to the gate to let them in. The driver met me at the front door. I could tell by the look on his face that he was expecting a servant.

"Good afternoon, Ma'am," he stammered.

"Good afternoon. Please forgive me for being so forward, but what is your name?" I inquired.

"It's Howard, Ma'am." He bowed and tipped his hat.

"Howard, I'm in a bit of a hurry. I want to take the Rolls Royce. I believe my driver leaves the key under the mat. If you would be so good as to bring the motor car around, I'll meet you at the bottom of the front steps in five minutes."

"Very good, Ma'am." He bowed again and bounded down the steps and across the lawn to where the Rolls sat in front of the garage.

I flew up the stairs and shot into the closet, wondering which fur Georgie would choose to go with my ensemble. I spotted a white satin jacket with large cuffed sleeves. I pulled it off the hanger and decided not to put it on for fear of creasing it before I got to the police station. When I got to the front steps, Howard was already there with the door open. I handed him the key to the gate, and we were off. When we neared the police station, I instructed him on what to do. I put up the privacy screen and pulled the shades. When I felt the motor car slow and heard the sound of the powerful engine bouncing off the alley walls, I knew we were there.

When the door opened, police officers created a barrier so no onlookers could see who was arriving at the back door to the station. The same institutional green walls greeted me much the same as they had before. Officers crowded around, asking for my autograph, until the captain on duty ordered them back to their stations.

The same captain then personally escorted me to the private cell holding Regina Banks. She was in a standard issue prisoner's uniform. At first glance, I could have believed she was playing a movie role. That is, until she looked up at me. Mixed emotions rushed across her face. I could tell I was neither the person she expected to see nor anyone she wanted to see.

"How are you, Regina?" I asked, as gently as I could.

"I've been better," she laughed, but it was an empty laugh.

"I'm sure you have. Is there anything I can get you?"

"You could get me out of here."

"They have not set bail yet, or I would be working on that very thing."

"Why are you here, Theo? Did you come to gloat?"

"No, Regina, not at all. I came because I promised Charlie, I would try to help you. Somehow, everyone has begun to think I'm some kind of Sherlock Holmes. I must be honest with you though. I really haven't a clue what I can do for you. But a promise is a promise. So, I thought I would start by asking you... what happened? And, how did your fingerprint, in Mr. Foster's blood no less, get on that desk?"

"That should be obvious. I was in the room after poor Clayton was killed."

"Why didn't you raise the alarm?"

Regina was quiet for a long time. My father had trained me well. When one asks a hard question, one must shut up and wait for the answer. Because he who speaks first, loses. As hard as it was, I sat quietly.

"Oh, what the hell. It's only a matter of time before they find out anyway, and it will make me look even more guilty. I was angry with RC for firing me. You know that RC makes rash decisions sometimes, but I always called Clayton his conscience.

"You may not know that anytime RC has a party, you can always find Clayton in RC's office. He hides out there because he hates crowds. I do too, actually. That's how I discovered him years ago. So, at every party, I always stopped and talked with him. He was a great friend to me."

She began to cry. I sat beside her and put my arm around her, whispering, "Don't cry."

Pulling herself together a bit, she confided, "I slipped into the office and found him dead. It must have just happened because blood was dripping off the desk. The safe was open, and there was ten thousand dollars in cash sitting on the desk. I know it was ten thousand because that's what RC had agreed to pay me the next day. But before he would give me the money, I had to attend your movie premiere and the damned party.

"I lost my mind, I guess. I slipped out of the office, claimed my fur from the coat check girl, and slipped back into the office again. I ripped open the lining at the sleeve and dropped the money down inside my coat. It turns out that some of the cash had blood on it. In the process of tucking away the money, I got blood on my blouse. So, instead of just checking my coat like I'd planned, I decided to have Charlie take me home. That's when I ran into you and Hugo.

"I burned the blouse after I got back to my house. And I hung the coat, the money still inside, in my fur closet, which is on the third floor of my house. That closet was once a servant's bedroom in the servant's hall. I guess that's why the police haven't found the money yet. They just got lazy and didn't bother to search the servant areas. I guess they assumed I might think I was too good to go up there."

She gave a bitter laugh.

"What do you mean by that?" I knew I looked confused because I was.

"I know what everyone says. All of Hollywood thinks I've murdered five husbands, so now it's easy for them to believe I murdered Clayton." She was in tears again, but that switched almost instantly to anger. "They are all wrong. I loved each of my husbands very much. Not like I love Charlie, but I loved them all dearly. They knew what I was, where I came from, and they didn't care."

I was lost again, but I tried not to let on. I was hoping Regina would fill in the blanks as she went along.

"When I met my first husband Bernard, I was sixteen. I'd been on my own on the streets since I was thirteen, surviving by whatever means I could. And I'm sure you know what I mean by that. Bernard was the kindest man I'd ever met.

"The first night I met him, I thought he just wanted to bed me, and I was hoping to turn a couple of dollars for it. But he took me back to his house, the one I still live in today. He had his maid help me bathe and get cleaned up, and she gave me fresh night clothes and put me in one of the guest rooms for the night. The next day, he had his driver fetch my things from the flophouse I'd been living in.

"His wife died nearly twenty years before, and he had three grown children he said were just waiting for him to die so they could get his money. All he asked from me was companionship. Much to his children's dismay, he married me, and we had three short but extremely happy years together.

"For a wedding gift, he put his house in my name, and he gave me three-hundred thousand dollars. I wasn't allowed to spend any of it until his death. Anything I wanted I had. He was the one who introduced me to RC, and he backed my first two movies. After those two movies, RC had more backers than he needed, and I was officially a starlet. He told me that he would be leaving me nothing in his will. That everything I had at the time of his death would be mine, but everything else went to his children. He did that to make sure they could touch nothing he'd given me. I wasn't even twenty yet. I was young and stupid. He knew he was dying. He even introduced me to my second husband. Gerald was in much the same situation as Bernard; he was looking for a companion.

"When Bernard passed away two weeks later, his children descended on me like vultures. But Bernie had been very wise. He left them millions, but they still wanted the house and the jewels he'd given me. But the courts denied them. Everything was in my name, and it appeared as if I was even paying all of the bills. Even though everyone knew it wasn't true, on paper it looked as if I was allowing Bernard to live in my house. And all the receipts for any of his gifts to me were in my name as well. The cash in the bank had been there for nearly three years. They could touch nothing. And to support me through it all Bernie had even given me a new man to replace him.

"I know it sounds horrible, but each husband connected me to the next one shortly before he passed away. Each man followed Bernie's same pattern. Theo, I have to tell you, I learned so much about business and how to handle money from each husband that I have carefully managed my own money until now I'm a multi-millionaire. That's why I say, I lost my mind. I didn't need or really want the money I took from RC's safe. I wanted my career back. It is the only thing I've ever felt I really earned for myself."

When she finished, she didn't cry or scream in anger. She slumped forward and let her exhaustion take over.

"How did they know the fingerprint was yours?"

She shook her head and looked up at me wearily. Her voice was raspy. It was if she were playing a character part.

"When you work the streets dearie, you tend to rub elbows with the police." And she gave me a hard wink.

"Oh," I said with resolve. "Like I told you, I'm not sure what, if anything, I can do, but your secrets are all safe with me."

"Thank you." Her head was hanging down, but she sounded like herself again. "I have to admit, it felt good to finally tell someone after all these years." Her head rose, and she stared pleadingly into my eyes. "Don't worry about me. But if there is any way at all, please find out who killed my friend."

She smiled at me. I rapped on the cell door, and the officer outside the door escorted me out.

# 20

Before leaving the police station, I asked one of the officers to telephone for a taxi, arranging for it to be at my house in twenty minutes. I wanted to make sure my temporary driver had a ride home once we returned to the house. The police gave me the same guarded walkway exiting the station house as I'd had on my entry. On the drive back to the house, I left the privacy shield up, but I opened the shades.

My mind wandered over the chapters of Regina's life. I had never much liked her, but that was only because of the way we met. She had perceived me as a rival for Charlie's attentions, and like all territorial creatures, she was prepared to fight for what she felt was hers. After hearing about her life, I certainly couldn't blame her. I had always lived a charmed life, filled with privilege. And now, as Theodora Desmond, I led a life of almost decadent opulence. One life I was born into, and the other simply fell into my lap. I hadn't earned or suffered for anything I'd ever had. I couldn't even begin to imagine how difficult Regina's life had been, or especially to know that, everywhere you went, you were disliked. Colleagues, fans, and I was betting even those she counted as friends, called her a black widow, thinking she had murdered her husbands.

I was shaken from my trance when the Rolls pulled to a stop at my front gate. I could see the taxi waiting at the curb. I picked up the speaking tube. "Howard, please have that taxi follow us up to the house. I had an officer at the police station ring for it. I didn't want you to have to wait around for a taxi on a Sunday evening."

"Thank you, Ma'am. That was very kind of you."

Howard got out of the car and walked over to the taxi driver. After speaking with him, he proceeded to the gatehouse, and in moments the gates were swinging open. The taxi followed behind us up the drive. When we reached the house, the taxi pulled in front of the Rolls. Howard helped me out.

"Do you wish me to escort you up to the house Ma'am?"

"No, I think I can manage it. Thank you for taking a fair bit out of your Sunday afternoon and evening to drive me."

"Absolutely no problem, Ma'am. Simply doing my job. I told the taxi driver I'd need to put the car over by the garage before we left. Here are your keys back Ma'am. I won't be able to close the gates, just so you know."

I jingled the keys he'd just handed me. "I can take care of that from inside the house."

"Very good Ma'am." He tipped his hat and got back in the car as I started up the step. By the time I had reached the front door, he had skillfully backed the big motor car along the driveway and turned onto the large gravel pad that stood in front of the garage. The taxi driver followed, driving in reverse as well. It was like watching one of those auto daredevil shows.

Just before Howard climbed into the taxi, he saw me looking and called out to me. "I put the keys back under the driver's mat." Then he waved, climbed in, and the taxi pulled away.

After closing the gate, I thought about a nice peaceful

evening at home. The house was quiet. Silent as the grave, actually, but my mind was relentlessly racing. I was on my way to the long gallery when I suddenly felt tired. I could see no reason that I needed to stay dressed. Instead of stopping at the door to the long gallery, I walked on down the hall to my bedroom. In the little sitting area, I sat in the chair usually claimed by Claudette and started to remove my shoes. I looked up and there was Reggie.

"You had a sinister mind. Who do you think killed Clayton Foster?" I asked the portrait. Reggie's visage of course didn't answer. He simply stood there looking defiantly out at the viewer. "A lot of help you are."

As I got undressed, I was tempted to leave everything where it lay. I never really felt right doing that, however, so I put everything in its place. My body felt free after removing the foundation garment that, believe it or not, I had gotten used to wearing. I stood at the closet door, silently wishing I could hear the shower starting up for me. I realized that if I wanted a shower this evening, I was going to have to start the process myself.

*Damn, Eddie, you have become unquestionably very spoiled.*

After my shower, I sat back down. The western script was still lying on the table. I picked it up and started to thumb through it. I remembered Seedy saying there were notes in the back, so I flipped to the back page. There were actually several blank pages permanently bound into the copy. There was nothing on the very back page, so I thumbed forward. The notes were on the very first blank page, directly across from the last page of the manuscript. I knew that, because the previous page had the words "The End" in a much larger font in brackets.

There was only one page of notes. Written violently in bright red ink across the entire sheet was a single word, "Rejected" with not one but three exclamation points after it. I say violently because the word had been overwritten several times, as if emphasizing the point, NO. Who in the world but some villain in a pulp fiction magazine would even own red ink? I guess I had my answer to that question. Studio heads owned red ink and used it too.

I went on to read the note under the angry expression in red. "Roddy," it began, the name followed by a comma as if the writer were penning a letter. Roddy? Why would RC's personal secretary, or his attorney for that matter, depending on whichever hat Mr. Foster was wearing at the time, start what was very obviously his professional opinion with what sounded much like a pet name or term of endearment?

*Roddy,*

*This is a fantastic script for the studio. My bet is that it will be quite profitable. Tommy would be perfect for the lead role. He has the smoldering eyes of Rudy Valentino combined with the rugged good looks of Doug Fairbanks. His deep rich baritone would be well suited for the masculine role of the western cowboy, very well suited indeed. He will truly shine in this new popular movie classification. He stands well over six-foot-tall and has an amazingly athletic form, due in great part, I am sure, to his training as an aerialist in the Grambling Brothers Circus.*

I read the note over several times. It appeared only to be an assessment of the script and of an actor Mr. Foster thought would be ideal for the role. Why had RC reacted so vehemently? I again, turned my attention to the portrait of Reginald Montgrieve, standing there in his tartan kilt. I thought of him performing at the Drakestone for one of their monthly floor shows. And I laughed out loud at how angry he'd be to believe that anyone would ever even consider that a possibility for such a lady's man as himself. The clock in the long gallery struck seven. I looked in the mirror on the dressing table just across from me.

"Why not. I could go as Eddie Standish. After all, I am Eddie

*Standish."*

I jumped out of the chair, shot through the bathroom to the bedroom on the other side, and went to the closet. It was almost empty. Georgie had wanted to use it as my overflow, but I hadn't allowed it. In this closet hung the last vestiges of one Edward M. Standish, BOY. These were the clothes that had been in my closet at Mrs. Haskin's boarding house. I pulled on a pair of standard men's drawers instead of the restrictive garments that I had grown so accustomed to wearing. I was amazed at how liberating they felt. There was utterly nothing binding me down. I had a rather dapper cream linen suit that I purchased two summers ago for a boating party that I ended up not attending. Therefore, the suit had languished in my closet. I wouldn't wear the jacket. I would wear a crisp white shirt, bow tie, and a lightweight sleeveless argyle sweater in beige, light gray and baby blue. I tied the laces on my two-toned brown and white saddle oxfords, and I was ready to go. It was then that I felt a sinking feeling. I was all dressed up, and I had no way to get to my destination other than drive the bright red roadster. And I couldn't do that. It would raise too many eyebrows.

I could take a taxi. But there was no way I could have them pick me up here. I could, however, meet a taxi at the bus stop at the end of the lane at the bottom of the hill. I made up my mind. There was a coin operated telephone at the bus stop corner as well, so I could telephone a taxi from there. But this late on a Sunday night, I wasn't sure how long it would take them to arrive. Since it was already seven-twenty, and it was every bit of a half hour taxi ride to the Drakestone, I decided to just risk telephoning from the house. I placed the call. I was told that a taxi would pick me up in ten minutes, so I had to hurry.

I grabbed a fist full of cash from my top dresser drawer, snagged my keys, and shot out the door. I was never before so happy to have the electric gates. When I heard them clang back in place, I was already within spitting distance of the bus stop. I got there a little breathless from the exertion, and I hadn't yet caught my breath before the cab pulled up.

When I told the cabby where I wanted to go, he just looked at me in the rearview mirror with disgust. "So, you're one of those, are ya? But I guess your money's as good as any. You're lucky tonight's a slow one."

I wasn't sure what to think about the comment, but I knew one thing for sure. There would be NO tip forthcoming.

# 21

It took right at twenty minutes to get to the Drakestone. The place didn't look nearly as bad at night as it did during the day. The façade was well lit; however, there didn't appear to be anyone about. No one was outside the building, nor was anyone wandering around the lobby like at the Ambassador or the Beverly Hills Hotel. The minute I paid the driver, he sped off. I walked to the front revolving door and pushed my way into the building. The big fifty year out-of-date lobby was empty except for two people. Madam Rochelle was behind the front desk. Tonight, her cigarette wasn't hanging from her lips as it usually did but was in a stylish black holder. She appeared to have no beard stubble, and she was dressed all in lace. If I hadn't known she was a man, I would have thought she wasn't unlike so many other heavy-set women. She was clad in black, doing her best to appear slimmer. Standing next to Madam Rochelle was Tiny, a very tall muscular man. The first time I saw Tiny, he was dressed in a men's bathing costume, wearing sunglasses, and sitting in a deck chair out in front of the hotel. Tonight, in a tuxedo as well-worn as everything else in the hotel, he looked every bit the gangster enforcer.

"Hey, honey. There's a twenty-five- cent cover charge. Our

acclaimed Lady's Club is performing tonight," growled Madam Rochelle.

Her cigarette may have been in an elegant holder, but she still clinched the holder between her teeth when she talked. I pulled a dollar bill out of my pocket and pushed it over to her, getting a ticket and three quarters in return. I held up the ticket as if questioning.

"Tiny will tear it for you. Give the other half to the bartender. Your first drink is on the house." I nodded, turned to Tiny and presented him the ticket. He tore it in half and shoved his portion into the side pocket of the badly rumpled tux jacket.

"Down the hall on your left. You can't miss it." I had forgotten how his high squeaky voice didn't match his bulky frame.

As I moved down the hallway, I could hear music and voices, lots of voices. I reached a large set of double doors. The frame was black marble, and the doors were painted a shiny black with long polished brass handles. I pulled open one of the doors. The odor of alcohol, cigarette smoke, together with a variety of inexpensive men's and women's perfumes permeated the already-stale air. The solid wood doors had acted as a sound barrier, and the noise as I entered the darkly lit room was thunderous. A five-piece band was playing, and the club was crowded with people.

"Good God!" I heard Georgie bellow over the crowd. He was at my side in a moment, which was no small feat since he was forced to work his way through a throng. "I never for a minute thought you'd come. Come on down and sit with Randel and me."

He tugged me by the arm through the mob until we reached a table near the center of the room. In front of us was the dance floor — packed with dancers — and beyond the dance floor was a curtained staged. Small tables for two or four people surrounded the dance floor all the way up to the edge of the stage.

"Can you believe who showed up?" he asked Randel.

"I'm sorry," Randel said looking up at me. "I don't believe we've met."

Georgie clapped him hard on the shoulder. "You know, it's Eddie."

"I don't, I've never met Eddie. You forget I don't move in your same social circles." He had a broad smile on his face.

"Good evening Randel. Thank you for allowing me to sit at your table. I'm afraid I'm feeling a little bit like a duck out of water."

"If you feel that way now, just wait. It gets worse."

Georgie went to slap him on the back again, but this time Randel caught his hand. Georgie's hand promptly went slack, and Randel kissed the back of it. "I'm sorry babe, but you know I don't much care for these things." Randel pulled him down into the chair, where he sat sheepishly and began to sip his drink. His quiet subservience didn't last but a moment.

"Oh!" he said excitedly. "I've got someone I want you to meet." He popped up. "He knows a lot about diamonds and jewels, and you've certainly got a lot of diamonds and jewels!"

He said diamonds and jewels as if they were two different things. I smiled.

Randel seized his arm before he could leave the table. "Eddie here," he nodded over in my direction, "doesn't own any diamonds or jewels. Remember?"

"Oh, that's right. But I still want Eddie to meet the man." He turned to me. "He's very handsome." He slipped out of Randel's grip and was swallowed up by the crowd.

"He means well. I'm wagering that between the two of us, we can keep your secret." Randel winked at me.

Randel was always calm and laid back. The only time I had ever seen him anywhere near out of control was the night Georgie had been arrested. Seems Georgie was Randel's Achilles' heel.

When Georgie returned, he had Ezra Blum in tow. Georgie had been right when he said the man knew a lot about gems.

He pulled Ezra to the table. "Abe Blum, this is Eddie. Eddie Stan..."

Randel jumped to attention. "Abe this is our good friend, Eddie Stand-er-ford." He mumbled the last name. Randel looked hard at Georgie.

Georgie only allowed the stern look to affect him for a moment. "Eddie, I was telling Abe you were close friends with Theodora Desmond."

I visibly cringed. Georgie just could not keep a secret.

"I've met her, you know," Ezra said.

"I have known her for about a year," I said, smiling up at Ezra, then turning my gaze to Georgie with an angry glare. If it registered on him at all, he did not show it.

"I am in town because my family is investing in her next movie. I am hoping to arrange a private meeting with her as well."

"A private meeting? Whatever in the world for?"

At that precise moment, a drum roll silenced the room. The house lights went almost out, and the stage lit up. The curtain opened, revealing a grand piano to one side. A tall, slender man with round horned rimmed spectacles sat at the keyboard, and standing with her hand on the piano was Madame Rochelle. She had changed from her all-black frock to one of silvery brocade. She wore a blond wig and held a long red scarf in one hand. Although not a look-alike, no one would have any problem knowing she was imitating Sophie Tucker. She launched into one of the bawdy songstress's comedic routines, "Last of the Red Hot Mamas." Tears streamed down my face as the hefty gravelly-voiced impressionist performed.

While she was singing, a waiter dressed as a lady came by and wanted to know if I would like anything to drink.

"I'll have a Beefeater Gibson, please."

She laughed. "Honey, we haven't had that spirit here since prohibition started. And we ain't got no onions either. How's about a martini?"

"How about champagne?"

"If you want bubbly, I've got beer."

"Then great, I'll have a beer." I handed her my half ticket, and she moved on.

Randel leaned over next to my ear and whispered over the music, "Wise move. All the gin is bathtub gin, and all the whiskey is rotgut. I'm guessing you've figured out that the Drakestone ain't the Coconut Grove." He snickered.

After the surprisingly good first performance of Madame Rochelle, the others quickly fell flat. Most of the impressionists were moving their mouths while a Victrola played scratchy popping records somewhere off stage. Ezra and I walked back away from the stage to the bar.

"I'm sorry, did Georgie say your first name is Abe?" I asked.

"Yes, he did."

"I must confess, I've seen your picture in *Variety*, and they had your name as Ezra." It was a little white lie. But his picture had been in *Variety*.

"You remembered me from a picture in the paper?" He brightened considerably. "Yes, my name is Ezra. Ezra Abraham Blum. I hate Ezra, but my family is set in their ways. So, when I'm not around my family, I use Abe. It sounds so much more American."

"So then, Abe, Georgie also said you know a lot about gemstones."

"I do know a lot about gems with an emphasis on diamonds. My family owns Blum Brothers Jewelers. I doubt you've heard of it. We're located in New York City, and most of our clients are wealthy society members."

We talked about jewels for nearly an hour and a half. I found Abe fascinating, and he had a wealth of knowledge. At the intermission, the band struck up, and the dance floor filled once again. Ezra asked if I wanted to dance, and I accepted. I found it odd dancing with a man when I wasn't dressed as a woman—unusual but delightful. Something that I gleaned quickly was that most homosexual men could easily switch from lead to follow without any issue. And in fact, during the four songs that we danced together, we switched up every song.

The drum rolled again, and we moved back to our seats at the bar. Madam Rochelle opened the second half of the show, this time singing Sophie Tucker's "Makin' Wicky Wacky Down in Waikiki." I turned to watch Madame Rochelle, bracing myself with one hand still on the bar. I felt Abe's fingers slide through mine. His thumb rubbed gently but probingly along my fingertips. When Madame Rochelle finished, I lifted my hand away from his to applaud.

"Abe, you are a nice guy…"

"But, you don't like Jews," he finished, his words flat as if he'd spoken them before.

"It has nothing to do with you being Jewish. I'm in love with someone else."

"I'm sorry. Georgie told me you were single."

"It's a really long story. I am single but—I'm in love with a man who likes girls."

"I wish I could say I didn't know what that feels like, but I've been there too. You understand, you will only get your heart broken."

"Oh, I think I'm already to that point."

"Then couldn't we just have a bit of fun?"

"Sorry, Abe, it just doesn't work that way for me." Changing the subject quickly, I asked, "Why do you want to meet with Theodora?"

"Selfish reasons, I'm afraid. She has a world-renowned jewel collection, and I would like her to work with our jewelers to build some of the pieces that she is having done locally. It would help us both. With the type of collection she possesses, if she decides to become more of an investor, we could counsel her in what to buy and what to sell. It's a very lucrative industry."

"I believe that might be something she'd be very interested in. I'll put a bug in her ear."

Abe and I had talked all through the second half of the show as well, and we danced to several more songs before I decided it was time to go. I said my goodnights to Georgie and Randel, then started to go call a taxi.

"Hey, Eddie!" Randel called. "We're ready to leave too. I believe we might live near you if you'd like a ride," he said with a wink. It seemed Randel looked at Eddie and Theodora as two separate people, which was fine by me.

"Sure, I'd love a ride."

The three of us climbed into an old black model A Ford, with me in the backseat and Georgie cuddled next to Randel as we set off for home.

"It sure isn't your Daimler," Georgie yelled over the road noise.

"I don't own a Daimler. I take the bus, trolley or a taxi wherever I go."

"If you ever find yourself in a pinch, this car is always parked at the back of the estate in a garage that leads into the alley. You wouldn't see it from the yard because it's part of the gardener's shed and hidden from view on purpose."

"Thank you, but I would never feel right using your car."

Instantly, the old model A was filled with Randel's deep rich laugh.

"Then the joke's on you, Eddie. Theodora owns this car too!"

"In that case, that's good to know. You'll have to show me how to find that hidden garage."

Randel gave me a big thumbs-up. Soon we pulled up to the front gate. Georgie got out, opened the gate, and waited for us to pull through. He turned the key again and ran to beat the gate's closing. Randel let me off at the door, reaching in to help me out.

"We'll see you in the morning," I said, as I started for the stairs.

"I'll be here to greet Miss Desmond bright and early. Will Miss Desmond want to use the Rolls tomorrow, do you think?"

"Most assuredly, she will." I mounted the stairs without looking back. I slipped inside the house and made straight for my bed and some much-needed sleep.

# 22

I woke startled from a fitful sleep. I leaned over and grabbed the clock to see what time it was. Ten minutes until six. I had planned on rising early this morning, but not for another forty minutes. I was wide awake and grumpy about it too. I put the clock back on the side table, sat up to stretch, and nearly jumped out of my skin once again, catching sight of Reggie standing at the end of my bed.

"Damn you Reggie!" I bellowed. I leaned over the side of the bed, picked up my shoe, and threw it at the portrait.

I immediately regretted losing my temper. Luckily for Reggie's visage, I don't throw many shoes, and my aim was poor. The shoe slammed into the frame instead.

"Damn!" I spat out. The shoe had cracked the side of the frame near the top. I got up to inspect the break but found that due to the height of the picture itself and the height at which it had been hung, the broken spot was well over my head. I needed a chair to stand on. Before I could get one, the door burst open.

"*Mon, Dieu*! What has happened? Are you alright?" I heard.

Claudette and Seedy stood framed by the door. Apparently, they were on their way to my room with morning coffee when I erupted at Reggie's portrait. They both looked panicked. Coffee had sloshed out of the pot and gotten all over the tray as well as the saucers.

"I'm sorry ladies," I laughed, unable to help myself. "Reggie frightened me, as he seems to every morning. I got mad and threw my shoe at him."

Claudette set the tray on the table hurriedly and turned to survey the picture for damage.

"*Dieu merci*, you did not harm the painting of that handsome man with his legs, *magnifique*," she said, rolling her eyes. "But I see you did break the frame," she added, pointing to the spot.

"I am aware I broke it, but when I tried to inspect the break, it was out of my reach." I lifted my arm and jumped up to illustrate. "When you burst in, I was just about to get a chair and inspect the break."

Claudette turned to clean up the mess with the serving tray. Seedy and I moved one of the chairs over in front of the frame. I was about to climb into the chair when we heard a quick shout of *"Merde!"* Whenever Claudette got flustered, she returned to her native French tongue. Seedy and I both turned to Claudette.

"What's wrong?" Seedy asked.

"I was wiping up the coffee spill, and some of the coffee splashed onto the two scripts lying here," Claudette replied, dabbing at them with a napkin. Then she turned to me and asked, "What would you like me to do with them. It's just a few drops on the covers."

"I'd like to say burn them, since I dreamed about both of those scripts all night," I replied.

"Why would you dream about those two scripts? Neither of them was written with Theodora in mind," Seedy said.

I knew right then that Seedy had read both manuscripts.

"I'm not a fan of the western," she continued, "but I liked *A*

*War Within Him* a lot. Why didn't you like it?"

"My new movie will introduce Zelda Kravitz in a romantic supporting role. *A War Within Him* will be her second picture, this time as the female romantic lead. Who would be the ideal actor already under contract to Colossal Studios to play the male romantic lead?"

"Hugo, of course," said Seedy. Then it dawned on her. "Oh My God! You're jealous!"

"I wouldn't say jealous."

"Then what would you say?" Claudette chimed in.

"I would say, the note in the back of the western script is what has me really puzzled." Claudette picked up the western manuscript, opened it to the back and looked for the note. By the time she located the right page, Seedy was standing next to her, reading along.

"Who's Tommy?" Seedy asked.

"I have no idea."

"Well, it looks like notes on the script. And someone with excellent penmanship thought that Tommy, whoever he is, would be perfect for the part."

"There is a new western actor at Monumental Pictures named Thomas something," Claudette added. "I saw it in *Variety.*"

"You're right. Thomas... Thomas..." Seedy thought out loud, tapping her finger on the top of her head. "Thomas Hicks!" she shouted.

We each snatched up a filled coffee cup and began to deliberate.

"Thomas Hicks was at the opening night party," I offered. "My father recognized him and went over to speak with him. Father called him an 'up and coming western star,' but told me that RC had rejected him. Father was perplexed because he couldn't figure out why he'd turned him down?"

We talked until the clock in the long gallery struck seven.

"Oh, lord!" I put down my coffee and jumped up. "I've got to be at RC's house at ten o'clock. I'm meeting Hugo and Detective O'Flaherty."

"What on earth for?" Seedy asked.

"I have an idea about the murder itself, and I'm hoping to be able to prove it." By the time I finished my sentence, I heard the shower running. "We'll talk about it later. I've got to hurry."

I passed Claudette coming out of the bathroom as I was going in.

"I will take the coffee things down and be back to dress you," she explained. "Be quick about your bath."

I was in and out of the shower in less than ten minutes. I was toweled off, in a black foundation garment, and all battened down in another three. I slipped on my robe and was just about to sit down, when I noticed the chair still sitting where I'd placed it in front of the picture. Since Claudette was not back yet, climbing up onto the chair, I thought I'd have a look at the frame. The break was still above my head, but I reached up high and ran my hand along the edge of the frame. The crack felt like a clean break. The frame must have been made in sections. That made sense to me because of the intricate pattern. It was carved with birds perched on tree limbs, and they completely encircled the frame. I thought it would have been much easier to carve in sections, then piece together. The broken part seemed to jut out just a bit. I thought if I could just push it back in for now, I could have a carpenter fix it properly another time. So, I reached back up and pushed the section back in, and it clicked.

*"It clicked?"*

When I first found the portrait hanging in Reginald Montgrieve's closet, it was in front of a doorway, completely hiding it. To unlock the door, I discovered, one simply pushed in on the bird's eye in the upper right-hand corner.

*"I wonder?"*

I reached up and followed the fine line that I could now see ran slightly above one of the birds. I pushed in on the bird's eye, and there was that click again. I gently pushed outwardly at that point on the frame. The section slid free of the rest of the frame. A box, for that was what that piece of the frame really was, dropped into my hand. Just at that moment, Claudette and Seedy reappeared to help me dress.

*"Mon, Dieu*! Did you completely break it, trying to fix it? It just goes to show you are not a handyman." Claudette was smiling.

"Oh, no, I haven't broken it. Reggie and his picture frames. It seems that this one has a hidden compartment." I looked inside the box. It was lined with black velvet, but I couldn't see a thing. When I shook it from side to side, there was a dull thud. I turned it up and shook the contents out and into my hand. In the back of my mind, I was expecting a sparkling gem like the ones in the last picture frame. Instead, I now held a huge, slightly pinkish chunk of rock.

"Not what I was hoping for, but...." Then I remembered a snippet of the conversation I had with Abe. "Last night Ezra Blum told me that if the average person saw a diamond in the rough, even one as big as a goose egg, just lying on the side of the road, he'd pass right by it and not give it a second thought. He would think it was a rock." I held it out for them to look at. "Do you think we are looking at a huge diamond in the rough?"

They both looked closely.

While looking down at the stone, Seedy asked, "Why were you with Ezra Blum last night?" And after a pause, she added, "I know you weren't home when I got here, and that was late. So, question number two is, where were you with Ezra Blum last night?"

I turned beet red.

"*Mon, Dieu*," Claudette laughed. "When he turns this red, you know the answers to your questions will be the best kind of juicy gossip."

"It is some of the juiciest, but I don't have time to spill it now. Right now, I'm pretty sure I have my investor issue solved. And I've got a new idea about the murder. Let's get me dressed."

Twenty minutes later, Claudette was helping me shimmy into my original Coco Chanel black dress. It was the very first dress of Theodora's I ever wore. Claudette had laid out every mammoth jewel I owned—at least those set into jewelry anyway; I still had a bagful that had not. Florence McCarney had told me to wear enough jewels to scream "you're rich." When I told Claudette that, she disagreed.

"I was with Miss Desmond the day she visited the House of Chanel, in Paris," she explained. "Molly almost passed by this dress. She said it was too simple, said she wanted something flashier. Coco Chanel, herself, overheard her. I will never forget what she said: 'Dress shabbily, and they will remember the dress; dress impeccably, and they will remember the woman.'"

In the end, I wore simple pearl studs and the large aquamarine pendant with the brother and sister diamonds attached. I picked up the humongous pink rock, banking on the fact that it was indeed a diamond, and dropped it in yet another monstrous black leather handbag. I wore no hat, no gloves, and no fur. Today, I was simple, elegant, and all business.

# 23

"Good morning, Miss Desmond," Randel greeted, as I slid into the backseat of the Rolls Royce.

"Good morning Randel."

We were back to business. I really did appreciate Randel's ability to separate business from personal. If Georgie had been my driver, I would have been peppered with questions about how I enjoyed last night? What did I think of Abe? What did we talk about? And the juiciest tidbit of all, would I be seeing him again? If Randel had any desire to know, he didn't ask. I knew that would be very much to Georgie's dismay, because I was confident that task had been assigned to Randel this very morning. I arrived at RC's house at nine-fifteen.

"Good morning, Miss Desmond," Samuel greeted as he opened the door and stepped back allowing me to enter.

"You will excuse me, Samuel, if I get right down to business. Would you please unlock the door between the stairways? I want to look at Mr. Foster's desk again."

Samuel was silent for a long moment. Although very subtle, I saw a range of emotions quickly cross his face. The final one was resignation.

"Yes, Ma'am." And he moved towards the hidden door.

He unlocked the door and followed me in. He opened the elevator door and down we went without saying a word. When we reached the bottom floor, I made for Clayton's desk. The day Seedy and I had been down here before, while Seedy had been reading through the investor prospectus, I had picked up and thumbed through the only other thing on Clayton's desk top. It was another movie script. At the time, I had wondered why it was on his desk, but after talking with Edwina and Seedy, I now knew Clayton made script recommendations. The manuscript was entitled, *"Women of Distinction."*

I turned to the storyline synopsis just after the title page. The story was of two women. It was set in England during the reign of King Edward IV. Both women had been given, as child brides, in marriage to much older men on neighboring estates. When both husbands die within days of each other, the two women form an alliance and decide to take over the running of their households. Since society dictated that they must relinquish their husbands' titles and estates to the next male heir, and both women had born only daughters, the ladies lay their husbands to rest in secret and continue on as if they were still very much alive. The story was of their struggles as women in a man's world and the deep, abiding, life-long friendship that resulted through their tribulations and triumphs.

After having read through the synopsis, I turned to the back to see if Clayton had made any notes. Across from the end page was Clayton's beautiful and orderly penmanship filling what had once been a blank page.

*Roddy,*

*This script would be amazing for our two tantalizing temptresses!*

*I know you don't feel that the studio can support two women in this position, but I must disagree. Since so many women are entering the work force, this movie could ignite single women around the world, and it just might create an entirely new movie-going audience. What are your thoughts?*

Had RC fired Regina because he didn't feel the studio could support two women in the role of temptress? It would appear Clayton was thinking of Regina and me not solely as temptresses, but more along the lines of formidable women like Florence McCarney and Gwennie Hawthorn. Strong women, winning the battle of women in power in a man's world. Having seen one of those ladies in action first-hand, I had to agree with Clayton, it could spark a whole new audience of movie goers.

I opened my enormous purse, folded the manuscript and pushed it inside. I was lost in thought as I turned back around to Samuel. I looked up at him, and as I started to speak my eyes were drawn to the parlor behind him instead. The vast space was now perfectly symmetrical. Six sofas with their six coffee tables surrounded the massive rough granite fireplace with its enormous opening. On one side of the fireplace hung the portrait of a younger RC Crawford, looking toward the fireplace. On the other side hung the matching portrait of a boyish Clayton Foster, also looking towards the center. Had the paintings hung side by side, the two men would be looking fondly at each other.

Above the fireplace itself was yet another portrait, one painted much more recently. It showed the two men in a very casual pose—RC seated, and Clayton with his arms wrapped around him. Their cheeks were almost touching as they smiled out. The three pictures together told the story of a long and much cherished love. I now knew why RC Crawford was devastated. I looked around the room. The scale of everything was so big. Then my gaze stopped at the two chairs by the radio. The very place I had found RC sitting after Clayton was killed. Two matching chairs. One for RC and one for Clayton.

"This is their private quarters, isn't it?"

"Yes, Ma'am."

"I'm surprised there isn't a bedroom," I said with a nervous chuckle.

"There is Ma'am, behind that mahogany panel. It's another hidden door. There is also a third elevator that goes up to RC's room on the second floor and Mr. Foster's on the third. They never used the entrance we've been using. They always came down the back way."

I looked at the clock on the mantel. It was ten minutes to ten.

"We'd better get back upstairs. We sure would not want the police back down here today. Besides, I have a murder to solve."

Samuel suddenly looked very concerned.

"Don't look so worried. I'll keep everybody's secret," I assured as I started for the elevator.

Samuel didn't move. "What do you mean by that, Ma'am?"

I turned back. "I'm guessing that you clean this room yourself, that none or at least very few of the other servants have ever been in these rooms. RC and Clayton guarded their secret carefully. They must have had complete faith in you before they ever divulged their secret. And there is only one way they would have trusted you that much."

I walked over and patted him gently on the chest.

"Now let's go."

We got back upstairs and into the foyer just in the nick of time. Mary was on her way to open the door as we emerged. She held off until we'd closed the hidden door and came around the large table that stood in the center of the room.

When the door opened, Detective O'Flaherty and Hugo were laughing and talking very animatedly. Animatedly, that is, until they saw me standing in the hall.

"Miss Desmond, would you be so kind as to tell us why you've summoned both Detective O'Flaherty and me here."

*"The nerve of Hugo taking that pretentious tone with me,"* I thought, but I put on my best pose-for-the-camera smile.

"I have asked Detective O'Flaherty, Sean... May I call you Sean?" I inquired.

"You sure can, Miss Desmond."

"Oh, please call me Theo. I asked Sean here today, to avoid any embarrassment over wrongfully arresting a very wealthy, very public figure. I just knew he would prefer that over a press conference."

Sean's smile disappeared. He started to speak, but I held up my hand.

"I summoned YOU here, as you say, Mr. Wainwright, out of common courtesy."

"See here Miss Desmond, we have the right person in custody. We have her fingerprint in the blood of the dead man."

"I'm sorry, Detective, but you don't. Follow me please."

I languidly sauntered with one hand on my hip to the office door, knowing full well exactly where both men's eyes were planted. I opened the door and gestured for the two men to follow me in.

"What the devil?" I wasn't sure which man said it first. It must be an ordinary policemen's term of surprise.

"How did that get here?" Sean asked, staring at the massive throne.

"A better question detective, is how did the hole in the back of the chair disappear? Oh, and the blood."

Both men looked hard at me.

"There happen to be two identical thrones. They were created for a movie that was never made. I had the second throne sent over from the studio this morning. I needed it to prove my point."

"Then I suggest you do so, Ma'am," O'Flaherty said flatly.

"Very well. Hugo, could I get you to play the part of Mr. Foster?" I extended my arm toward the chair.

Hugo moved around the desk and sat heavily onto the throne. For a moment, I was reminded of the first time I ever saw him, in his rumpled black suit, sitting in this throne's brother.

"The police are saying Regina's motive was robbery. Have you found the money?"

"No, but it's simply a matter of time."

"Am I correct in my assumption that all you really have is her fingerprint in the dead man's blood?"

"Yes, and I'll wager it's enough to send her to the electric chair."

"All it proves is that she was in the room after Mr. Foster was killed." He started to protest, but once again, I held up my hand. I stepped behind the desk far enough to be behind the chair.

"If the killer was standing here, would you both agree that Mr. Foster knew his killer?"

Two heads bobbed in affirmation.

"All right then, let us say I'm Regina Banks. She's a bit taller, but not by much. Would either of you say she was more physically fit than I am?"

I got a quick "NO" from both.

"I see the money on the desk, and I want it. I snatch the sword," I pulled the remaining blade free from its scabbard, knocking the stand over and letting the sheath fall to the ground. "At this point, would I still have the element of surprise needed to then run over, seize Mr. Foster by the neck, and pin him against the chair before driving the sword through him? Oh, and remember, I have to bring the sword thrusting down, not pushing up. Therefore, I'll have to jump up in the air while holding him tightly around his neck. And of course, let us not forget the arch in Mr. Foster's back, an arch that was completely free of blood. She could not have done it. It is not humanly possible." I re-sheathed the sword, set the stand right again, and placed the ancient weapon back in its place on the shelf.

"The other alternative, of course, is if I grabbed Mr. Foster by the neck first. Do you mind?" I asked Hugo.

Now intrigued, he indicated for me to proceed. I stepped behind the throne. Once there, I could not be seen over the top. I reached around the throne and tried to slip my arm around Hugo's neck, but my arm was decidedly too short for me to stay centered behind the chair. Once I got myself in a position where my arm finally reached around Hugo's neck, I stretched my other arm out as far as I could for the sword on the shelf. My hand, however, barely stuck out from behind the throne. I was still a good foot and a half from the blade.

"This won't work either," I said, peeking around the throne with my arm still wrapped around Hugo's throat, and winked at Sean. He couldn't help but smile.

"What would work?" asked Sean.

"Trade places with me."

I stood back next to the doorway to look at the scene.

"How tall are you, Sean."

"Six foot two."

Mr. Foster was a little bit taller in the waist than Hugo.

"Sean, hand Hugo one of those encyclopedias off the shelves behind you to boost him up about two inches." Hugo gave me a cross look but sat on the book. "Now Sean, lean over the chair like you are talking to a lover."

Both he and Hugo's heads popped up. "What?"

"Just do it."

Sean leaned over the chair.

"Look up, Hugo."

When Hugo leaned up, his back arched naturally.

"My back just arched," he said with surprise.

"Sean, slide your arm around his chest as if you were being playfully affectionate."

Sean looked at me and rolled his eyes, then he slipped his arm around Hugo's chest.

"Sean, lean forward even more like you are going to kiss him. And Hugo, lift up your head more, so your lips can meet his."

The two men were smiling as their faces drew only a breath apart.

"My back is arched even more," Hugo murmured.

"Now, Sean, slide your arm up around his neck and hold Hugo tight against the back of the chair. Can you reach the sword?

Sean reached out and easily clasp the handle of the sword. He pulled it free and raised it.

"Enough, Sean! I don't want my leading man skewered over a demonstration," I laughed. "You were right Hugo, when you said the murderer was a man." Sean gave Hugo an inquisitive look.

"Sean, both Hugo and Samuel," I pointed over my shoulder to Samuel, who stood just outside the doorway, "surmised before you arrived the other day, that Clayton Foster had been murdered by a man. They were correct. Gentleman, your murderer is one Thomas Hicks, who has recently signed with Monumental Pictures as their new western actor. RC had just released him, I suspect because his voice didn't test well."

They looked perplexed, so I said, "Let me explain. I think that, unbeknownst to Mr. Crawford, Clayton Foster had already put Thomas Hicks under contract. I bet you'll find that Mr. Foster was seduced by Mr. Hicks. My guess is, Mr. Hicks was to Mr. Foster as a mistress would be to any other older man. You will also find his contract release in his possession. You see, Monumental Pictures would have required a copy before they could sign him. My thoughts are that Mr. Hicks had prostituted himself to Clayton Foster in order to obtain a contract with Colossal Studios, then he became angry when it was canceled. He was at the opening night party. Remember, Hugo? My father went over to talk to him."

"I'll have to check everything out," Sean said.

"I bet those unknown fingerprints on the sword are his," Hugo said.

"You might be right. We will certainly see."

"You know," I threw in as an aside, "Clayton Foster had been RC's employee for over twenty years. RC trusted him implicitly. RC felt betrayed when Mr. Foster signed an actor without his knowledge, that on top of feeling grief at the loss of a close business colleague, is there any wonder why he fell apart. Sean, is there any way Regina might be released, even if it's just on bail?"

"Let me see what I can do. It's pretty evident, at this point, that Regina could not have murdered Clayton Foster."

"Thank you, Sean. And if you're not able to release her outright, I'll post her bail. Please let me know, and I'll arrange for my driver to pick her up. That way, her picture won't be splashed across every paper's front page with her looking like she's been in jail for the last three days. Now, gentlemen, if you will excuse me, I have a meeting to prepare for. Oh, and Hugo, don't forget about your second summons this afternoon at three."

I turned and walked from the room. Samuel had the door open before I could get to it. He followed me outside and closed the door behind us, holding on to the knob.

"Bravo, Miss Desmond! That was terribly naughty of you to make those two men reenact the crime."

# All That Glitters

"Yes, it was." I smiled and left it at that, as I slipped gracefully into the buttery soft leather seat of RC's Rolls.

# 24

As I was taking the stairs to the second floor of the only administrative building on the Colossal Studios lot, I wondered why a man, with not one but three elevators in his personal home, did not have one up to his own office. Arriving on the second floor, I turned down the hallway that led to RC's offices. When I reached the door to the suite, I smiled. In large gold letters under Colossal Studios, I read "Theodora Desmond, Chief Executive Officer." I opened the big glass door and went in. Down the short corridor, I could see Edwina busy at her desk. Along the hallway leading up to her desk were two rooms. One was the conference room where I would soon be meeting with the investors. Across from that was a well-appointed windowless room that served as the studio's private screening room.

"Hello, Edwina," I greeted as I strode down the hallway.

"Good morning, Miss Desmond. You look stunning today."

"I'm hoping I look all business, today. Please, thank your husband for getting the lettering done so promptly."

"Like I told you, he jumped at the chance to quit ironing. I took the liberty of also having him create a new nameplate for your door."

"I hadn't even considered that. Thank you again."

"I take it your morning appointment went well."

"It went amazingly well. I hope by this afternoon that all charges against Regina will be dropped and she'll be released from jail."

"Oh, my goodness, however did you manage that?"

"It hasn't been managed quite yet, but I feel quite confident it will. However, in case the police don't drop the charges, please make sure the studio attorneys can help her post bail."

"Yes, Ma'am."

"Where would I find Regina's sound test?"

"Normally, it would be in film storage, but it's actually still here in the screening room. Mr. Crawford was watching it the day *Samson and Delilah* premiered. I'm the one who'd send it to storage, and I just haven't done it yet."

"Good. Do I need to have someone to come over and set it up so I can see it?"

"No, Ma'am, I can get it ready for you."

"Great! I'd like to watch it as soon as possible."

"I'll have it ready in just a few minutes for you."

"Thanks. And around noon, I'm expecting Mrs. Florence McCarney and possibly her daughter, Estelle. Would you please make sure we have a light lunch ready to be served in my office?"

"Would Watercress sandwiches and lemonade work?"

"Perhaps we should have something a bit more substantial. Mrs. McCarney is a rather robust lady," I added with a smile. "When the investors arrive, please put them directly in the meeting room. I don't want to greet them until the meeting starts." I started into RC's...well, I guess, my office now and turned back. "Oh, and Edwina, is there any way you could find some of that delightful prohibition booze?"

She looked at me oddly. "You mean like rot gut and bathtub gin?"

"The very same."

"Yes, Ma'am, that will be easy to do."

"Good. Replace all the liquor in the conference room with that, please — before the investors arrive. And instead of setting the decanters back on the sideboard, put them on the table near the seat reserved for Mr. Housley Overholser."

"Yes, Ma'am," she said hesitantly, looking at me like I might be a tad bit crazy. "Would you like me to set up and start the projector now?"

"That would be splendid." I changed directions and followed Edwina into the projection room. She loaded the film in the machine in minutes, then switched on the projector and switched off the lights as she left.

The screen before me lit up. The image counted down, three-two-one. Suddenly, there was Regina's face, and a male voice spoke in the background, "Regina Banks sound test, dramatic reading." The camera pushed in on Regina, and she began to run the same lines I'd learned for my sound test. Each reading, nine in all, came one right after the other. When it was done, I came to an entirely different conclusion than RC—Regina's sultry voice ideally fit her smoldering looks.

*What was RC thinking?*

I switched off the projector, because the now loose film end was flapping around noisily. On the way back to my office, I asked Edwina to please locate all of RC's information on Regina and bring it to me.

Shortly before noon, Florence McCarney arrived. She was again dressed in a deep, almost blood red. The neckline of her dress had been cut very low, only to be filled with a pleated white raw silk with a rather high collar. It was apparent that the dress had been designed to show off her gigantic gold necklace. I wasn't sure whether to call it a necklace, or maybe a collar. The first thing that came to mind was a lavish adornment worn by an Egyptian Pharaoh, made of solid gold and reminiscent of the sun. It was so incredibly large that it seemed to envelop her, and I could only guess as to its weight.

"How are you, my dear?" said the bountifully Rubenesque woman, thrusting her arms out to embrace me and nearly bowling over poor Edwina as she struggled to hold the door open for her.

"I am well, Mrs. McCarney," I said, returning the hug. "I hope this day finds you well too."

"Yes, Yes."

"Please sit down. I've had Edwina arrange a luncheon for us. I'm hoping that is all right with you."

"Do I look like a woman who turns down lunch?"

I knew better than to answer. I just smiled and motioned for Edwina to serve the meal.

Edwina rolled in a cart filled with a beautiful display of small ham sandwiches, little pickles, and a yellowy potato salad.

"It looks wonderful, dear. Thank you for going to all the fuss."

"Oh, it was no fuss," I said, truthfully. After all, Edwina had done all the work.

She filled her plate with four of the small sandwiches, a small handful of the pickles, and a generous dollop of potato salad. Holding the plate daintily, she reached up and patted her gold collar. "I saw you looking at my necklace when I came in. It was made by Blum Brothers. It was not their finest hour, but I can't fault them. They were dealing with Aloysius. It was the very first piece of jewelry he bought me after we struck it rich. God love him, his heart was in the right place. The blasted thing weighs nearly five pounds. It's like toting a sack of potatoes around your neck. Over the nearly twenty-four years I've owned it, I've had sixteen different dresses designed to wear it with. I know young Mr. Blum will recognize it because his grandfather said it was the ugliest piece of jewelry ever designed for a lady." She roared with laughter.

"It is certainly impressive. Is it made with gold from the Lucky Scotsman mine?"

"You are the first person, in all these years, to ever asked me that. Yes, it is. Aloysius took two bags of gold nuggets all the way to New York City. He told them he wanted a big gold necklace for his wife, and he wanted them to use it all. This was the result. You can see why, even if it is the ugliest piece of jewelry ever designed for a woman, it means more to me than any other piece I own. And I own a lot. That said, those are a pretty impressive set of rocks you're wearing too."

"Thank you, so much. The hanging teardrops are called the 'brother and sister' diamonds because they were cut from the same stone. They are my favorites. They were not designed by Blum Brothers, but I'm not worried about Mr. Blum pulling out after our conversation at the Coconut Grove. I also want to thank you for your influence with the ladies in the equestrian world. Mr. Chesterfield is maintaining his investment as well, unless something unforeseen happens. So, our only challenge should be Mr. Housley Overholser. And I have a couple of ideas there as well."

"Good! I knew once you were able to sleep on it, things would become clearer. You merely allowed Mr. Overholser to bully you last time. And the two others were like sheep following along. In this round, you will become their shepherdess and expose Mr. Overholser for the wolf in sheep's clothing that he is.

The intercom beeped, its green light flashing. "It is one o'clock Ma'am," came Edwina's voice. "All three gentlemen are here and in the meeting room."

I sat on the corner of the desk, leaned over, and pushed the green button down. "Did you set the new booze near Mr. Housley Overholser?"

"Yes, Ma'am, I most certainly did."

"Thank you. Oh, and Edwina, bring your pad and accompany us, would you please? I need you to act as stenographer."

"Yes, Ma'am."

I sat up straight on the corner of the desk and rubbed my hands together. "Are you ready to head into battle, Florence?"

"Most assuredly!" She was as giddy as a school girl. "This is absolutely my favorite part of business. I think you'll do great, but if you feel you're losing control, I'm here to help. But only if you need it."

We both hopped up and moved towards the door. Just before following Mrs. McCarney through, I pulled the large rock, the one I suspected was a diamond, out of my purse. I had placed it in a small black velvet pouch, one that typically held one of my bracelets. I slipped the pouch into one of the file folders I was carrying. It was a bit bulky, but it would have to do. We added Edwina to our little entourage as we passed her desk, and together the three of us marched down the hall toward the meeting room.

The moment I opened the door and stepped through, Housley Overholser was on his feet and began protesting loudly, "Before we collect our hats, Miss Desmond, I hope you have the authority to have your secretary write us a check!"

Just as quickly, a voice bellowed back, "Sit down and be quiet, Mr. Overholser!" Everyone in the room jumped. The voice had been my own. Overholser didn't sit, but he did close his mouth.

"Sit down, Mr. Overholser," I said again, with a great deal

more aplomb. He sat.

"Gentlemen, I would like to introduce Mrs. Florence McCarney. Mrs. McCarney and her husband, Aloysius, own the Happy Scotsman gold mine. She is sitting in today as a possible investor herself. Also, my secretary, Edwina, will be transcribing our meeting so there will be an official record."

I motioned for Mrs. McCarney to have a seat next to Overholser. Then I moved to the far end of the table, putting Overholser on my left, and Ezra on my right, who was next to Chesterfield. Edwina had a chair at the far end of the table nearest to the door.

"I apologize for the rocky start to our meeting," I said, looking straight at Overholser. "Understand, Mr. Overholser, I will not tolerate being screamed at. Do you understand?" He fumed up at me but said nothing. "When last we met, I gave each of you a portfolio outlining how the funds of your investments will be used. I'm sure as savvy investors you've taken the time to read it, even though it was not presented to you in the manner I had wished. Therefore, this meeting should be brief. Are there questions about the portfolio that I can answer for you? If I am unable to answer your questions now, rest assured I will obtain the answers and get back with you quickly."

"Miss Desmond," Overholser interrupted, "I say again, we wish to withdraw our investments." His voice was civil, but the look in his eyes was murderous.

"We, Mr. Overholser? Do you have a mouse in your pocket?" It was one of my grandfather's favorite sayings when one of his employees was trying to speak for another. "I am only hearing you asking to pull out. I do believe that Mr. Chesterfield has decided to go forward. Am I right, sir?" I looked at Grady Chesterfield.

He nodded with a smile.

"Mr. Blum," I continued, "would you mind if I call you

Abe? A dear friend of mine tells me you prefer it."

Abe beamed. "Yes, Miss Desmond, I do prefer it. And yes, you may most certainly call me Abe."

"Wonderful, Abe. Have you decided to keep your investment in place?"

"I had never planned on pulling out, Miss Desmond."

I turned back to Overholser. "It would appear that only you wish to pull out, Mr. Overholser. Edwina, please write Mr. Overholser a check for the amount of his investment less a twenty percent administrative fee."

"What?" He was bellowing again, but this time I expected it.

"It is simply the cost of doing business."

"I will sue this studio for every penny it has!"

"I seriously doubt that, Mr. Overholser. You see, I am aware of your current situation with the United States government. I cannot see you wanting to give them any reason to look closer at your business dealings than they already are. And, of course, in the spirit of full disclosure, we — the studio that is — would feel compelled to inform the judicial system about your varied, and somewhat rather dubious income sources. Or you could keep your investment where it is and make lots of good CLEAN money. The choice, of course, is yours."

"Why, you bitch, that's blackmail," he spat out at me.

"Why, you disgusting, foul mouthed bastard, you might be right," I replied in a sickly sweet syrupy tone infused with a beaming polite smile.

Overholser harrumphed. He reached over, grabbed a decanter from the tray sitting next to him, poured a large whiskey, and shot it down. He coughed, sputtered and gasped for air.

"What the hell is that?" he coughed out.

"I was only trying to be hospitable. That is some of the

finest liquor in Texas. It's whiskey from your own distillery. I figured, if it's good enough for your oilmen, it should be good enough for you."

Overholser stood up. "I'm going to keep a close eye on you," he said, pounding his index finger on the table.

"Well, Tex, I'm easy to find. Just buy a ticket to your local theater. I'll be the one on that big silver screen putting money into your pocket."

Overholser stormed from the room.

"Dear God, I wish I could do that!" Abe exclaimed, expelling a deep gush of air, once Overholser had departed.

Everyone, including Abe, laughed loudly, releasing the tension in the room.

The meeting was promptly adjourned. I apologized again to Mr. Chesterfield, thanking him for taking the time to talk with me at the Coconut Grove.

Then I asked Abe to wait in my office. "There is something, I wish to discuss with you. Edwina, would you please show Mr. Blum to my office?" Abe followed her out the door.

"Florence, I can't thank you enough for all your help and for taking time out of your day to come and support me. I'm not sure I handled that well, but he didn't pull out."

"And that is what really matters." Florence said, smiling.

I winced. "You didn't think resorting to blackmail was going overboard."

"Hell, NO! He's the type of man who only responds to force. I understand calling him a foul name after he called you one is the biblical eye for an eye, but in the future, you might refrain from that. Men sometimes react violently. But other than that, you handled everything as though you'd been dealing with 'hard to get along with' people, all your life." She smiled and gave my hand a tight squeeze before walking out the door.

After seeing her out, I went back down the hall. Edwina

was just coming out of my office. I gave her a hug. "Thanks for taking care of me today. I asked for a lot of things at the last minute. I hope I didn't frighten you too badly when I screamed at Mr. Overholser."

"I did nearly jump out of my skin," she grinned. "Mr. Crawford himself could not have handled that better."

"I will take that as high praise indeed." I pulled the pouch from the folder, shook the heavy rock from the pouch into my palm, and opened my office door.

# 25

"Think fast!" I called, as I tossed the heavy stone underhanded towards Abe.

The young man quickly turned in his chair and fumbled to catch the stone before batting it to the ground.

"Good catch," I chuckled, moving around the desk, while Abe dropped down on all fours to retrieve the stone. "What do you make of it?"

Abe rose up on his knees, cupping the big crystalline lump in his hands. His eyes were filled with wonder. He lifted the stone carefully and held it high in the air between his two index fingers and thumbs, almost as if it were an offering to some revered deity. It was then it registered on me, he was holding it to the light, looking deep within it.

"This cannot be real," he whispered incredulously.

"That is precisely the question I'm putting to you," I replied. "My speculation, however, is that it is most definitely authentic."

"If it's authentic, I would wager it just might be the largest pink diamond ever discovered. Is this one of the stones in your collection?"

I hadn't really given that any thought. Since I was awarded Reggie's jewel collection and this was still another of

Reggie's gems, then it wasn't too far a leap to lay claim to this one as well.

"Yes, it is."

"Miss Desmond, the reason my family decided to invest in Colossal Studios is that we were hoping to build a business relationship with you. After the announcement of your jewel collection, my father approached Mr. Crawford about investing. He had planned on coming to California himself. But a few months ago, Mr. Crawford contacted my father and insisted he send me instead. My father was furious. You see, although I'm very well trained in my trade and feel I'm am an excellent craftsman, I'm the youngest son. And of my father's three sons, he considers me to be, well, lacking in business acumen."

*More likely the fact that you like men over women,* I thought to myself. But instead I asked him, "Do you want my jewelry business?"

"Yes, Ma'am we do."

"Why in the world would already renowned jewelers in New York City want my business?"

"Why, Ma'am, with the jewels you now own, the pieces created for you will become the jewelry of legends."

"I'm not sure I completely understand."

"Miss Desmond, when you found the Rose of Kintyre, everyone around the world became interested. People love pictures and stories of large jewels. Our firm created the new necklace that now holds the Rose. The Rose in its new mounting is breathtaking. But when it was finished, we thought we were done. The piece was delivered to the Duke, and like so many large gems in private collections, it was once again destined for obscurity.

"But then you wore it at the premiere of your new movie. You cannot even imagine how many inquiries we've had since that premiere. And it's still been less than a week. My father knew it would create a sensation if someone famous wore the necklace in public. And who better to wear it than the movie star who found it. That's why he planted the seed in the Duke's mind and encouraged him to allow you to wear it. Now every time the Duchess wears her famous necklace, she'll be the talk of the town. But only because the necklace was worn first by someone just as famous as the ancient ruby itself.

"Every piece you wear after having worn the Rose of Kintyre will be watched by others. Wealthy men will want jewels like the ones Theodora Desmond wears for their wives, sweethearts, lovers, and mistresses. We have already had several requests for a two-teardrop diamond pendant like you're wearing today. And to the best of my knowledge, it has only been seen in public two, maybe three times. But it's been seen in all the right places by all the right people. Yes, Miss Desmond, Blum Brother's wants your business. We are prepared to offer you a deeply discounted rate on your creations if you will allow us to publicize them as having been created by Blum Brother's Jewelers."

"Done! As soon as I can, I'll arrange to travel to New York City. You and I will work on this project together." I nodded towards the diamond in his hands. "I'll have my secretary contact your father. I want him to know that no one else but you will handle my account."

Abe looked stunned, but then a broad smile set his face alight. As he started getting to his feet, I became cognizant he had been on his knees during our entire conversation. He stood and stuck out his hand to shake mine. When our hands met, he looked down at them and ran his thumb over my knuckles, a gesture just like that night at RC's party when Overholser had held my hand. Before letting go, he looked me hard in the face, then he turned my palm up and dropped the big pink rock into it. I slipped the stone back into the little black velvet bag.

"Miss Desmond, when you see Eddie next, please tell him I said thank you. And let him know I'd enjoy spending another evening with him." He smiled. He didn't wait for my reply before moving through the door and closing it behind him.

It was two-forty-five, and I only had about fifteen minutes before my meeting with Hugo and Zelda. I put the diamond back in my handbag and pitched the purse into RC's big leather chair. I leaned over the desk and pushed down the toggle switch and the green light glowed.

"Edwina, would you please come in?"

There was no reply, only a quick knock before Edwina slipped through the door.

"Yes, Ma'am."

"Do you know if Zelda and Hugo have received copies of this script?" I held up my coffee spattered copy of *A War Within Him*.

"Yes, Ma'am. They both received copies about a week ago. They were sent by messenger. I could look up the exact date and time if you'd like."

I shook my head. "What if anything, do you know about this movie?"

"Mr. Crawford was talking about shooting your new movie, *Raptured Love*, the one that introduces Zelda, and this movie simultaneously," she said, pointing to the manuscript. "*A War Within Him* will star Hugo, with Zelda as co-star. He wants to release the two movies within six months of each other. His thoughts are that it will be Hugo's third film, so he will be the main draw for *A War Within Him,* and it will allow Miss Kravitz to hold her own as an actress. Her contract is temporary until after this second film."

"Thank you, Edwina. Please let me know once both Hugo and Zelda arrive."

"They are both already here, waiting outside."

"In that case, show them both in."

Edwina opened the office door.

"Miss Kravitz, Mr. Wainwright, won't you please come in?"

Edwina stood back and allowed both actors in before closing the door behind her as she left.

"Please, both of you come and have a seat," I said. I motioned to the two chairs in front of the desk.

"Hugo, have you heard anything regarding Regina?"

"No, I have not." He offered no further information.

I moved to sit on the corner of the desk again, only this time I crossed my arms over my chest. For some reason, it helped me feel in control.

"I have no desire to take up a great deal of your time, so I will be brief. As you both know, I have only recently taken over as head of the studio. I'm working diligently to bring myself current with the studio's activities. Now that I have moved from the roles of ingénue to temptress in my acting career, it is paramount that we replace the ingénue as soon as possible. Mr. Crawford has selected you to be that replacement, Zelda. However, we do feel, the V and Z combination in your last name is too harsh. We have decided you will become Zelda Warren."

Her face when instantly sour. "I do not wish to change my name, Miss Desmond."

"Zelda, unfortunately, that is not your decision. It is the studio's. Just ask dear Hugo here."

"Wainwright isn't your real last name?" She looked at him with amazement.

"Wainwright didn't used to be my last name, nor was Hugo my first. At least you'll be left with a little bit of your old self."

"I am certainly not happy about it."

"You'll get used to it. We all have," I said, uncrossing my arms. "Now that we have dealt with that, let's get on to the main reason I called you here today. It's about publicity. I want to start immediately playing up a rivalry between Miss Warren and me for the affections of Mr. Wainwright. After all, you win his loyalty in our next movie, although I win his heart. In *A War Within Him*, you win him back from both drink and war. The role of the ingénue is always a battle. Hers is always the virtuous fight. And in our film together, we need the fans to want you to triumph over me.

"I want to start this rivalry with the studio sponsoring a star-studded dance marathon. They seem to be all the rage right now. I will enlist the aid of my personal secretary, Cecelia Schofield, and my office secretary, Edwina Sullivan, to get the ball rolling. I want it to be in two weeks' time at the Coconut Grove. Miss Warren, I would like you to work closely with both of those ladies. Edwina knows almost every person in the movie industry, and Seedy is a master of organization. This will give you the opportunity to meet many of the people with whom you will be working closely in the future. Do either of you have any questions or concerns?"

"I only have one question at the moment. Why am I starring with Zelda? I thought RC planned to shoot several movies with you and me as a team?"

"I cannot and will not speak for RC, but it seems simple. Our next film together will be your second and should cement your new role as the male romantic lead. In *A War Within Him*, you'll be the star and Zelda the co-star. You will be the main audience draw. It should be a barometer as to your audience appeal. I hope RC will be back in command before then, and what movies we make or don't make will be up to him. If there are no further questions, we all have a lot of work to do. Miss Warren, Mr. Wainwright, you are being paired together for the dance marathon. Miss Warren, you will need to set an appointment with my haute couture."

"By that, she means, dressmaker," Hugo interjected smiling at me.

"He's right. His name is Georgie Herndon. Edwina will give you his contact information. I want you to be a vision in white."

They both stood, and I ushered them towards the door.

"Oh, and by the way, I'm entering the contest as well. So, the best you can do is second place."

Miss Warren's eyes grew wide.

"We'll just have to see about that." Hugo winked and gave me a mischievous grin.

I walked both of them all the way out to the front door of the offices.

"Your name looks good in big gold letters," Hugo said, pointing to the door. "But if I know you, you will always prefer your name on a marquee in lights."

I gave him a wink before stepping back inside the office. I could feel Hugo's eyes on my back through the glass door as I walked toward Edwina's desk, but I didn't turn to look. When I reached Edwina, I stopped and informed her of my dance marathon plans and how I thought it should work. I told her to call Randel and have him bring my car around. It had been a very long day, and I wanted to get home, get out of these clothes, and be Eddie at least for a little while.

# 26

Randel and I rode in companionable silence back to the house. As we pulled towards the front gates, they began to swing open. I leaned forward, saying, "Stop at the gatehouse please, Randel."

"Yes, Ma'am."

I rolled down my window.

"Good evening, Mr. Truman. I wanted to ask how you were getting along with the electric gate system?"

"Couldn't be much easier Ma'am." His face bore a wide grin.

"Wonderful. Please, give my best to Mrs. Truman."

I tapped Randel on the shoulder, and he drove on towards the house. When I stepped from the motor car, I noticed the bright blue Mercedes roadster parked just in front of the Rolls.

"It appears you arrived home just in time, Ma'am. It seems you have a guest."

"So it would seem."

The door was already opening when I reached the top of the steps.

"Good evening, Ma'am. I have shown Mr. Wainwright and Detective O'Flaherty to the long gallery."

"Thank you, Wallace."

*So much for getting undressed.*

I climbed the stairs to the long gallery. When I entered the room, both men stood, each with a drink in his hand.

"Good evening, Detective, and fancy seeing you again today, Hugo. I see both the former officer and the current policeman are embracing the laws on prohibition. I think I'll have a drink too, if you don't mind."

I walked over to the decanters, but before I could pour myself the drink, Hugo was at my shoulder.

"Allow me," he offered. "Scotch?" He already had the crystal glass in his hand, and his other hand was moving toward the ice bucket.

I gave a quick shake of my head in the direction of the ice tongs he now held and sighed, "It's been a long day. Make it neat."

"Neat it is." And he poured two fingers, then started to tilt the decanter up.

I took a finger and pushed the decanter back down, saying, "Make it three." I cocked an eyebrow, and he smiled as he handed me the now much fuller glass. "Well, gentlemen, I assume this isn't a social call, so to what do I owe the pleasure?"

"John, I mean Hugo, insisted we bring you up to date on what's happened since we last spoke this morning."

I raised my glass to Hugo and nodded my thanks.

"The police searched Mr. Hicks' apartment," Detective O'Flaherty continued. "Just as you predicted, we did find the signed release of contract. We also found a tuxedo covered in blood, dumped in a neighbor's trash can. It turns out Mr. Hicks' fingerprints were already on file. His name isn't really Thomas Hicks, but Cecil Barrow. The police suspected him of killing another older gentleman to whom he was romantically linked, but we could never prove it. Unfortunately, it seems that Hicks is now on the lam.  Most likely, he's using the money he stole to make his getaway.

"Also, we released Regina Banks this afternoon and have dropped all charges.  I'm sure you knew that, since it was your driver who fetched her from the station house." I didn't let on, but I had no idea that Regina had been released from jail.

Both men had evidently said what they had come to say, and they quickly finished their drinks and took their leave.  I stood at the window and watched them both vault into their seats.  Hugo steered the bright blue roadster down the long driveway.  Mr. Truman was ready for them, however, and the gates were swinging open long before they had reached him.  Hugo turned onto the road, and they were gone.

I looked after them for a long moment, missing Hugo and the fun we'd had together.  But that was the way it had to be.  I shrugged, set the nearly still full tumbler of scotch back on the drink cart, and made my way toward my bed chamber.

Looking around my bedroom, I decided the best place to keep the giant pink diamond was right where I found it.  I kicked off my shoes and climbed up on the chair.  I reached up and pushed on the bird's eye, and the box popped free from the rest of the frame.  I wedged the large stone back inside its velvety niche, then snapped the box back into place.  I'd just gotten down and had the chair back in place when Seedy and Claudette came in.

"You certainly have taken your new role as 'Empress on High' seriously," declared Seedy.  "I've been on the phone with Edwina for the last two hours.  And just so you know, that poor woman was terrified when you commanded her to organize a marathon dance contest—and to have it at the Coconut Grove, of all places—in just two weeks.  You do understand that events like that take months or often as much as a year to plan?"

"Empress on High?" I asked. "Commanded her to organize? I wonder then, how RC can fill a room in a matter of hours."

"It could be that he's the head of a major movie studio and has a great deal of influence."

"Exactly! Two weeks should give her more than ample time." I stuck out my tongue at Seedy.

"'Empress on High' fits you much better than 'Chief Executive Officer.' And Edwina is not accustomed to your ways. You tend to have an idea, spew it forth, then leave it for someone else to bring to fruition. Seems that RC always supplied her with copious notes from which she could easily work. You, however, require people to think for themselves. She's very capable of doing just that, but she's never been given such an opportunity before."

"She'll do fine."

"On another front, I knew you were busy dealing with the investors, so I told Randel to bring Regina Banks here instead of taking her directly home. I telephoned Georgie, who brought over something for her to wear. And Claudette put her in the guest bath, where she could freshen up and change before Randel drove her home. Afterward, Randel said that her house was mobbed with reporters and photographers, so she was glad she didn't arrive looking like she'd been in jail for several days. She sends you her thanks."

Claudette immediately spoke up, "The black widow may not have killed Clayton Foster, but that doesn't mean she didn't kill five husbands!"

I halted Claudette's tirade with a raised hand. "This really isn't my story to tell," I said. "But if you'll sit down calmly, I'll tell you what Regina told me."

When I finished, both ladies had tears in their eyes.

"And come to find out, she is only two years older than Charlie. She seems much older only because she's been a wife and public figure since she was in her mid-teens. And she is very much in love with the Viscount too. I'm going to encourage her to tell her story to the Duchess. I think it will ease both the Duke's and Duchess's minds regarding their future daughter-in-law."

"Daughter-in-law?" gasped Seedy. "Do you really think the Viscount is going to ask her to marry him?"

"He's totally besotted with her, and she with him. So, yes, I think he will."

The telephone rang. Claudette hopped up and answered it.

"Desmond residence, Claudette speaking. Certainly Samuel. I will let her know. *Au revoir*." She hung up the telephone and turned to me. "Monsieur Crawford's private rail car has just arrived. He is coming directly here to speak with you. He should be here in less than an hour."

"Great! Maybe, I can finally get some answers."

# 27

I reached the long gallery at the half-hour mark. I had just gotten comfortable and had the newspaper in hand when I heard a gentle rap at the door. It opened, and Wallace stepped in.

"Good evening, Ma'am," he said, softly. "Truman telephoned from the gatehouse. It seems Mr. Crawford is on his way up the driveway."

"Thank you, Wallace, for the advance warning." I folded my newspaper and set it aside. "When he arrives, show him right up."

I walked to the window to watch his approach and found that one of the studio's limousines was already in front of the house. In moments, there was another gentle rap as Wallace admitted RC into the room.

"Good evening, my dear," he greeted brightly.

Typically, he would have rushed across the room and kissed me on the forehead. Instead, he turned to Wallace and said firmly, "Please see that we are not disturbed. BY ANYONE!"

"Yes, sir," Wallace said with a slight bow as he slipped out the door, closing it securely behind him.

I looked quizzically at RC.

# All That Glitters

As if to answer my implicit query, he said, "What we are about to discuss is for our ears only." With his pronouncement, he walked over to the cart with its two crystal decanters, one bourbon and one Scotch. He chose the Scotch and poured two fingers into a glass; then, to my surprise, he poured another two fingers into a second glass. Picking up both glasses, he walked over to me and held out one of the tumblers. Again, I looked puzzled. "Trust me, my dear," he confided, "you're going to want this."

I took the proffered glass.

"Why don't you sit down?" He motioned to the chair I'd just been sitting in near the fireplace. I walked back to the chair and sat. I set the Scotch on the table next to me as RC began to pace. I sat quietly waiting for him to collect his thoughts. He stopped with his back to me, his shoulders squared, and he stood a little taller. I knew he had gathered his resolve when he turned.

"My dear, I owe you a huge debt of gratitude. One I'm quite sure, I will never be able to fully repay."

Still, I said nothing.

"Theodora, you are a great actress, but I've been around many great actresses for a great many years. We have come to the point when we need to dispense with pretense. I know it was through your efforts that my name was not linked to my dear Clayton's..." he hesitated, "in a romantic nature, that is."

I started to play the fool, but he raised his hand with his palm out, gesturing for me to stop.

"I met Clayton when he was twenty and I was forty-one. He was applying for the job that he held until his death." RC's eyes glistened now, seeing only into the past. "He'd just graduated with a degree in business. He informed me that he would like to work for me for only the next three to five years; he said he wanted to save enough money to attend law school. He wanted to be a lawyer. Can you imagine anyone *wanting* to be a lawyer?" he said with a slight laugh.

"I was impressed with his honesty and his determination. I wanted to see if he could really stick to that plan, so I hired him. He worked tirelessly and accomplished any task I ever set before him." He paused to take a small sip of his Scotch.

"On the anniversary of his third year of employment, I called him into my office. I asked him how he had advanced on accomplishing his goal of saving enough money to attend law school. He beamed, thanking me sincerely for remembering our conversation of so long ago. Indeed, I was amazed that simply the recalling and verbalizing thoughts of another, thoughts held as essential, could make them so happy. He went on to excitedly explain that it would still take him another two years to save enough, and that he hoped he could remain working for me.

"I informed him, however, that no, he could no longer continue working for me. That my situation had changed, and that I needed a personal secretary who already held a law degree. But I asked him to come back when he had obtained his law degree, that I would hire him again. He looked crestfallen.

"You see, Theo, I had already lost my heart. When his face fell and his shoulders slumped, I couldn't bear it any longer. I told him why I had called him in that day. That I wanted to pay for his education. That I would find someone else to take his place while I sent him to any law school in the country. All he had to do was choose. I suggested the law schools of either Princeton or Harvard. Either one would ensure that he could secure a position with any of the formidable east coast law firms. I expected him to be excited. A young man, still well under thirty — I thought the offer would thrill him. But instead, he looked hurt. To tell you the truth, I was baffled.

"He asked me if I thought he'd been doing a good job. He

hoped I had. He said he had been giving it his all. I commended him on doing a superb job. I even explained to him that was precisely why I was offering him this opportunity. I'll remember the look on his face and what he said next until my dying day.

"He said, 'Sir, I am a very frugal man. Working in your household, I've never had to purchase a meal or pay any type of rental for my lodging. And today was the first time I've been less than one hundred percent honest with you. I would like to clear that slate. The truth is, sir, I have had enough money to attend law school for over a year now.'

"I remember his eyes filling with tears. I knew by the look on his face that inside he was at war. And finally, he made the decision to tell me.

"'The truth is sir, I love you. I know it is considered wrong and a sin, but there you have it. I will be more than happy to leave now, as not to demoralize you any further.'

"He started to rise. I was in shock. I thought this couldn't be happening. I'd wanted him since the first day I ever laid eyes on him, and somewhere along the way it had turned into a love for me as well. I couldn't imagine a day without him in it, working alongside me. By the time I came to my senses, he was standing at the door ready to walk out of my life forever. I don't remember going to him; I just remember leaning against the door to bar his exit, then throwing my arms around him and pressing my lips to his.

"I remember pulling apart long enough to whisper in his ear, 'I love you too. With all my heart.'

"Then I said a silent prayer, 'Dear God in heaven, help us. The road ahead will be filled with trials and tribulations. Please, dear God, let us weather these storms together.' And he did, you know. God answered my prayer."

He suddenly seemed to relax, relieved of an enormous burden. And for the first time since he entered the room, he was smiling.

"My brother, Norbert, owned a home in Los Angles near Loyola Marymount. I'd just broken ground on the house where I live now, and it was going to take four years to complete the new home. So, I made arrangements with Norbert to use his house. It was rarely used by his family anyway, since they spend most of their time back east close to my sister-in-law's family.

"My brother didn't keep any staff at the house, so we lived as lovers. I used a staffing agency and rotated hired staff members to help keep our little secret. Like this house, there was a master's chamber and mistress's chamber; and like this house, the rooms connected through the bath. With his belongings in one room and mine in the other, it was easy to keep our secret. It was the most incredible four years of my life. Clayton earned his law degree at Loyola University, and with his new degree, he was invaluable to me."

Instantly, RC's expression changed from sheer bliss to that staggering, lonely, lost feeling that accompanies the loss of a beloved spouse. "Now the love of my life is gone. Killed by me and my jealous heart. You see my dear, there comes a time in every man's life when he is no longer a boy or the epitome of manhood, but he isn't yet old or withering either. When that time arrives, men long to feel connected to their younger days once again. That was the point Clayton had reached in his life.

"Along came Tommy Hicks, who made Clayton feel young again. Just like Clayton had done for me all those years before. I'm sure it all would have blown over if I'd gone along with Clayton's plan to feature him in a movie. After all, the boy was a pretty face, but he couldn't act. It would have been his only movie.

"But I was jealous, so I refused to have the boy under contract or even put him in front of a camera. I had no clue how unhinged the young man was. I imagine there'll be a hole in my heart for the rest of my life. I'm certain I'll mourn Clayton's passing for a very long time to come."

RC closed his eyes hard, clenched his teeth and firmed his chin, willing himself not to cry. Once he regained his composure, he shrugged, sniffed once, and he was back to business.

"But life is for the living, and for the time being at least, that includes both you and me. Now is the time for us to be candid. I've known Theodora Desmond since before she was Theodora Desmond."

I looked puzzled.

"That's right. I've known Molly, or should I say known of her, ever since Bertie sent her mother back to Oklahoma all those years ago. Not much gets past me, my dear. When he brought Molly to California and worked so hard to get her screen test in front of me, I felt that any man that would work that hard for a child he'd barely known certainly deserved a break. So I made up my mind. I'd watch the screen test, and then I'd be brutally honest with him.

"I had the movie reel sent by messenger to my home. The night it arrived, Clayton and I played the short reel downstairs in our private theater. When it was finished, I didn't say anything. Clayton turned to me with a look of amazement. He told me, 'I think you just discovered America's newest sweetheart. The camera loves her.'" RC slowly shook his head and gave me a slight smile.

"Clayton could always pick a star. And he was right, as usual. Theodora Desmond indeed won the hearts of moviegoers everywhere. She was an astonishing actress."

He kept talking about me — at least me when I was Theodora — in the past tense as if I were the one who had died, not Clayton. I was beginning to feel a knot of anxiety in the pit of my stomach. I was sincerely hoping it wasn't showing on my face.

"To the best of my knowledge, Bertram Standish only has two children. Molly, the daughter who seemed to be a secret — a secret that is, to everyone but me. And he also had a son, the light of his life, Edward. Edward seemed destined to follow in his father's footsteps. I believe until recently that he was enrolled in the Bentley School of Business, right here in LA, and carrying very high marks."

I sat frozen in place.

"Can I share something with you, my dear?" he asked quietly.

"Why of course," I said, forcing my tone to be calm and pleasant.

"Molly, as Theodora Desmond, was a wonderful actress. But Edward as Theodora Desmond, to choose a single word, is phenomenal, both as an actress and as a businessman. Or perhaps you prefer businesswoman?"

I picked up my almost forgotten Scotch and drained the glass. It burned wickedly going down.

"I told you, you were going to want it," he laughed.

"How long have you known?"

"From the moment you were introduced to the Duke. Molly would have never known to call him, Your Grace. Then when you flipped Reggie, I was one hundred percent certain. You see, young Edward, may I call you Edward?" he asked.

"Call me Eddie; almost everyone does."

"You see, Eddie, your father was always talking about his son and how he was working his way up to a tenth-degree black belt. How he was going to be the youngest man in the state of California to achieve such a high honor. I really do listen, especially when it comes to people talking about the things they love. It can be a great bargaining chip. I always know what to offer when I want something in return.

"And that brings us to where we are, Eddie. You are a master at the illusion of Theodora Desmond. In fact, I would use the term chameleon. A chameleon who can turn that illusion into any person they so desire."

I said nothing. I wasn't sure what to say—or even what he meant for that matter.

"*Samson and Delilah* will be an astronomical success in just weeks. It will catapult you into a realm of stardom held only by the rare few. People will flock to Theodora Desmond movies in droves, just because it's Theodora Desmond.

"You can create this youthful illusion now. But what happens when you begin to age? Actors usually have three choices as they get older. They either take on less important mature roles, become character actors, or they retire. As I see it, you only have one option. You will need to retire." Then he wagged a finger at me, adding, "and I'm guessing you will *want* to retire. You don't seem like the type of man who will want to live the rest of his life as a woman."

He picked up his glass again, musing, "I've been pondering this dilemma for a while now. I'm not concerned about any future movies within your three-year contract, but beyond that I am concerned."

He took a long sip of his Scotch, then looked at me with what looked like candor. "With Clayton's death," he continued, "I was not in any condition to work with those three investors. And there was only a short window of opportunity to forge a trusting relationship with them too. I knew that Eddie as the actress Theodora was outstanding, but not really sustainable. So, I wanted to see if Edward Standish was anywhere near the businessman his father is. I thought you'd simply negotiate terms with all three investors. Instead, you formed powerful new alliances and scared the hell out of at least two of those men. Your father could never have pulled that off, and he is one of the best, if not the best in his field.

"You, however, have already surpassed his abilities. You got an actress to agree to change her name. Take it from me. That is no small feat. And you decided to have a dance marathon of famous and wealthy people to generate a rivalry between you and another actress. Sheer genius! That's why, starting immediately, I am going to pay you eight thousand five hundred dollars a week, and one percent of the box office take. The only actor making more is Charlie Chaplin. Then in three years, Theodora Desmond will retire and take up life as a recluse. At the same time, Edward Standish will become the acting chief executive officer of Colossal Studios."

I cocked an eyebrow.

"Forget it, Bertie junior. This offer is beyond incredible, and I won't go a penny higher," he said chuckling.

"Why would you do this?" I stammered.

"For starters, because you saved my reputation. But mostly because you're exceptionally talented and your uncanny business skills will make both of us wealthy beyond our wildest dreams."

He looked at me and chuckled again, rubbing his hands together.

I grinned, let the offer hang in the air a couple of seconds then I looked him straight in the eye, "Throw in the Rolls Royce, and you've got a deal."

"Deal then!" And we shook hands. Then RC smiled as he added, "Oh, and act surprised when Bertie tells you about his amazing negotiating skills."

He finished off his Scotch, set his glass down, and started for the door. He had just reached for the knob when he turned back to me.

"The ability to create an illusion like yours is rare indeed." Then raising a finger in my direction, he added, "Rare, but not unheard of. And you are not the first. Illusionists such as yourself tend to have a seductive, alluring aura that surrounds them. They draw people to them like moths to a flame. Some of the people drawn can become very dangerous if they ever see through the illusion. And you, my dear, have a propensity to attract murder. Have a care, Theodora, that it's not your own."

And with that ominous warning, he slipped quietly out the door, closing it behind him. I stood, walked to the drink trolley, poured another two-fingers of Scotch, shot it back and let it burn its way down.

*Here I am. I've just become the second highest paid entertainer in the movie industry. I was already one of the wealthiest women in the country, maybe even the world. I have a loving family and amazing friends. Half the known civilized world knows who I am, and most of those are adoring fans. And right now, at this moment, I feel more alone than I ever have.*

"What can I do about that?" I asked myself out loud.

I heard my father's voice echo inside my head, "Get that smile in place. It's show time!"

I smiled and moved toward the door. I had to telephone Abe Blum. I needed a partner. I had a dance contest to win.

# 28

The next morning, I awoke early once more. I was sitting in my robe with my feet propped up on the coffee table, just finishing up my reading of *"Women of Distinction,"* when Seedy and Claudette arrived with morning coffee. I moved my feet, so that Claudette could set the silver tray bearing the silver coffee pot and its robin's egg blue cups and saucers on the coffee table. I leaned back and pitched the movie script on to the dressing table behind me, as Claudette filled the cups.

"What is up with you?" asked Seedy, concern in her voice. "You look like someone who has the weight of the world on his shoulders."

"And a weighty world it is today," I replied.

"Oh my, and we are feeling sorry for ourselves too. Okay spill. You weren't in this dark mood last night before you met with RC, therefore, it must be something he said."

"No, not really, it's that I have a lot on my mind. Now that RC is back, I'm unclear as to what to do. I'm sure he will want to resume his position as head of the studio. You see, the thing is, I've come to enjoy being studio head.

"At first, I was totally lost, but over the last few days, I've started several projects I'd like to complete. And during my conversation with RC last evening, he never once brought up immediately going forward. So, now I'm at a loss as to how I should proceed."

"There is no need for you to be at a loss." Claudette said emphatically. "If Monsieur Crawford, said nothing to the contrary, then you will continue doing the same job you've been doing.

"We will finish our coffee and you will get dressed for the office just as you have for the last several days. He thrust the job on you, and he will need to be the one that takes it away again."

"I must agree with Claudette. If, RC Crawford had wanted you to step down, he does not seem like a man to mince words. He would have informed you he was usurping your authority," Seedy added.

The telephone rang. Claudette hopped up to answer it.

"Desmond residence Claudette speaking." She listened. "Let me give you to her personal secretary." She handed the telephone to Seedy.

"Good Morning, Cecilia Schofield speaking." She listened. "Yes Mr. Blum." She smiled over at me broadly. "She does have an opening today. She could see you at 1:30 this afternoon in her office at the studio or, if you would prefer, she could do a 12:00 lunch."

I was busy shaking my head no. But Seedy was paying me no heed.

"Lunch at noon it is then." Seedy listened again. "That is perfect, sir. I will let her know and she will meet you there. Will the reservation be in your name? Spectacular then. Good-bye." And she hung up the telephone.

"What was so spectacular and why in the world did you schedule a luncheon for me?"

"What is spectacular is that Mr. Blum is staying at the Ambassador Hotel. He suggested you dine at the Coconut

Grove. You remember the concierge that you told us about, the one that nearly broke his neck trying to get to you and the Duke? Since, you will now be there for lunch with Mr. Blum, you might take the opportunity to inquire as to having your dance marathon there. Edwina and I each called the Coconut Grove yesterday and they have flatly refused to host the event."

"Why in the world would they do that?"

"Because, according to the gentleman we spoke to yesterday, 'It would be detrimental and deleterious to the reputation of the Coconut Grove and the Ambassador Hotel."

"Detrimental and deleterious? It will involve a great many of their current clientele. I cannot see it being detrimental in the least."

Claudette must have slipped into the bath, because I heard the water come on in the shower. When she returned to the room she was like a woman on a mission.

"Get yourself out of that chair. The only thing that has changed since yesterday is that RC Crawford is back in town. You have no time to mope. Get in the shower and we'll get you dressed."

Seedy crossed her arms and nodded in agreement. I went. When I came back into the room, Claudette had my clothes lying on the bed and Seedy sat in her chair reading the new script.

"Sit!" Claudette commanded. I sat.

"I really like the premise of this new script. I think it would be perfect for you and Regina." Seedy said, looking up from her reading.

"Have you looked at the notes in the back?"

"No, I haven't," she replied, immediately flipping to the back of the manuscript.

"Wow, this is Clayton's handwriting, isn't it?"

"Yes. The manuscript was lying on his desk. I saw it while

you were busy with the prospectus."

"After reading this, do you think RC sacked Regina because he didn't think that the American movie going public would support two movie sirens? And if that is the case, why do you think he ever cast Theodora as temptress to begin with? I'm mean, he had an acclaimed movie siren already, who is far from past her prime, and he also had an adored block busting ingénue. Why turn his ingénue, Theodora Desmond, into a temptress at all? Doesn't that strike you as odd?"

"That's a very good question. The night Theodora became a movie siren was the first night I became Theodora. RC must have already had it planned for Molly."

I mentally added that to a growing list of questions I had made up my mind to ask RC. I had started the day lost for direction, but now I had a plan.

I would go to the studio office. My gut told me, that almost without a doubt RC would be there. I would speak to him about Regina and the possibility of filming *Women of Distinction*.

Then I would meet Abe for lunch at the Coconut Grove. I chuckled to myself. Just a few days ago, I was searching for a reason to go to the chic hot spot, and now it seems, I'm headed there every time I turn around.

Today, I was again wearing the chocolate brown worsted wool suit with its robin's egg pinstripe and matching fleur-de-lis embroidered lapels. Around the collar of the barely blue silk blouse went on three strands of pearls. Fastened around my throat was a single strand diamond choker with the brother and sister pendent dangling from its middle. To go along with my five-inch heels of robin's egg blue, I seemed to have acquired a matching mammoth handbag. I folded the script Seedy had been reading and slipped it easily inside the purse. Claudette had softened the look of the business suit with a white fox fur draped over one shoulder.

I stopped by my office on my way to the front door. I wanted to pick up the dossiers on the three investors. I needed to return them to RC. I pulled out the movie script, laid the three brown envelopes on top of it, and folded them all in half. It was a tight fit, but I got them all into the big purse. I was very glad that it was the largest one I'd carried yet. I picked it up and it weighed a ton. *Oh well, at least I don't have to carry everything tucked under my arm.*

I shot out to the front steps where Randel was waiting with my door to the Rolls held open. I smiled as I descended the steps. *My Rolls-Royce.* I thought, as I slid in and was immediately cocooned within the confines of its burgundy leather luxury.

# 29

When I entered the building, a string of movers were all in a row one behind the other, marching down the stairs like a line of ants carrying what I presumed to be the large leather chairs that had once occupied the meeting room upstairs. When I had worked my way past them, receiving whistles and catcalls for my efforts, and arrived at the top of the stairs, I could see a man working diligently on lettering the glass door. I knew at once, although I had never met the man, this must be George, Edwina's husband. I figured he was removing my name and replacing it with RC's, but when I drew near, I found that my name remained as well as my title. However, below that George had added RC Crawford's name, and beneath that, was the title, Founder. Seems I was to remain Empress on High. *Well, question number one answered.*

The man lettering the door looked up as I approached and smiled.

"You must be Edwina's husband George," I said extending my hand.

"That I am, Miss." He took my hand and gave it a quick pump. "How are you this fine morning, Miss Desmond?"

"I am very well, thank you for asking. Any way I can slip

through the door?"

"That is absolutely no problem, Miss. I am almost done here," he laughed. "I would have been done an hour ago if it hadn't been for the movers." He stood up and held the door for me to enter.

I could tell as I walked down the hall, yet another army of ants was shifting furniture in here as well. It would appear that RC was transferring his office into the former conference room. Edwina quietly sat behind her desk watching the proceedings as she sipped a cup of coffee. She smiled at me. When I reached the reception area in front of Edwina's desk, I spotted RC in conversation with a very colorfully dressed woman with very large spectacles. She had what looked like fabric swatches in her hand. They all appeared to be in pastel colors, with pink shades being predominant.

When RC looked up and saw me, he looked relieved. He smiled and came running my direction. He kissed me on the forehead.

"My dear, I am so glad you have arrived. I've got someone I would like for you to meet." RC took me by the elbow and moved me over to the woman standing just inside what I guessed had just become my permanent office. "Theodora Desmond, I would like to introduce Clara Foxworthy. Mrs. Foxworthy is a home decorator. Clara, may I introduce Miss Theodora Desmond." The two of us shook hands and greeted each other.

"Theodora, I have enlisted Clara's aid. I wanted her to supervise the moving of my office and to add or subtract anything that didn't fit the new space. I also, wanted her to design your new office as well.

"But we have run into a slight difference of opinion as to the flavor of your new decorations. Clara thinks that you will most likely want something in the French style, one of those numbered Louie's, or maybe, the Napoleonic era, covered in pastel colors and chintz. I told her that you didn't seem like the chintz or pastel type to me."

"Oh RC, thank you so much for consulting with me before you proceeded," I said beaming at him. "Mrs. Foxworthy."

"Clara please," she replied. The woman had an overly large mouth with thick lips, and currently, those big thick lips were painted a brilliant red.

"Clara," I started again. "Although I very much enjoy a good chintz," I lied, "I would like this office to be furnished with very comfortable furniture. I enjoy William Morris and the Craftsman styles."

Clara looked horrified. "But my dear Miss Desmond. Both of those styles are very masculine. Surely you wouldn't want an office that looks like a man?"

"Dear Clara, normally I would agree with you one-hundred percent, and if I were designing an office for my personal rooms, there is nothing I would like better than Napoleon III furnishings, upholstered in those breathtaking chintz prints you're holding in your hand. However, my new position as Chief Executive Officer means I will be conducting meetings that will often be comprised solely of men."

I took Clara by the elbow and led her deeper into the now almost empty office. "This room also has a very unique view, that sense we are a movie studio, I would like to capitalize on." I looked over at RC, and then I drew Clara even closer to the windows with their backlot view.

I leaned in close to her and whispered conspiratorially, "Now you know Clara, we ladies have operated all our lives in a man's world. Going into a man's office doesn't make us feel out of place at all, but I'm sure in your profession you know how men are." Clara nodded in affirmation. "They would rather spend an entire day toiling in a field, even pulling a plow, rather than spend one hour in any room that's decorated for ladies." This time her head bobbed up and down almost as if she had an affliction.

"One of my primary jobs as CEO is to obtain and work with investors. To date, those are all men. So, I am sure you see why I want the furnishings of the room to be large and masculine."

At that moment two of the movers came in to move out RC's desk. Both men were large in girth and muscles. After removing the drawers, they hefted the huge desk in the air and then turned it sideways to fit it through the door. "Take great care not to scratch the desktop." Clara barked out.

After the two men had passed through the doorway carrying the desk, I again leaned into Clara, "I see you, too, must work in a man's world. Can you imagine either of those gentlemen sitting for a meeting in a Napoleon III chair?" I could tell by the look of horror that had just formed on her face that she had pictured one or both of those movers plopping down into one of the expensive antique gilt spindly leg chairs and watching that chair crumple to the floor under their weight, taking its occupant with it.

"Oh, Miss Desmond," she gasped. "I had never thought of it like that. I will create for you a masculine office with very sturdy, but beautiful furnishings that will compliment your unique view."

"I cannot wait to see what you come up with. I've taken enough of your time. I will leave you to monitor your movers and ponder this space." I turned and moved back toward RC. "I was hoping to speak with you this morning, but everything seems to be in utter chaos."

"That it is, my dear, but if you like, we can sequester ourselves in the screening room. I've already found it to be the only space here that offers any type of quiet." He motioned for me to follow him.

* * *

# All That Glitters

I smiled at poor Edwina quite literally caught in the middle of the mess. It was evident she would not be accomplishing anything today.

# 30

Once we were inside the screening room, RC closed the door. The sounds of the melee in the rooms beyond vanished entirely. RC turned and rapped on the wall with a grin. "I had this room soundproofed so that a movie could be viewed without disturbing the whole office. I discovered this morning that it works both ways."

He walked over to the two comfortable leather lounge chairs that sat on either side of the projector. They were currently facing the silver screen mounted on the wall at the far end of the room. He turned the two chairs so that they were facing, offered me one, and then he sat in the other.

"Now my dear, what's on your mind?" RC asked, then leaned back giving me a beatific smile.

"RC, I wanted to talk with you a bit about Regina."

"I assumed you would," was his reply.

I must have looked puzzled because he pointed to the projector. "The last time I was in this room before this morning," he began, "was the day of the *Samson and Delilah* premiere. I had been watching Regina's sound test. I especially, remember putting the film spool back in its metal canister. I made sure to do it so that Edwina would know I was finished with it and could send it over to film storage.

"This morning, the film was back on the projector, and it had not been rewound. That's how I knew it had been viewed. I assumed there would only be one person who would have even given the sound test more than a passing thought. Then I had to ask myself, why would you be thinking about it at all? The only answer I could come up with was that you had spoken with Regina and she had told you something that set that mind of yours to spinning."

He again sat quietly smiling. He was unquestionably a clever old cuss. Indeed a master at getting people to open up to him, he had fed me just enough information to force me to talk. I wasn't certain where I should start. I had no clue if Regina had ever told him about her life, so there was an exceedingly long pause in our conversation.

It was RC who took the initiative to speak first. "Did Regina by chance tell you of her first husband, Bernard?"

"She did."

"Did she tell you about each of the subsequent husbands, too?"

I nodded.

RC smiled, shaking his head. "You really are amazing, my dear. I know the entire story, but not because Regina has ever shared it with me. Regina's first husband, Bernie, Bernard Winslow and I had done business together many times over the years. He actually was the financial backer for her first two movies. About a week before he died, he and I had a long chat. He told me the entire story, including the part where he had found Regina his own replacement. I know each subsequent husband followed suit."

I nodded and told RC, "Regina also revealed to me that she was more than financially secure, so she didn't need to work. But she values her career above all else. She told me that she felt it was the only thing she had ever truly earned herself.

"When you terminated her contract that day, she was

beside herself, not to mention angry with you. She went to your office the night of the party to talk with Clayton. She said he hated crowds and always hid out there when you were entertaining." RC smiled and nodded in agreement as I continued, "She wanted him to talk to you on her behalf.

"When she entered the office and found his body, she panicked. She didn't want to have anything to do with the police because of her, shall we say, somewhat checkered past.

"Hugo and I saw her immediately afterward because we were involved in a conversation with Charlie. She seemed out of sorts for sure; but at the time, I thought it was because you had sacked her.

"She asked Charlie to take her home, using the excuse that she had caught a chill. They left the party immediately after that. At first, I thought you probably fired her because her voice didn't test well. But the more I thought about that, the more I knew that couldn't have been the reason why. I needed to judge for myself.

"That's why I asked Edwina about her sound test. I watched it and knew that you couldn't have dismissed her because of her voice. Her sultry voice perfectly matches her smoldering looks. I was baffled as to why you would have let her go. Then yesterday I think I figured it out.

"The other day, when my secretary Cecelia and I went down to your private quarters with Samuel to retrieve Clayton's copy of the investor prospectus, I noticed a movie script lying on Clayton's desk. While Cecelia reviewed Clayton's notes and numbers, I thumbed through it."

RC's face bore a look of confusion, but I continued. "I dismissed it at the time because we were in a hurry. But after pondering the possibilities, yesterday I went back and retrieved the manuscript." I opened my enormous purse and pulled out the screenplay, flattened it out from where I had folded it in half to fit into the purse, then handed it to RC.

"Are you familiar with this manuscript?" I asked. As RC opened the cover and began to read the synopsis, he shook his head.

"I'm not sure where Clayton acquired it," I explained, "but I discovered yesterday that his notes are in the back. They interest me almost as much as the script itself."

RC flipped to the back. I sat quietly as he stared at the page for a long time. Then he ran his fingers down the page, touching the words as if trying to touch Clayton through them. When he finally looked up, a tear streaked his face.

"He was one of the most insightful men I have ever known. I had counted on Regina going to talk with him. She made a point to speak to Clayton at every party she attended. That's why I made attending the party for the premiere a requirement for getting a payout on her contract.

"After reading this," he said, pointing down at the script in his lap, "and knowing how fast your mind moves, of course I will entertain all of your questions and answer them to the best of my ability." RC sat back and rested both hands on the arms of the chair. He seemed to be bracing himself for a battery of questions.

"All right then, why turn Theodora into a temptress to start with? You already had a very popular box office draw in that department, as well as Theodora filling theaters as your ingénue?"

"I didn't anticipate you opening with that question. You really are a deep thinker, my dear."

"Actually, I cannot lay claim to the question. It was my secretary Cecilia, who posed the query to me after she read Clayton's notes. However, after having given it a good deal of thought, it seems like the most important question to have answered."

"Believe it or not, that's where almost everything started. Regina would have made a marvelous Delilah, but she had become increasingly melancholy. You see, one of Regina's most significant marketing assets is her nefarious reputation as a black widow. It was actually husband number three, Homer Jasicutt, who came up with the idea. One night at a party, he said, 'You know RC, if the American movie-going public actually thought your movie star siren — in real life — killed the older men she married, they'd flock to see her movies.' And he was absolutely right. They did.

Regina knew about the marketing ploy from the outset. But as time went on, as the papers and tabloids played it up after each husband's death, the ruse began to take its toll on Regina. Moviegoers did line up to see her movies, and they still do. But the press, as the press tends to do, would not let go of the black widow angle. Eventually, she came to despise the hand-crafted reputation."

I nodded. "You are one-hundred percent correct; Regina does hate that reputation."

"I didn't know what to do. It wasn't the reputation that needed to change; besides we couldn't do that even if we'd wanted too. The cat was already out of the bag. What needed to change was Regina's attitude. I sat down with her several times and discussed her outlook on the black widow story, but it never seemed to help.

"It was Clayton's idea to make Regina think she was about to be replaced. He felt it might jolt her into rethinking her attitude, or at least working in that direction anyway. I thought it was worth a try.

"I did not want to hire a new actress I didn't really intend to feature, though. Clayton came up with the idea of using Theodora. I wanted to try out the new talking movie equipment as soon as possible anyway. I never expected Molly to finish shooting the picture. Molly was the perfect ingénue, a real-life goodie-two-shoes. I had no expectation of casting her as a temptress, plus I knew she had become pregnant." I looked aghast. RC only shook his head, rolled his eyes, and smiled. "I thought, Molly would come to me and confess before the actual shooting of the picture started. Then, I would have been forced to replace her with Regina.

"Never in my wildest dreams did I think Bertie would find a solution to the dilemma. And who knew that the new Theodora would be a better actress than the old one. Then you went off script — I'm guessing just so you could kiss one Mr. Hugo Wainwright— and with one kiss and a single line, delivered with heartfelt emotion, you created a movie sensation. I knew it the minute I saw it happen." RC smiled.

I felt my face heat, and I thought I might actually be blushing.

"Regina's attitude had worsened instead of getting better. Two days before *Samson and Delilah* was released, I had a pre-screening of the movie for about twelve people. I asked the Viscount and Regina to be members of that group. When I play a movie at a pre-screening, what I'm really watching are the viewer's faces, not the film. I could tell before we got to your now *famous*, or maybe I should say *infamous*, line that we had a hit.

"But that ending set Regina off. After the screening, she came to my house, stormed into my office, and exploded. I overreacted and fired her. I had decided to recant even before her limousine passed through the gates of my estate, but I wasn't going to do it until after the premiere. I thought I'd let her stew a while, then she'd go visit with Clayton at the party.

"But before I had a chance to talk to her again, my world crumbled. Clayton was killed, and I was in ruins. Then the police arrested her for Clayton's murder, and I didn't know what to think." His eyes puddled again, and he looked down and wiped his eyes with his shirt sleeve.

I gave him a moment to compose himself. When he looked back up, I asked, "RC, would you consider allowing me to talk with Regina?  I could rescind her termination and give her a copy of that script.  I've read it and think that she and I would be perfect for the roles.

"It also might bolster her reputation.  She would be deviating from her usual role as the siren, which might give the movie-going public a new perspective on Regina as a truly grieving widow.  I think Clayton also may have been right on target about how it would play to the working woman."

RC's eyes were rimmed with red.  He sniffed and laughed.  "My dear, you are gutsy as hell.  You do know that she doesn't like you, don't you?"

"I am aware of that yes, but her dislike might not be as intense as it once was.  And if I champion her, perhaps we can achieve a level of, if not friends, at least colleagues who work well together."

"Then, you most assuredly have my permission," he said with a chuckle.

"I have just one other question."

"Only one?"

"Yes, for now anyway," I said smiling.  "And it doesn't pertain to Regina, either."  I once again picked up my mammoth handbag, opened it, and removed the three dossiers.  I flattened them out as best I could before handing them to RC.  "These came in very handy.  I learned a great deal from my new ally, Florence McCarney.  My question is regarding Abe, oh, Ezra Blum.  Why did you request he come to California instead of Jacob, his brother who usually handles those talks, or his father, who most assuredly wanted to meet with me?"

A broad smile split RC's face.  "That was Clayton's idea as well.  While you were solving the Montgrieve murder case for the police, I could tell that you and the then Detective Lister were becoming close.  I was very concerned that you would be discovered. And discovered by an officer of the law, nonetheless.

"I told Clayton of my concern, and he suggested we find you a new man, particularly one who preferred the company of another man, even if he was dressed like a woman.

"We weren't having much luck until the courts awarded you Reggie's jewel collection and it was made public. That's when the Blums contacted me about investing in Theodora Desmond movies specifically. I knew what they really wanted, but I am always looking for new investors, so I authorized a detailed background check with the Pinkerton Agency. They are very thorough, as I'm sure you've noticed."

He removed the contents of the brown envelope that contained the Blum dossier. He looked up at me as he tried to smooth out the document and pictures. "For your next opening night gift, fur capes are out. I'm going to get you a good executive valise," he said with a wink. He then pulled out the picture of Abe with the older gentleman. "It was this picture, or perhaps more relevantly, what is written on the back, that caused me to ask specifically for the young Mr. Blum." He flipped the photograph over.

I remembered now that it was the only picture in the file that had anything written on it. It said, "Both Lavender Gloves."

"I remember seeing that, but I'm not sure what it means."

"It is a reference to Oscar Wilde. I guess you would say it's a reference to men like us. Unless I am going blind — and I can assure you, my dear, I am not — Mr. Ezra Blum is a very handsome man." He flipped the picture back around so that I could see Ezra's smiling face." Then he pursed his lips.

"You and Clayton were trying to play matchmakers?" I asked astounded. Then I laughed. "He is not only handsome, he's a wonderful guy too. He's about to be my dance partner in the marathon, but I have no romantic designs on him."

"Too bad, he is very handsome. and very well-moneyed too. He would be quite the catch."

I just shook my head and stood up. RC followed suit. He leaned over and kissed me on the forehead. For some reason, I gave him a hug. He smiled down at me and made his way towards the door.

"Good luck with Regina, my dear," he called over his shoulder. "I'm afraid you're going to need it. And you might rethink Mr. Blum as well," he added, raising his hand in a wave, then glided quietly out of the room, closing the door behind him.

# 31

When I went to retrieve my handbag, I noticed that RC had left the script for *Women of Distinction* lying in his chair. I picked it up, folded it in half once again, and slipped it into my purse. I then headed out the door to ask RC one last question, and hopefully to glean an approximate time frame from Mrs. Foxworthy for the completion of my soon-to-be newly re-furnished office. When I exited the screening room, I looked between the two offices for RC.

"You won't find him," Edwina called with a grin. I looked over at her from the doorway of RC's new office. "He fled," she chuckled.

"Fled?"

"Like a rat from a sinking ship. Mr.Crawford has never been able to deal with pandemonium. He has always liked everything nice and quiet in the office. I guess it's because, with all the other drama he deals with, he has always considered this his sanctuary. If it is okay with you, Miss Desmond, George and I will head out to lunch. I don't often get the opportunity to have lunch with my husband during the work week."

It was only then that I noticed George sitting in one of the chairs aligned along the wall of the reception area. I moved towards Edwina's desk.

"That will be fine. But before you leave, I'd like to leave this with you." Once again, I fished the now bowed manuscript out of my purse. "Would you know if the studio currently has any other copies of this?" I handed it to her.

She looked down at the title on the cover. "Where did you get this?" She looked at me, with a look that might have been astonishment mixed with bewilderment.

"It was lying on Clayton's desk. That's why I thought there might be other copies. Do you know something about this manuscript?"

"Yes Ma'am, I actually do. I'm not sure how Clayton got hold of it."

Now I was intrigued. "Got hold of it? Do tell."

Edwina seemed to hesitate, staring down at the screenplay. I kept quiet. The silence stretched on, but finally, she said softly, "I wrote it."

"You wrote it?"

"Yes, Ma'am. Writing radio scripts and screenplays are, well...a hobby of mine. But I've never seen it bound and typeset like this. I only have the typewritten copy in a three-ring notebook. How would Mr. Foster have gotten it, and all done up like this, I wonder?"

"I wouldn't have the foggiest idea. But, Edwina, it is marvelous. I just talked to RC about producing it. I want Regina Banks and me to play the lead roles."

Edwina look so stunned I had to tell her, "Breathe!"

She sucked in a deep, audible breath. I smiled at her as she sat shaking her head. "I can't figure out how Clayton got hold of it," she said, for I think the third time. When she looked up at me, a tear was sliding down her cheek. "And you want to make a movie out of it?"

"Yes, I do. I finished reading it this morning, and I love the story."

I don't think I'd ever seen anyone look so amazed in my life.

"It was me, Eddie."

I jumped, then spun around to face the voice. I had completely forgotten that George was sitting there. My brow furrowed as I wondered how this man could know who I really was.

Finally, relief flooded through me, as comprehension dawned. He was talking to Edwina. His pet name for her must be Eddie. It was my turn to take a deep breath, and I did just that.

George looked first at his wife then at me. "You see Miss Desmond, I read everything Eddie here writes, and there are a lot of those manuscripts, but this one was my favorite," he said, as he rose and moved over to the desk. He looked lovingly down at Edwina, then back at me. "I tried to get her to give it to Mr. Crawford a few years back, but she said it wasn't good enough.

"Then about a month or so ago, I was downstairs in Mr. Foster's office doing some lettering for him, and he was telling someone on the telephone how he'd like to find a movie script that featured a powerful woman in the lead role, but not one that was a harpy or a siren.

"I immediately thought of Edwina's screenplay. It not only had one powerful woman, it had two. I went home that very night and found the notebook that had her finished pages. There are so many, I knew she wouldn't notice it missing. I took it to a printer and had it typeset and bound.

"The printer told me that if I was creating a manuscript for submission, it needed a synopsis. I had to ask him what that was. When he told me, I wasn't sure what to do, 'cause I don't write none too good. He said if I could write down what the story was about, he knew someone who could make it look good, a lady who was an English teacher. So I did it.

Then the English teacher, Mrs. Riley, got it all fixed up for me. When it was done, the printer said he had even put blank pages in the back for notes, just like the professionals do.

"I went back to see Mr. Clayton and gave him the screenplay." He punctuated his confession, by saying, "And I made sure to tell him who wrote it too." It seemed George had said his piece. He beamed down at Edwina with pride.

Edwina still looked shocked, but then her face began to take on a stern look. Before she could be cross with him, I clapped George on the shoulder.

"You did the right thing George." I turned to look at Edwina, adding, "and you were very wrong. This script is more than good enough. And what's more, I want you to stack up all your notebooks filled with screenplays and get them to me. I want to see how many others might be perfect for the big screen.

"Oh!" I exclaimed, then tapped my finger hard on her desk. "And send that back out to the printers and have five more copies made." I paused. "I'm not sure what printer we use, but I want you to contact the printer that helped George here. I think we need to do business with businesses who make customer service like George received a priority." I winked at George.

"But first, go have lunch with your amazing husband. Dang!" I exclaimed. I've got a luncheon myself." I looked up at the clock. "Edwina, please call for my auto."

"Randel is already downstairs. He rang the office about ten minutes ago."

"Great!" I said, as I turned and shot out of the office.

# 32

When I flew out of the building, Randel was there standing next to the Rolls with my door already open. He smiled and tipped his hat. I slid into the auto, he closed my door, and in moments we were underway.

Just before we arrived at the Ambassador Hotel, Randel asked, "Ma'am, now that Mr. Crawford is back in town, do you want me to arrange to return the Rolls Royce? I have to tell you; I am sure going to miss it."

"Well then, Randel, I've got good news for you. RC and I struck a bargain, and I am keeping the Rolls. So, you won't have to miss it after all."

"That is wonderful news, Ma'am," he said as we pulled into the driveway of the hotel.

The valet opened my door and helped me from the automobile. In a moment I was inside the building. It looked like Seedy was in luck; the same young man was working the concierge desk. Once more, he was out of his chair and hastening in my direction.

"Good day, Miss Desmond," he greeted, rushing over and holding out his hand. I hadn't asked the man's name when I was here with the Duke. But today, he was wearing a name badge, Oscar Burbridge.

"Good day, Oscar." His face lit up.

"Mr. Blum has left word that you would be arriving. He got caught on a call to New York and will be down momentarily."

"That's perfect then. It will give us a few minutes to chat." Oscar looked perplexed as too why I would want to speak with him. "Shall we go back over to your desk?" Now he really looked baffled, but he did as I asked. He sat down on his side of the desk, and I took one of the two guest chairs. "Oscar, I was hoping to speak with you about renting out the entire club for an event I am putting together."

Oscar lit up. "Would that be an after party for one of the Colossal Studio's movie premieres?"

"No, it would be a dance marathon."

"I am so sorry Miss Desmond, but the hotel expressly forbids those types of activities. They are considered bawdy, and the hotel considers them to defile its reputation."

"Even if it is a charity event?"

"I'm afraid so, Ma'am."

"Oscar, please understand that I am not trying to impugn your honesty or character, but I would like to speak to the hotel manager."

"Miss Desmond, you are not impugning my integrity at all. I only state hotel policy. If you will pardon me for a moment, I will be happy to fetch Mr. Hobbnorton for you." He stood, smiling down at me.

"Before you depart, could you please give me Mr. Hobbnorton's given name?"

"That would be Sebastian, Ma'am."

"Thank you," I said, and he move quickly towards the front desk.

Oscar was gone for several minutes before I saw him striding back across the lobby, and hot on his heels was a fit older gentleman with silvery hair. I assumed that gentleman to be one Sebastian Hobbnorton.  As they approached, I stood.

It was Mr. Hobbnorton who spoke as they drew near. "Please, Miss Desmond, there is no need for you to stand."

I didn't sit back down; instead, I put out my hand to shake his, as any businessman would.  Again, he looked taken aback.  I'm sure he had expected me to proffer the back of my hand to him; none the less, he slid his hand into mine, and I gave it a shake.  Perhaps it was a bit too firm, because it triggered a widening of his eyes.  I felt the corners of my mouth turn up.

"Mr. Hobbnorton, may I call you Sebastian?"

"Why yes, Miss Desmond, you most certainly may."

"Sebastian it is then."  I gave him my best pose-for-the-camera smile. He smiled back congenially. "Sebastian, I am certain that Oscar has apprised you of my request. I wanted to speak with you personally in hopes that you and the hotel would make an exception to your policy, being that the event is to raise money for a charity."  I again gave him my best Theodora smile.

"My dear Miss Desmond, I wish that I could.  However, that particular policy has absolutely no room for leniency. The hotel considers that type of function detrimental and deleterious to its reputation."  He smiled sympathetically back at me.

It was at that moment, I caught sight of Abe walking briskly in our direction.  I only had a minute left in this conversation, and I had not been able to sway the manager at all.  Seedy, Edwina and I had never discussed charging an entry fee that we would in turn donate to charity, but having just implied it, I thought it would be an excellent idea.  Then another one of my father's sayings popped into my mind. "Fear of loss, is a terrific motivator."

I looked at Oscar as Abe approached.  "Oscar, would you

call for my limousine, please?"

The man looked puzzled.

"Your limousine?" He looked over at Abe as he stepped up to the little group.

"Yes, please."

I turned to Abe. "Hello, Abraham," I said brightly. This time I proffered the back of my hand. Abe took it. I slipped in, and in the European fashion, I kissed him on the cheek facing the two men and then move to the other cheek. Instead of kissing that one I quickly whispered. "Follow my lead." I could feel the smile on his cheek more than see it, as I moved away from him.

"Miss Desmond, I hope you will please forgive my tardiness," Abe said with an apologetic nod.

"Most assuredly, my good sir. And I hope you will forgive me for asking this. I know we were scheduled for lunch here at the Coconut Grove, but I was trying to mix business with the pleasure of your company. However, I was unable to conduct my business with the Ambassador Hotel and the Coconut Grove nightclub. I had hoped that we could host the dance marathon here."

My mind raced to think of a charity that everyone would feel bad about not championing. Children! Children's Homes. Crippled children came to mind next, but I just couldn't do that. Seedy and Edwina would simply have to find a Children's Home to receive our donation. I turned to Sebastian and Oscar to explain, "Mr. Blum here is going to be my dance partner for the charity event to benefit Children's Homes in Los Angeles."

I smiled excitedly at the two men, then turned back to Abe. "Abraham, the hotel feels that it would be.... What did you say, Mr. Hobbnorton? Oh yes, detrimental and deleterious to their reputation to host such an event."

I had to give Abe credit. He was a good actor. The look of

shock that flew across his face was worthy of the stage.

"I'm thinking," I continued, "the best alternative would be the new Beverly Wilshire Hotel. It is the only location exclusive enough to house the event and large enough to handle the rooms for the participants and their guests. Would you mind if we took our lunch there?"

"No, my dear. In fact, I think that is an excellent idea."

Oscar and his manager both look dumbfounded.

"Oscar, did you call for my Rolls?"

"No Ma'am, but I will immediately," he sputtered.

"My dear, this won't cause an issue with the publicity and advertisements the studio was planning to run, will it?" Abe threw in, looking concerned.

"No, I'm sure it won't, we've made the change early enough before the planned date."

Oscar was on the telephone when Abe offered me his arm. I slipped my arm through his, as we glided towards the big glass door. Randel pulled up only moments later, and we climbed into *my* beautiful Rolls-Royce. As Randel pulled away from the hotel, Abe began to giggle.

"Where to, Ma'am?" Randel asked.

It wasn't a question I was used to hearing from him. He usually knew our destination. And I was laughing so hard I could barely speak. I looked at Abe.

"I guess we should have lunch at the Beverly Wilshire, don't you?"

He dried the tears from his eyes on his jacket sleeve. "Yes, I guess we should."

"That's where we're going, then, Randel. The Beverly Wilshire Hotel."

"How long do you think it will take that bombastic ass to call your office?"

"I would wager, he was doing it before we could get into the Rolls."

"You are awful, my dear. I didn't realize the marathon was a charitable event," Abe said, beginning to sober.

"Neither did I until just a few minutes ago," I chuckled, and Abe was lost in laughter again.

"You'd better warn both of your secretaries," he replied, wiping his eyes again.

I instantly sobered. "Oh my, you're right!" Alarmed, I hurriedly said, "I don't want either Seedy or Edwina to spill the beans. Randel, please pull over at the next pay telephone you see." When the sleek automobile pulled to the curb, I started to get out, but then I realized I had no change.

"Abe do you have any pennies so I could use the pay telephone; I have no change."

"I hate to carry change," he explained. "It jingles in my pocket."

A snort came from the front seat as Randel fished change from his pocket and handed it back to me. Then he was out of the Rolls in a flash, opening my door and helping me out. "There is a pay telephone inside that drug store to your right," he informed me. I looked toward the store and instantly noticed that the sign on the window read "McPherson Drugs," one of my grandfather's drug stores. I smiled and hurried in.

# 33

I had the operator connect me with the house first. It was Seedy who picked up the telephone.

"I figured this would be you. Exactly what Children's Home will the dance marathon be supporting?"

I laughed. "Since you already know and covered for me, let me call you back." I didn't wait for her to answer. I clicked for the operator and had her ring the office.

Edwina answered the telephone. "Colossal Studios, Edwina speaking."

"Has the manager from the Ambassador Hotel called you yet?" I asked the minute she had identified herself. There was a long pause. I could tell she wasn't used to calls like this and she was processing the information.

"No Ma'am, he hasn't."

I breathed a heavy sigh of relief. "That's excellent news. I was scheduled to have lunch at the Coconut Grove. Since they already turned both you and Seedy down as a site for the dance marathon, Seedy thought I should talk with the hotel manager directly. I did, and he turned me down as well. But my lunch appointment, Ezra Blum, and I put a little indirect pressure on him. I told him that the dance marathon was to offer financial support for a Children's Home charity.

Seedy can fill you in on all the details, but I wanted to let you know just in case the hotel manager calls you. He's already called Seedy, so you may not actually receive a call, but forewarned is forearmed, as they say."

She giggled on the other end of the line. "Working for you, Miss Desmond, is so much fun. That is, when you're not scaring the devil out of me."

"I'll take that as a compliment." I started to ring off, but Edwina continued, "I'm glad you called, as a matter of fact. While George and I were at lunch, he wanted to show me the location of the printer who helped him, actually it was very near the sandwich shop where we ate. Since we were standing in front of the printer's shop, I went in and met Mr. Martin, the owner. I informed him I would bring back the manuscript so he could make five more copies.

"He laughed and explained that typically, when a writer orders copies, they print a run of at least ten for the author to send to various studios, hoping for at least one of them to be interested. He said his apprentice failed to read his note about just one copy, so he printed ten. Since the other nine were done, he kept them just in case. I took all nine, and he packed them up that very minute. They are on my desk right now."

"Please deposit another penny to continue your call," the operator cut in. I deposited another penny.

"You're on a pay telephone?" she asked.

"Yes, it's a long story, and I'll fill you in on the details later. Right now I need one of those scripts sent to Regina Banks. And enclose a handwritten note with it. I want it to read:

*"Regina,*
*Read through this manuscript. I'm thinking of you and me.*
*Call me if you have any interest*
*Theo*

"Also, I want two other copies sent out, one to Florence

McCarney and the other to Gwendolyn Hawthorne. You should have Florence's address already. Send Gwendolyn's in care of Hawthorne Textiles in New York City. I think both of these women might be great investors for a movie that deals with strong women."

After just a couple of seconds, I said, "On second thought, hold off on sending the one to Mrs. Hawthorn. I don't actually know her personally; I just know of her. I'll want to open a dialog with her first."

"Yes, Ma'am," Edwina replied. "I'll have the one sent over to Regina within the hour, and I'll mail Mrs. McCarney's and get the other one wrapped and ready to go."

"Oh, and Edwina, is Mrs. Foxworthy, the home decorator, still in the building? If so, I want an estimated date she might be finished with my office."

"No Ma'am, she's not. I can tell you, she feels like your office is going to be a huge challenge."

"Really? I wonder why. I would think she does offices for executives on a regular basis."

"The challenge seems to be your request of a craftsman interior that complements the view. She stood in your empty office muttering and tutting to herself for a long time. Then she confided that, if you had only chosen Art Deco with splashes of Art Nouveau, she could have done something spectacular."

"I love the new Art Deco style," I replied, intrigued. "I wouldn't mind that at all. I just don't want pink chintz and gilt French furniture."

"I can certainly understand that. I wouldn't want that anywhere, much less in a business office." She giggled again. I was guessing she did not giggle when having conversations like this with RC.

"Then call Mrs. Foxworthy immediately and tell her Art Deco with a splash of Art Nouveau will work perfectly. Tell her I wouldn't want to miss out on something spectacular." This time Edwina quite literally guffawed. I rang off and shot back out to the Rolls, where Randel was waiting patiently.

I slipped in and apologized to Abe for taking so long. I then disclosed that Mr. Hobbnorton had indeed telephone Cecilia already, but that she had covered for me admirably.

It then dawned on me that I had failed to call Seedy back. I'd just have to call her from the Beverly Wilshire.

# 34

After my lunch with Abe, I had Randel take me home. My feet were killing me, and for some reason I felt like it had been a very long day, even though it wasn't even five in the afternoon.

Mr. Truman started the gates swinging open when he had recognized the Rolls motoring up the street, but I asked Randel to stop at the gatehouse. When we pulled to a stop instead of continuing through the now-open gates, Mr. Truman came out to check on us.

I cranked down my window. "Good afternoon, Mr. Truman."

"Good-day, Miss Desmond," he said, smiling and tipping his hat.

"I just wanted to let you know that Mr. Blum will be dropping by in an hour or so."

"That's perfect, Ma'am. I will send him right on up to the house. The two of you practicing your dancing tonight?"

"Yes sir, we are. We are hoping to beat out Hugo and Zelda in the dance marathon."

He grinned. "Dance marathons are a lot of fun. The Missus and I have danced in three already, but the best we have finished so far is the top ten."

"You and Mrs. Truman have danced in marathons before?" I must have looked amazed because he broke into a laugh.

"Yes Ma'am. We may be old, but we are pretty active. The Missus has always loved to go dancing, and she is usually game to try anything that involves a dance floor."

"Mr. Truman, would you and Mrs. Truman like to dance in this dance marathon?"

"We'd love to, but I doubt we could afford the entry fee for a dance marathon like your puttin' on."

"To be honest, right now there isn't an entry fee at all. But I tell you what. If there ends up being one, I'll cover it for you."

"Oh Ma'am, I couldn't let you do that."

"Mr. Truman, there is no need to stand on old fashioned principles. If there is a registration fee, I will very happily pay it."

"In that case, yes Ma'am, we would love to dance in your dance marathon."

"Great!" I said, smiling back at him. "I'll make sure Seedy gets your name on the contestants' list." I motioned to Randell, and he drove on through the gate.

Once inside the front door, I kicked off my shoes. My feet ached from wearing heels, yet I had agreed to dance practice with Abe. I climbed the stairs to my bedchamber and opened the door, finding Claudette standing there patiently waiting. I was holding my shoes as I trudged into the room.

"From what I hear, it sounds like you have had a whirlwind day," she said.

"That's putting it mildly. And it's not over yet. Abe will be here in about an hour, and we are going to practice our dancing."

"Let's get you in the shower then. I know it will refresh you."

"No, I think it would put me to sleep. But please, find me

some comfortable shoes to wear."

She took the shoes and handbag from me, then headed into the closet. She was back in an instant and began helping me out of the woolen suit.

With a knock on the door, Seedy popped into the room, paused just a second, then with that "cat that ate the canary" grin on her face announced, "Well, Miss Desmond, you did it. The Coconut Grove will be hosting the dance marathon. But please act surprised when Edwina tells you in the morning. It would seem that Mrs. Edwina Sullivan is coming out of her shell."

"Oh really?" I asked.

"Yes. The snotty manager from the Coconut Grove called back later this afternoon. I wasn't available. So, rather than wait for me to return his call, he called the studio and spoke with Edwina.

"She said he wanted her to let you know that the hotel would be considering your request and would get back with you. She then informed him that she wasn't sure if Miss Desmond was still considering the Coconut Grove, that she did know, however, that you had spent all afternoon at the Beverly Wilshire talking with them."

Then with an even bigger grin Seedy added, "Edwina then told him if Miss Desmond still has any interest, she would get back in touch with him. If not, then of course, she's already booked the Beverly Wilshire instead. And with that, she thanked him for his time and hung up. She said it hadn't been five minutes before he called back and told her that, yes, the Ambassador would love your business."

Shaking her head with a laugh, Seedy continued, "Edwina then told him, if he wanted to host the event, that she would send over a list of everything that you expected from the hotel, and then he could submit a bid.

"She sent our list, and he got her the figures about thirty

minutes ago. The only thing I know you are not going to like is that the hotel's first available Saturday is three months from now. Otherwise, all she needs now is for you to sign off on it."

I smiled. "I told you she could do it."

"You do know she thinks you are a half a bubble off plumb, don't you?" she said with a grin.

"No she doesn't."

Seedy then flipped open her note pad. "This afternoon I received a call from Regina. She received the script from Edwina, and she said she has not been able to put it down since. She loves it. She wants to set a meeting with you at your earliest convenience."

"That's wonderful news."

"Did you send her, *Women of Distinction*?" Seedy asked.

"Yes, I did. Try to set up something for tomorrow if you can. I also sent a copy of the script to Florence McCarney, and I'm going to mail one to Estella's mother-in-law as well. I love the idea of a group of female investors. And this manuscript will be an ideal place to start. Did Edwina, mention *Women of Distinction* to you?"

"No, why would she?"

"Because she wrote it," I announced.

Both Seedy's and Claudette's mouths dropped open.

"It would seem that writing radio shows and now screenplays has been her hobby for years," I confided. "Her husband George gave that first copy to Clayton Foster without her knowledge."

The red cradle telephone rang. Claudette answered it. "I will tell her. Thank you, Wallace." She hung up. "Mr. Blum is here."

I winced. "You will need to get Edwina to tell you the story."

"I'll call her at home tonight."

# All That Glitters

I slipped into a silk pajama and a pair of shoes, but with only three-inch heels, and made my way down to meet Abe in the ballroom.

# 35

Seedy had set up a luncheon for me with Regina. It, of course, had been at my new regular haunt, the Coconut Grove. It would seem that the manager, Mr. Hobbnorton, and I had become best friends now that the hotel and club had been booked.

It would also appear that Mr. Hobbnorton enjoyed leaking information to the press in order to inflate his own self-importance. That meant that the day of my luncheon with Regina, the front of the Ambassador Hotel teamed with a small army of press and photographers.

Regina had arrived before me. She seemed to be thrilled to be back in the limelight, as she stood smiling for photographers and chatting with reporters. I wasn't as keen to be blinded by flashbulbs in the middle of the afternoon. Besides, I had a busy schedule and I wanted to get down to business. So, when Randel helped me from the Rolls, I walked briskly through the throng, slipped my arm through Regina's, posed for a few volleys of flashes, then promptly turned Regina around so we could make our way into the hotel.

We were, of course, greeted at the door by Mr. Hobbnorton, who tried his best to be caught in a photograph with Regina and me. He escorted us back to our table in the Coconut Grove.

Our luncheon had been brief and to the point. Regina loved the idea of changing her movie image to that of a strong-willed woman thriving in a man's world. I discovered that she already knew Gwennie Hawthorne and was more than willing to make the introductions.

We finished our meal, and I thought our business had been conducted, when suddenly Regina reached across the table and placed her hand on top of mine. "I will never be able to repay the debt of gratitude I owe you," she said. "You cleared me of criminal charges, found the man who murdered my friend, and gave me back the one thing in my life that means everything to me, my career."

"I hope that last statement is inaccurate." I said smiling. "I hope your career always takes a backseat to your relationship with Charlie. He's a wonderful man. He sought me out and asked me to help clear your name. He knew you couldn't have murdered anyone. Before you told me your story, I wasn't so sure myself because I had only Hollywood gossip to go one."

"I know he loves me, but I'm not confident how that is going to play out with his family. I did as you suggested and told his mother, but I'm not convinced she took the news affably."

"I don't know the Duchess well, but I do know that she loves her son and wants him to be happy. I'm sure it will be much easier for her to accept you as a woman wealthy in your own right, not a gold digger known as a black-widow."

Regina smiled, but I could see how those words still stung for her.

"I have one other issue. I still have the ten-thousand dollars I took from RC's office the night Clayton was killed. I'm not sure what to do with it. I don't feel I can openly give it back because RC would certainly shun me then. I don't want to keep it either, since he's not buying out my contract with it."

"RC, along with the police, thinks the money was taken by Tommy Hicks. And, I agree that returning the money wouldn't help anyone at this point. You might, however, consider donating the money to a children's charity by sponsoring a couple in the dance marathon."

"I suppose that you would like that to be you and your dance partner." She said with a grin.

"Actually, no, I wouldn't. Everyone in that contest is wealthy in their own right, save one couple. If you agree, I would suggest Mr. & Mrs. Truman. The Trumans are an elderly couple. Mr. Truman is, in fact, my gatekeeper, and I am paying their registration fee. However, if they don't win the marathon, that donation alone would secure them an honorable mention for collecting one of the largest donated amounts."

Regina's smile grew even wider and she gave a firm nod of her head. "Then my money is on the Truman's to win!"

I had to smile myself. "Oh Regina, it's not like betting on the ponies."

"It is in my book. I have no desire to dance in one of those ridiculous tests of endurance. But I will be there to cheer for my team, the Trumans."

"I'm sure they will love having you on their side."

# 36

It had taken Edwina several weeks, but she had found a suitable children's charity, and the marathon's entry fee had been set at a staggering one-hundred dollars per couple. Engraved invitations, printed by the studio's new printer, went out by the boxful.

As word spread, some of the most prominent and influential people jumped at the chance to dance. Seedy had issued an invitation to Estelle Hawthorn. As it turned out she and her husband, Ernest Winthrop Hawthorn — Ernie — had already danced in two marathons. Seems dance marathons undoubtedly were the rage.

Seedy had also invited the McCarneys, expecting them to decline. She was totally surprised, however, when Florence McCarney herself telephoned me to accept. With each passing day, the contestant list continued to grow.

With RC back at the helm, now as founder, things flowed much more smoothly. The reason for the marathon, of course, had been to pit Zelda against me for the affections of one Mr. Hugo Wainwright. RC had brought the three of us together before the official beginning of the movie filming, and we shot several scenes that he had spliced together to create a very compelling movie trailer.

# Nick Hillard

Several of those scenes would end up on the cutting room floor before the movie's release, but the trailer itself put moviegoers across the nation on pins and needles, waiting for the release of the new feature.

Once the trailer had been released in theaters, the exploding interest of the press in a dance marathon, pitting the new up and coming American sweetheart against the now proven temptress, was a given. In fact, it would have been next to impossible to keep them away.

Now that I was one of the highest paid entertainers in the industry, I decided it would be wise to do some investing. Down the street from the sparkling new Beverly Wilshire Hotel, developers were creating a shopping plaza, and I thought I knew a business that should open there.

I had talked Georgie into opening his own fashion house, the House of Herndon. The biggest obstacle to overcome, as it turned out, had been Georgie himself. Randel had told him that he would need to look the part of a successful fashion designer and not walk around unshaven in a dress. He had stormed into my study that afternoon in a rage with Randel right behind him, trying to rein him in.

Taking an obstinate and combative stance, Georgie practically shouted, "With all your big ideas and fancy talk, you never once told me that I would have to become one of those lifeless, unadorned laborers! You are trying to kill my creative spirit! I won't let you do it!"

I was taken aback. I had no clue what he was ranting about.

"I'm sorry Ma'am," Randel cut in. "We were talking about the new studio. I was telling him, that if he were going to be a successful businessman, he would need to look the part. That he needed to start shaving before he went to work and not wear dresses at the new place."

"I'm not going to do it.    I wear dresses because they

inspire me." Both hands jumped to his hips, his head turned to the side, and his very Romanesque nose shot into the air. In that pose, he looked every bit the diva he truly was.

"Randel," I scolded. "Why on earth would you tell Georgie that?"

Randel looked stunned.

"Georgie, of course, you can wear a dress at the new studio. However, I can see Randel's point with regard to shaving. If you are going to wear a dress, and you are selling dresses to an upscale clientele, who are for the most part women, you surely want the product you are wearing to be displayed in its most beautiful form, don't you?"

"Of course I do."

"Then would you agree with Randel and me that shaving is a must?"

"Yes, I guess you are right. I hadn't thought of it that way."

"Great! So, you can wear your dresses. I remember the first time I saw you in your studio; I simply thought you were a quirky bohemian eccentric." The look on Georgie's face was priceless, and I had to work doubly hard to keep a straight face. I knew that Georgie certainly did not see himself as quirky, bohemian, or eccentric. "There, we have our problem solved. Are there any other concerns you might have?"

"No, I don't think so," he said, rather shyly.

"Well, then if that's all, I am expecting Abe over in about fifteen minutes to practice our dancing." I started to usher them out the door when I remembered there was something else I'd wanted to discuss with Georgie.

"Georgie, I almost forgot. I want to chat with you about my dress for the dance marathon. I know you are aware by now that the studio is trying to create the illusion of a rivalry between Zelda and me." He nodded with a quizzical look on his face. "I would like you to create not only my dress, but a dress for Zelda as well. I want her to be angelic, all in white, with maybe a slight touch of sweetheart pink. With my new status as the wanton tramp, I will be wearing all red."

"Oh dear God," he exclaimed. "No, you won't! You would look like a hardened Jezebel."

"That's the point," I said.

"No, that is not the point," he replied. "You need something different. You want to look like a seductress, a woman desired by all men. A woman, that at the mere sight of you, causes their bodies to react instinctively with heated desire and passion. I will create something so spectacular for you that it will instantly generate a stiffening in the trousers of every red-blooded man in viewing distance."

Wallace suddenly announced that Abe was on his way up the driveway, so I immediately agreed to let Georgie have his way. Both Georgie and Randel turned to leave, but Randel gave me a thumbs up and a wink behind Georgie's back just before he slipped his arm around Georgie's shoulders and pulled him in close.

The day the House of Herndon opened, Georgie looked impeccable in his navy pinstriped suit. And it didn't seem to block the flow of his creative spirit at all. On the day of the official grand opening, I arranged to meet the now Zelda Warren at the salon so Georgie could measure her for her new angelic look.

I arrived at the salon well before Zelda. Georgie and I were both chatting from behind the front counter, looking out the storefront windows, when Zelda arrived in a taxi.

"Since this will be the first time you will measure her," I said, nodding toward the pretty young girl now climbing out of the taxi, "It is my sincere hope that you won't strip her naked from the waist down." I grinned over at him.

"My dear Miss Desmond, she doesn't have as much to hide as you do." He made a quick grab for my crotch, but I was faster.

"I dare you, sir." I feigned indignation.

"You should never dare me," he said as he winked.

From the day the doors opened on the new salon that bore Georgie's name, he had become even more impossible to live with. Georgie had Zelda's arm up in the air with a measuring tape under her armpit stretched up to her wrist within minutes of her walking in the door.

"I wanted to thank you, Miss Desmond. I have come to love my new last name. It never occurred to me how easy Warren is to spell. I've spent my entire life spelling Kravitz to almost every person I've ever met."

"Your welcome. I'm glad you like it. It sounds very wholesome, and since you are playing the sweetheart, it seemed an appropriate name."

"It does, indeed. What would you think about me changing my first name to Sally Mae?"

"Sally Mae Warren. You know, I like it. In fact, I like it a lot. We will need to get with RC before the new trailer is released. Hopefully, it won't be too late to change it. And, of course, he will have to bless it with his seal of approval. He does, after all, outrank me."

While Georgie finished measuring her, I slipped into the backroom and telephoned RC. Edwina put me right through to him in his new office. RC loved the name. He said it had an innocence about it, and I agreed. So, when the trailer for the movie was released, Zelda Kravitz officially became Sally Mae Warren.

It took nearly six weeks for Mrs. Foxworthy to decorate my new office, but it had been worth the wait. RC and Mrs. Foxworthy had wanted it to be a surprise, and I hadn't been in the room for the last month.

When they opened the door for me the first time, I don't know who gasped louder, Edwina or me. It was beautiful.

And there sitting on the top of my two-tone art deco desk was yet another gift from RC — a black leather executive valise.

Abe and I had had many conversations regarding the big pink diamond after our luncheon at the Beverly Wilshire. I agreed to allow him to send it to New York. His father had deliberated for nearly two months, deciding on how to cleave the stone. In the end, the giant pink lump became eleven sparkling diamonds. Abe's father had informed him that the largest of the stones, which tipped the scales at one hundred and ten point two-three carats, would be used as an investment gem since it was too big to wear mounted in anything other than a crown or carried in a scepter. He assured his father that he didn't feel I would have any qualms about wearing a crown. However, it would be the sixty-seven-carat stone, the second largest of the eleven, and it's much smaller eight-carat heart-shaped sibling that would be the first to make their public debut.

I had sent the monstrous diamond to New York on one condition — that Blum Brothers would open a Beverly Hills location and allow Abe to stay in California to manage the store. There was a lot of opposition at first. I assumed it was because the family didn't trust that Abe could do the job. As it turned out, however, it was because his mother had not wanted him to move so far away. So at first, his father had flatly refused.

When his father said no, I spoke with Abe about opening his own jewelry business with me as his backer. When the elder Blum got word of that proposal, and it registered with him that he would not only lose his son from his business, but also the wealthy clientele from the west coast, he quickly reconsidered.

Within two weeks of the opening of the House of Herndon, the Beverly Hills location of Blum Brother's Jewelers opened next door on Rodeo Drive, and their first commission was the mounting of two of the eleven sparkling pink diamonds.

# 37

The night of the dance marathon finally arrived. I arranged for Howard, the studio's driver, to pick up my Daimler and ferry both Sally Mae and Hugo to the Coconut Grove. I wanted them to arrive together, assisting the press in jumping to the conclusion that our sweet, innocent Sally Mae was winning the race for Hugo's affections. The two had been seen in public quite a bit lately, most times intentionally, as were Hugo and me. I hoped to thoroughly confuse the public.

Seedy, Edwina and Mr. Densmore were charged with signing in all of the contestants, making sure each dancer wore a team number on both front and back so the judges could easily spot them.

Georgie and Claudette had been in my room at five o'clock to help me dress. The dance didn't start until eight, so I thought five a bit early, but I had already come to learned that it took much longer to become Theodora than I usually thought, especially whenever Georgie had something special planned.

Tonight, Georgie had gone above and beyond. My costume, and it was quite the costume, was solid black and served a two-fold purpose. To be practical, Georgie had foregone a plunging neckline down to my navel, and used drop cap sleeves instead; they bared the tips of my shoulders while still covering most of the upper torso, thus making the garment durable enough to dance in. From my scooped neckline to my waist, the fabric was so sheer it appeared to be made of gossamer. There was nothing of my form left to the imagination except for strategically placed bugle bead work covering the naughty bits.

A skirt that dropped to the floor encircled my waist. It was pure silk with a thick black satin band which wrapped the bottom of the gown and ran up and down the brazenly wide-cut split that traveled from the floor almost to the top of my hip. There would be no fur tonight, just a shawl of the same gossamer fabric as the bodice, also trimmed in black satin. I was a very white blonde tonight with a Marcel wave, adorned with a seed pearl headband.

Abe had dropped by earlier, bringing my two new jewelry pieces in preparation for their world premiere tonight. Thanks to Blum Brothers running full-page newspaper ads, the public already knew about my pink diamond choker. Blum Brothers had dubbed the emerald-cut triangular-shaped pink diamond the "Silent Star." The massive diamond triangle was mounted point down. It was like an arrow pointing to my décolletage — or, well, where it should be anyway. The stone rested in the hollow of my throat, held in place by a five-strand choker of American beauty-cut white diamonds. I loved the piece.

Randel was waiting at the bottom of the steps at six-thirty. Abe had changed at my house and looked very dapper in his black tuxedo. When we arrived at the Coconut Grove, the queue out front was almost overwhelming. It reminded me more of the red carpet at a movie premiere than a dance. I shouldn't have been surprised, since most of Hollywood was on the guest list. From my position, I could make out the

Daimler about four cars in front of us. It took nearly fifteen minutes for the Rolls to pull up to the door.

I turned to Abe. "It's show time! Get that smile in place. Always smile. Never close or cover your eyes, no matter how bright the flashes."

"You've got this down to a science, don't you?"

I pondered that for a moment. "Yes, I guess I do."

I could see Hugo and Sally Mae, arm in arm. Photographers were going wild. I felt a pang of jealousy. It was then I noticed there really *was* a red carpet. I made a mental note to ask Seedy if that had been her idea or the hotel's. The door opened, and the hotel valet's hand slipped inside. I turned in my seat as Georgie had once again instructed. I slid my bare leg, freed by the slit in my dress, out of the car first. A cheer rose from the crowd when they first saw my black-silk-stocking-clad leg glide into view. Then the cheer turned into a gasp as the crowd witnessed the first glimpse of the solid gold garter fitted snuggly around the top of the silk hose, followed by a good deal more bare thigh. Perched between my bare flesh and the black silk stocking, mounted on the clasp of the garter, winked the brilliantly pink heart-shaped diamond, now known as "The Heart of Desire." I stood, the pink diamond and my bare thigh both still very visible. Flashbulbs exploded.

In seconds, Abe was out of the car and at my side. When he took my arm, I feared the crowd was going to boo. Instead, they went almost silent as they tried to figure out who he was, and if he might be a better catch than Hugo Wainwright. But the silence didn't last long. I took the first step toward the door, and the diamond on my thigh caught the lights of the hotel portico. Instantly flashbulbs began popping again, and the crowd clapped as we made our way inside the building.

Abe and I stepped up to the registration table where Seedy,

Edwina, and Mr. Densmore sat.

"Well, aren't you looking demure this evening," Seedy laughed sarcastically. I didn't think she would ever forgive the studio for turning Theodora Desmond into a vamp. We signed in, and Mr. Densmore started to assist us in attaching our numbers both front and back. He pinned Abe's numbers to his tux while I chatted with Seedy and Edwina. When it was my turn, he stopped, staring straight at my chest.

"I-I-I think I should have Cecelia take care of this," he stammered, holding the cloth placard bearing our number, forty-eight.

"I think you are correct Mr. Densmore," I replied.

The man turned beet red. Seedy jumped up to help me, taking the placard from Mr. Densmore. The man stepped back, but I noticed his eyes were still fixed on my chest. A slight smile crossed my face as I wondered, *Was Georgie's prediction on target? Was the fixated Mr. Densmore tenting in his trousers?"*

"Georgie will kill us both if I snag this fabric," Seedy fretted, holding a pin in one hand and the number placard in the other. "Especially since this was the dress used in the publicity photos."

Throughout the last several weeks, Blum Brothers had been running ads in newspapers across the country announcing Theodora Desmond's newest addition to her gem collection, the "Silent Star." The photographer wanted a portrait of me modeling the choker. When I asked Georgie what I should wear, his answer was the same as Randel's had been—I should be wearing black. However, instead of wearing the black Chanel, he wanted to feature his own design. The morning papers had called him an "unnamed designer" after the opening of *Samson and Delilah*, and I think it still piqued him.

When the ad photo was made, however, the full dress

wasn't finished, so the photo showed only the bodice and the shawl. Below that, I was wearing pants Georgie had designed. The photographer captured me only from the waist up. Everyone loved the finished portrait, so much so that the day Theodora Desmond's picture appeared in the papers wearing her enormous pink triangular diamond, Abe received several new commissions. Furthermore, Georgie had telephone calls, telegrams, and even ladies stopping into the salon wanting evening wear. A couple of them even inquired about copies of the dress Theodora Desmond was wearing in the photo.

"I should agree to make them that exact outfit," he told Claudette, Seedy and me one morning when he joined us for coffee. "Then I'll make them the same black bodice and shawl and connect it to a pair of brown & cream houndstooth trousers. Who knows? It might turn into the new cat's meow." We all had a good laugh.

Finally, Seedy hit upon the idea of attaching strings to both the front and back placards, and I wore my number like a sandwich-board. Crisis averted, we made our way back to the club.

To perpetuate the rivalry between Sally Mae and Theodora, Edwina placed us at tables on opposite sides of the dance floor, but nearest the judges and onlookers. The crowd was huge, and every table was full, as were the bars on the floors above overlooking the club and its giant dance floor.

On our way to the table, I was taking in the nearly twenty-piece orchestra, with another twenty pieces seated in back as extras to spell their counterparts. The musicians were ready to play in teams, non-stop until the marathon had its winner.

Scanning the orchestra, I noticed that the piano player was the same one I'd seen playing for Madam Rochelle at the Drakestone. Since I supposedly organized the proceedings, I thought I should speak to the band leader and greet the band.

I made my way to the bandstand. Musicians were nearly spilling off the raised platform, there were so many of them. I introduced myself to the band leader, who assured me he knew who I was. I received waves from several of the other musicians too. I gave them my best pose-for-the-camera smile and waved back. I even signed a few autographs. Abe had struck up a conversation with the piano player, so I waited patiently for him, scanning the crowd—at least until I saw Hugo.

He was sitting very close to Sally Mae, and he was showing her something he had in his hand. She seemed very excited about it, whatever "it" was. Again, I felt that pang of jealousy. But my response to that feeling hadn't changed. *This was the way it had to be.*

"He's the one, isn't he?" Abe was at my side, whispering in my ear, drawing me back from my reverie.

"I'm sorry?" I asked.

"I said, he's the one."

"I'm sorry, I still don't get your meaning."

"Hugo Wainwright is the one. The man you love, but who is off limits to you. The one you told me about that night at the Drakestone."

I looked hard at Abe.

"Don't worry. I would never have known if it hadn't been for your hands." I cocked an eyebrow quizzically. "That night at the Drakestone, when I held your hand, I felt the calluses. They were in the same place on your hands as they are on mine. I knew you must be involved in one of the Asian martial arts practices. After the investors' meeting, do you remember showing me the diamond? When I handed it back to you, and you shook my hand, I felt the calluses again. I had to do a double take, but then I knew. Karate?"

"Judo."

"So, he's the one," he said again, nodding towards Hugo.

"He is," I said, feeling defeated.

Abe smiled at me. "If you ever have a change of heart, I'd love to apply for the position."

I gave a nervous laugh. "For now, I don't see that ever happening, but I will keep your application on file, should that position ever become available." And I gave him an appreciative grin.

"Your secret's safe with me."

For some reason, I knew it would be. As we made our way back to our table, I was utterly lost in thought. Abe had never questioned why or how but had simply accepted me at face value.

We hadn't even had a chance to sit down before the spotlights hit the dance floor and the announcer was greeting the audience and instructing the dancers. He asked the dancers to prepare to dance their way up to the judges' table. Edwina and Seedy had arranged the seating so the couples to first dance to the front was seated at the back, by the bandstand. With forty-eight couples, this process was going to take a bit, but it was all part of building anticipation. Couple number forty-seven was Hugo and Sally Mae, and Abe and I brought up the rear as couple forty-eight.

The rules were explained as the dancers began to stand. As the band struck up a waltz, all the dancers moved slowly to the back as each couple, from first one side, then the other, danced to the center of the floor. They took turns dancing past the judge's table. Each couple was introduced when they reached the spot in front of the judges, then they completed their introductory dance with some kind of flourish. Seedy and Mr. Densmore were by the bandstand, one on either side, to time the start of each couple, allowing enough time for the couple ahead to complete their dance just before the next couple arrived at the judges for their introduction. This made the process move much faster than I had anticipated.

In seemingly no time, couple forty-seven, Hugo and Sally Mae, started their run down the center of the dance floor. Sally Mae was a surprisingly good dancer, and it was quite evident to both Abe and me that she and Hugo had been practicing together, too. They were over half way down the dance floor when Seedy signaled us to take the floor.

"Ready?" Abe whispered in my ear as he put his arms around me.

I nodded, tilted my head to the side, and leaned back as he spun me onto the floor. We were nearly three-quarters of the way down the floor when the main spotlight fell on us. Our number was called, and we were introduced by name. In moments, we had reached the judges' table. For our final flourish, Abe's hand slipped from our frame, and moved to the hidden tab at my waist. As I spun out from his arms, he held the tab and my full-length black silk skirt tore away and dropped to the ground. In its place, spilling only a short way down to well above my knees, was a glistening black beaded fringed flapper's skirt. In the center of my right thigh, Georgie had omitted the fringe, creating a nearly three-inch gap allowing the twinkling deep pink *Heart of Desire* — along with its thick golden garter and a good amount of bare skin — to take the place of prominence. The onlookers cheered. Instead of leaving the dance floor like all the previous couples, Abe twirled me towards the center of the floor. The other couples were making their way back onto the dance floor, too. It was a tight fit, to say the least.

RC had appointed himself head judge. The judges weren't considering our dance skills, however. They merely made sure each couple followed the rules. There was really only one official rule: once the competition started, no couple could leave the floor. Any who did were out of the contest.

RC stood. "Is everyone ready?" he called and raised his arm. As he dropped his arm, the band opened with a Charleston.

An hour and a half in, the dance floor had emptied by nearly half. At the start, Abe and I were talking during the slower numbers. But at this point, even though each of us was still smiling, the conversation had ceased.

Once we reached the three-hour mark, my feet were throbbing. There were only nine couples left on the floor. I wasn't surprised that both Estelle and Ernie Hawthorn and her parents Florence and Aloysius McCarney were still dancing. Lord help both the misters in those two couples if they wanted to stop before their wives. Besides Hugo and Sally Mae, of course, the only other pair I knew, and the one that surprised me the most, was Mr. and Mrs. Truman. I would normally have considered them to be an elderly couple, but at that moment they were moving around the dance floor full of vim and vigor.

The McCarneys left the floor next. Then one by one, four other couples dropped out in quick succession. Then there were four. When the band picked the tempo back up, I felt sure the Trumans would be the next to go, but they were not. Instead, Estelle and Ernie threw in the towel.

Sally Mae was looking like the last rose of summer. Her face was ashen, and her hair had gone limp. Secretly, I couldn't help but feel pleased.

*"See what you will be waking up to every morning Hugo?"* I thought wickedly.

After two more songs, Mr. Truman gave me a salute as he and his wife left the dance floor. I looked at Abe, his face streaked with sweat. I could tell he was moving around the floor through sheer willpower alone. I looked across the floor, and I could see that Hugo was practically holding Sally Mae vertical. Her feet were stiffly ambling across the shiny wooden surface.

The band segued into the quickstep. I looked at Hugo. He looked back at me. We both knew this was the last dance. It would come down to which of our partners could hold out the longest. I appraised my partner. I needed him to rally, but I could tell, God love him, he had nothing left. I was going to have to lead and support him like Hugo was supporting Sally Mae. Abe was so tired, he didn't even notice when I took control. I looked up, and my eyes locked with Hugo's. It was if we were connected somehow. At the same time, each of us rolled our partners in. We were totally in sync as the two of us spun them out again away from us. When they reached their furthest point, we each let go. Poor Sally Mae and Abe careened towards each other, narrowly avoiding a collision.

I slipped seamlessly into the now empty void in Hugo's arms, snapped into frame, and we shot across the dance floor. The crowd went wild, while all the judges were busy trying to disqualify us. We paid them no heed as we bounced around the floor.

As if to echo our renewed determination, the band changed keys and picked up the tempo. Hugo matched their pace, and we were flying. The room was a blur. RC and the two other judges had given up. As we picked up speed, the crowd's cheers grew louder. I could tell the song was drawing to an end. We were right in front of the judges' table when the last notes sounded. Hugo dipped me deeply, and my right leg flew into the air.

A photographer shouted out, "Hey Hugo!"

Hugo looked up. That picture was the one in every newspaper in town the next morning. Hugo's smiling face only a breath away from the sparkling *Heart of Desire* and my bare thigh. The headline read: "Sally Mae Doesn't Stand a Chance."

Hugo righted me, and we took a bow to thunderous applause. Then it started.

"Say it. Say it," the crowd began to chant.

Hugo had already made it quite plain he didn't like doing the scene from *Samson and Delilah* that ended with a kiss. I started to pull away and move back over to check on poor Abe when Hugo tugged me back to him.

"It's my turn this time."

I was exhausted, and I wasn't in the mood to trade barbs. Hugo had one arm wound tightly around my waist. He pulled me hard against him with a jerk. He looked deep into my eyes.

"There is no one in this world for me, but you. I will love you until the end of time," he said gently, his eyes glinting with determination.

"That's not the line," I protested.

"It's my line. What do you say?" Still holding me tight with just one strong arm, he held out a closed fist. When he opened his hand, nestled in its palm was a thin platinum band encrusted with tiny diamonds. "Theodora Desmond, will you marry me?"

## The Book Review:

Book reviews are the life blood of any author. This is the second book of a series. If you enjoyed the first two books, please let others know. Reviews are available wherever you purchased your copy. Reviewing is also available on Goodreads. Your reviews are greatly appreciated.

## Join Nick's Mailing list:

## www.nickhilliard.com